To my husband.
Thank you for taking care of our home and its many inhabitants
while I follow this silly dream of mine.

DESCRIPTION

The graves are small, but they hide a big secret.

When The Preacher targets her family for his last kill, Winter Black is the only survivor. After recovering from the brain injury she received that brutal night, Winter single-mindedly pursues a career as an FBI agent, but not even her unexplainable talents, discovered after her coma, can prepare her for her first case.

After human remains are discovered in the woods, someone will go to lethal lengths to keep an old mystery buried. Special Agent Black is pulled into an investigation that hits too close to home. In the town where her parents were murdered, Winter needs to find one killer...while being stalked by the shadow of another.

Welcome to book one of Mary Stone's debut crime fiction series. If you love a page-turning thriller with mind churning mystery, unexpected villains, and riveting suspense, Winter's Mourn will keep you guessing until the end.

BEFORE

Pain was like a living thing as yet another contraction tore through the girl.

"Help me."

It was a whisper. It was a prayer.

It was ignored by the observer standing on the other side of the cage.

The burning between her legs intensified as she bore down, her young body seeming to know what to do. The pain faded, but it would be back, she knew. And it was.

How had it come to this?

A stupid fight with her parents. She'd been so cocky, so sure that she was a professional at life and knew it all. She was a grown-up. Heck, she'd even had sex with Scotty Jernigan, the captain of the football team.

At sixteen, she'd thought she had it all figured out.

"I hate you!"

Those were the last words she'd flung at the man and woman who'd brought her into the world as she stomped from the house, intent on doing things her own way.

"I'm so sorry," she whispered to the memory of their faces. And she was. So very, very sorry.

She wanted to say more, make them hear her pleas from the ether, and maybe by some miracle they would find their way to her now. Because she needed them. Not just physically but in every other possible way. But before she could ask them for their forgiveness, pain sank its fangs into her again.

She bore down, pushed, gritting her teeth.

In the movies, there was a nurse counting to ten. There was a husband lovingly holding up one leg. There was a doctor ready to catch, ready to know what to do if things went wrong.

And things were going very, very wrong.

"Help me," she said after the contraction abated.

The observer didn't react. Didn't speak a word. Didn't move.

The burning grew even stronger, and she looked down, sure that her private parts had burst into flames. But instead of a red glow...there was a head, dark hair swirling wetly over the crown.

Bursting into tears, she touched her child for the very first time.

A baby.

Even as her belly had grown bigger and bigger over the months, it still hadn't felt real. The sickness. The exhaustion. The cravings. The movements under her skin.

It felt real now.

The vice contracted around her belly again, turning her attention away from the miracle of what was happening and back to the pain. The terrible, awful, body-splitting pain.

She pushed again and again, screaming through the contraction, and the pressure increased. Swelled. Blossomed.

Then it was over.

Between her legs lay the bloody, squirming child.

A girl.

Reaching for it with shaky hands, she smacked its bottom, swept her finger in its little mouth. Her addiction to hospital TV dramas was paying off.

There was a cry. Soft at first. Then it grew stronger as the baby's anger and confusion at her new reality increased.

"Shhh…" the girl soothed, sticking a finger in the baby's mouth. She smiled as the little one began to suck. "That's right, sweet girl. I'll take care of…ohhh…"

The pain this time was a surprise. Wasn't that part supposed to be over? She had to stop herself from holding the baby too tight as she screamed through gritted teeth.

The baby wailed again, and she laid it down beside her.

Was there another child? Twins? Was that even possible?

But when she looked down between her legs, she saw that the only thing she was delivering was blood. A river of it.

She looked at the observer, her panic kicking in again. "Please help," she cried as agony and fear stabbed through her.

As she watched the key slide into the lock of the cage, heard the click of metal on metal as the mechanism opened, hope swept through her. Help was coming, after all.

"Perfect," the observer whispered, voice the very picture of awe. Gloved hands lifted her baby girl while shrewd eyes took in every inch. "Simply perfect."

The girl was weak now, but that didn't stop her from trying to reach for her child. "Give her to me."

Cold eyes turned her way, making her shiver.

As if that single shiver had triggered an avalanche of them, she began to tremble violently.

So much blood. So much pain.

Would it ever end?

She looked at the observer again, clutched at the long

black coat only inches from where she lay. "Help. Me." She swallowed back the tears. "Please."

As she watched, the observer laid the child down. Scissors appeared, as well as two plastic clamps, and she watched in fascination as gloved hands quickly took care of cutting the umbilical cord, effectively separating her from the baby. She nearly wept as the bond between them slipped away.

Those same hands then went to work wrapping her tiny baby in a blanket, placing a tiny pacifier in its mouth. All the time, there were the whispers of "perfect" and "I did it." Other mumbles she couldn't comprehend.

When she cried out again, the knife of pain growing even sharper, the observer turned to her.

"I won't let you suffer." Something was pulled from the pocket of the long coat the observer wore, a flash of metal that she immediately identified.

No.

Even as the word echoed in her mind, she looked at her baby one last time, then closed her eyes as the cold steel pressed to the back of her head.

A click. Then nothing.

The observer was right. She didn't feel anything anymore.

1

Winter's hand trembled violently before her fingers went nerveless, and they abruptly loosened their death grip on the fragile piece of evidence in her hand. The picture she'd been holding fluttered to the floor, landing face-up. A little boy's face stared up at her from the grungy, dark green shag hotel carpeting. Innocence and fear combined in his wide-eyed expression, captured sometime after his parents had been murdered, and he'd been taken by their killer.

She couldn't catch her breath.

Justin. Her baby brother.

Winter sank down on the bed behind her, the mattress sagging under her weight, trying to control her frantic wheezing. She bent at the waist, resting her forehead on her knees.

In, out, she told herself. *Slow. Calm. Breathe in. Breathe out.*

She needed to clear her mind. Focus.

But, right then, all she could do was mourn.

She waited until the black dots flickering at the edges of her vision cleared, and her panicked wheezing evened out into a calmer rhythm. She wasn't thirteen years old anymore. She wasn't a child. She was an FBI agent. Steeling her spine, she bent over and picked up the photograph again.

The photo itself appeared to be old. It was a Polaroid, and while Polaroid still made cameras and film, the colors in the photo looked faded. Yellowed. There was no inscription on the white strip at the bottom of the picture, but there was a tiny puncture at the top. Had it been pinned up on a bulletin board?

That thought almost made her lose it again. Did The Preacher take pictures of all his victims? Put them up on a glory wall so he could reminisce about the brutal murders he'd committed over the last twenty or thirty years?

In the photo, her brother's six-year-old face was pale, and she could make out a smudge of dirt on one cheek. Justin's blue eyes were wide and confused. He was wearing the same SpongeBob pajamas her mother had dressed him in after his bath before Winter left the house to spend the night with a friend.

"Night, Winter." She could almost hear his voice. "Thleep tight, don't let the bed bugth bite." He'd been missing both front teeth the last time she'd seen him, and she'd teased him with the mercilessness of a bratty older sister about that lisp.

The punch of grief came again, hitting her chest dead center with the impact of a body armor-piercing slug. Winter squeezed her eyes shut against the familiar pain. It didn't help. This pain was brutal.

She remembered the smell of Johnson's Baby Shampoo. Justin had thrown his arms around her waist and squeezed tight. She'd been impatient, ready to leave for her best friend Sam's house. They'd planned a long Friday night of binge-watching gory Halloween movies on the Syfy channel, stuffing themselves on greasy, extra-buttery microwave popcorn, and talking about boys.

So, instead of squeezing him extra hard, she'd just extri-
cated herself from his pudgy little arms, dropped a quick kiss
on silky dark hair still damp from his bath, and hollered,
"G'night, twerp," on her way out the door.

Another punch of pain. It had been the last hug she'd ever
get from her only sibling, and she regretted her teenaged
callousness.

So many times, she wished she would have stayed home.
If she had, though, she'd be dead. Butchered like her parents
in their beds. Or taken, like her brother.

Counselors had told her countless times later, in their
soothing, calm voices, that her absence from the house that
night hadn't changed anything. A stranger, a psychopath, a
serial killer, had targeted her family for some reason she
couldn't fathom, and Winter's presence wouldn't have made
any difference in the outcome.

She was fortunate to be alive, she was told over and over.
She'd nodded and let them think they'd convinced her. She
knew it was classic survivor's guilt, but she'd never forgiven
herself for walking out the front door that night.

Even though she'd come home, she'd still been too late.

She and Samantha had argued over a stupid teenage boy
whose name she'd only recently been able to remember.
She'd left Sam's house, walking down the windy, leaf-littered
sidewalk at two o'clock in the morning. Come into the
house, eerily quiet in the darkest part of the night. Seen her
parent's door ajar, dim light spilling out into the hallway.
Caught one horrible glimpse of the charnel house that was
their bedroom. Seen the red crosses on the walls. The Jude
14:15 in blood. Then she was hit hard enough in the head
from behind to cause a short coma and a lingering traumatic
brain injury.

Years later, Winter still blamed herself for not saving
them.

As if the memory of her head injury was enough to snap her out of her paralyzing grief, the details of the dingy hotel room around her burst from fuzzy gray to sharp, technicolor clarity. She hadn't been left helpless after that night. She'd come out of her coma with some new skills and a focus: catching the killer who'd destroyed her family.

Her mind coldly clear now, she studied the picture of Justin with deliberate detachment. With laser focus, she memorized the trees in the background—their types, sizes, what they might look like a decade later. She pictured the angle of the camera, adjusted an approximate time of day based on the shadows cast by the trees, and cataloged every minute detail of the picture until it was ingrained in her mind.

If she ever came across the place where this picture was taken, she'd recognize it.

DIDN'T she realize she'd left her curtains open?

Women these days had no shame.

I didn't even need the pinhole camera I'd set up earlier behind that godawful-ugly painting above the TV. From out here in the parking lot, I was able to see the expressions that chased across her face. Fear. Anger.

And through the binoculars I'd brought along, sadness.

Oh, those tears. They made my heart go pitty-pat in a way it hadn't for a long, long time. I wanted to lap them up. Lick that salty wetness right off her smooth, pale cheek. Savor the innocence those tears represented. The camera probably caught those silvery tear tracks in HD. I'd be saving that video for later. Later, when I could savor it properly.

The skinny little black-haired girl with the spooky blue

eyes sure had grown up pretty. Pretty as a picture, just like her momma. And now she was FBI. Seemed fitting.

Chuckling, I scraped a fingernail against my front tooth absently as I watched her study the gift I'd left just for her.

I was officially in retirement now. Had been for years. But watching that girl sitting up there in her lonely hotel room, I was tempted to pay her a visit. Bring it full circle.

But no…

Not now. Not yet.

When another hotel room door swung open, I dropped the binocs in my lap. A tall, broad-shouldered man with short dark hair stepped out, scanning the mostly empty lot. The FBI girl's partner. Now definitely wasn't the time.

Watching the FBI man walk toward Winter's door, I could see his knock get her attention, and she jumped up, her eyes wide before she bent over quickly like she was hiding something. Probably stuffed the picture under the mattress. I chuckled again, pleased, and my truck gave its usual growl and rattle of exhaust as I cranked the ignition.

That's right, girlie. Keep it a secret. Just between us. A family thing, so to speak.

I'd been watching her over the years, kept tabs so often that she surely felt like family at this point. The FBI man looked out the window, into the parking lot for a moment, before pulling the curtains closed.

I wasn't worried. No reason to be. They weren't here in Harrisonburg for me.

Would probably fornicate, the sinners. That would make me angry. Very angry.

That wouldn't do. Not yet.

I looked down at the scene playing out on my cell phone, watched the FBI man talk to the blue-eyed girlie for a moment, and wished I'd taken the time to wire the room for sound. Maybe another day.

Not now.

I shifted the truck into reverse, and the transmission clunked as I backed slowly out of the parking slot.

Tonight wasn't right. I had lots of things to do before I could meet my blue-eyed girlie again.

Lots of things to do.

NOAH FELT an itch at the back of his neck and closing the curtains hadn't done a thing to scratch it. He'd talked to soldiers, MPs, veteran cops over the years, and the itch was a real thing, not to be ignored. It meant something.

Just now, though, he wasn't sure what.

He studied Winter from his spot at the little table in the corner of the room. She looked paler than usual to him, and her eyes—such a cool shade of blue, deep and dark—were shadowed underneath, looking almost bruised. *Stressed*, he thought.

And why shouldn't she be? She was on her first FBI murder case, which just happened to be in Harrisonburg, the little Virginia town where her family had been killed a bunch of years ago. Investigating some old bones found in the woods that just might belong to her missing brother.

"You sure nothing's wrong, aside from the obvious?"

Winter nodded, a piece of that long black hair of hers coming loose from its prim knot at the back of her neck. She tucked it behind one ear and folded her arms, staring at him pointedly. It was plain to him she didn't want him in her room, but he didn't mind. He wasn't going anywhere.

"You know, I'd like to consider us friends."

She rolled her eyes at him, and he didn't miss the flash of...something that crossed her face at his words. Guilt?

"Sure, Dalton. We've been friends since I took you down in front of the Director of the FBI Training Academy."

I gave her a good-natured snort. "Darlin', you're remembering it all wrong. I took *you* down."

"My elbow in your sternum said otherwise."

"Fine, I'll be a gentleman and let you think you won." He needed to steer this conversation back on track. "Anyway, friends talk to each other."

Noah took out a well-worn deck of cards from his pocket and unwound the rubber band that held them together. He cut the deck with practiced ease, shuffling both stacks into one so quickly, they were a whispering blur. He'd found people were more willing to talk when they didn't think you were paying them your full attention. But it didn't take any attention at all to shuffle a deck of cards.

"We can talk to each other in the morning, Dalton," Winter huffed, exasperated. "We're meeting for a run in less than seven hours, remember?"

"What do you think of Officer Benton?" Noah cut the deck again, ignoring her rhetorical question.

"I think he's a douchebag. Is that what you came over here to ask me?"

"Poker?" he offered, riffling the cards for effect, keeping his face carefully neutral. "Doesn't have to be strip, unless you insist."

She just shook her head, sighed, and climbed up on the bed, propping pillows behind her. She grabbed the remote off the nightstand and flicked on the postage-sized TV across the small room. The soothing drone of a nightly news meteorologist's voice rolled out on low volume as he gave the weather report for the next day. The late-September warm stretch would continue. Partly sunny, high of seventy-five. Good day to visit an old crime scene.

"I knew Benton," she finally said. "In middle school."

"Small town. Figures you'd know some people. Was he a douchebag back then?"

She barked out a laugh. "Weren't all teenaged boys?"

"I wasn't. My mama told me so."

Winter clamped her hands over her face and sagged down into the pillows. "Why was I assigned to this case? Did you talk Max into putting me on this with you?"

He didn't bat an eyelash at her change of subject. Noah knew it had been bothering her. It was out of character for any Special Agent in Charge to put a rookie and a relative rookie on a case together, and she'd have to be dumb not to realize that. Winter wasn't dumb.

"Miguel Vasquez was going to take it, but his appendix exploded, and he'll be down for a couple weeks. I was his backup. Everyone else is tied up with that credible terrorist threat that came in last week."

Her hands dropped to her lap, her fingers twisting together in a rare show of anxiety before she pulled them apart. "Why didn't Max assign it to you, then? You're the one with four years of actual police experience. I've only got a degree. Why make me the case agent?"

"Because I asked him to." He held up a hand, forestalling her argument. Her eyes flashed in warning. "You did well with the jogger rapist. I'm still pissed you went off script on that one, but you got him. You need another win to cement your spot in the Violent Crimes unit."

"Jeez, Dalton, you're just as much of an FBI rookie as I am. Who are you to give advice to the SAC?" She turned off the TV and shot to her feet, pacing the narrow width of the room. It looked like steam would erupt from her ears any second, but at least she had some color now. She didn't look so haunted.

Noah shrugged, giving her one of his most irresistible grins. He tipped his chair back on two legs, knowing the cocky pose would rile her up even more. "I'm charming. Everyone likes me. Even you, and you don't like anyone."

"I don't like *you* much right now, either." She lashed a foot out to connect with one upraised leg of his chair on her way past him, and he teetered for a second, bracing a quick hand on the wall to keep from tipping over. "Did it have anything to do with the fact that these bones might be Justin's remains? The initial report said they belonged to a male. Probably between six and ten years old. And they've been in the ground for a long time. Years."

There it was. The wound was lanced, Winter's pain out in the open.

"Yeah," Noah said quietly into the stark silence that followed her words. "I thought if there was any chance it could be your little brother, you'd want to be in on it."

"You were right. But I don't need your Texas charisma or whatever," she waved one hand, "to smooth the way for me."

"I didn't expect you to thank me," he replied, sober as a judge. "But I could think of a few ways you could go about it." He gave her a lewd look and wiggled his eyebrows.

"No fraternizing, Dalton." A grin twitched at the corner of her lips, spoiling her severe expression just as he'd hoped it would.

"But what about that night you got tanked, and I drove you home—"

"Out. Now." To emphasize her point, she flung open the door, whacking it against his outstretched foot.

Laughing at her obvious discomfort at the mention of their one not-very-memorable kiss, he stood up and whipped the rubber band around his card deck. "See you in the morning. I'm right next door if you change your mind."

She snorted and locked the door behind him with a decisive snap.

The smile slid from his face the second the sound faded,

and he looked out across the dark parking lot. The itch at the back of his neck was mostly gone. So was the rusted-out blue Chevy that had been parked in the lot earlier. Curious, he jogged down the stairs that led to the main floor units and stepped off the curb, walking to the back row in the lot where the driver of the Chevy would have been. An oily spot marked the asphalt.

He looked up and could make out Winter's silhouette through the too-thin beige curtains. He hadn't teased her enough to pull her out of her funk. She was back to pacing again.

And if the man inside the truck was still there, he'd have had a perfect vantage point for looking in Winter's hotel room window, watching her work out whatever was bothering her.

2

Winter didn't sleep that night.

The photo under her mattress seemed to be burning a hole in the bed. The man who had killed her parents and taken her brother had been in her hotel room. The Preacher. What a hateful, hateful name. Sacrilegious.

How had the bastard known she'd be there, what room she'd be in? She had no idea. Did someone do it for him? Was he a Harrisonburg local? An adult she'd known growing up? His kills had been scattered across the country, so it wasn't likely. But she was sure the photo had been left by him, or at least at his direction.

Should she have told Noah? Turned the photo in for evidence? Instinctively, she knew there wouldn't be any prints. No one had managed to catch him in decades, and she doubted he'd resurface after all these years just to give himself away with a careless mistake.

Sliding the photo under her door had felt like a personal message. That was fine.

Finding and taking down The Preacher was a very

personal vendetta. An eye for an eye. She didn't plan on sharing that with anyone, either.

Rolling over, her legs tangled in the blankets, she punched her pillow, trying to get comfortable. The red glow of the alarm clock told her it was after three. She tried to shut off her brain, close her eyes, but it was impossible.

Winter finally gave up as the weak gray light of dawn began to illuminate the hotel room. She rolled out of bed and pulled on a pair of stretchy yoga capris and a loose tank top over a sports bra. She'd brushed her teeth and was tying her running shoes when Noah tapped on the door. She stepped out and locked up, tucking the key into the tiny inside pocket at her waistband.

Noah was big, handsome, and irritatingly cheerful for this side of six a.m. His dark hair was growing out from his short military cut and stuck up a little on one side where he'd been sleeping on it. He had on a pair of black basketball shorts and a wrinkled red Texas Longhorns t-shirt. If not for his sharp green eyes and wicked grin, he'd have looked about twelve years old.

Winter felt an unwelcome wave of affection. He really was a great guy. It was damned near impossible not to like him.

"Ready to rock and roll?" His tone was light, but he studied her face like he was searching for something. She stuck her tongue out at him and headed down the stairs to start stretching.

"We'll run to the park at the edge of town. Easy warm-up, just a few miles. One loop on the trail once we're there, and then first one back buys breakfast. That way you can't claim I've got home-turf advantage."

They set off at a comfortable pace. A light, cool breeze banished some of the previous night's cobwebs and the only sounds besides their rhythmic breathing came from a few passing cars and birds chirping their morning greetings.

"Sleep okay?" Noah asked, just into their second mile.

"Like a baby," she lied. "You?"

"Yep."

Winter, adjusting to the déjà vu feeling of being back in her hometown, didn't mind their companionable silence. They passed her fourth-grade teacher's house, a small brick bungalow on the main street, roses blooming on trellises next to the wide front porch. She wondered if Mrs. Jensen was still teaching. The woman had seemed ancient to Winter back then, but she'd probably only been in her late forties.

They passed the small town's only grocery store, the Shop N' Stop. The building had gotten a facelift since she'd last seen it. She remembered putting in her first job application there at the beginning of that last fall. She'd wanted to be a grocery bagger, had dreamed of having extra spending money.

Her dad, a quiet man with a kind, bearded face, had been an English professor at James Madison University. Her mom, sweet and vivacious with long black hair like Winter, had been a housewife. Winter had wanted the after-school job since her small allowance had barely kept her in Bonne Bell lip gloss, but never found out whether the grocery store would have hired her or not.

The sun was just rising when they reached the park, the playground deserted.

The merry-go-round was the same, warped steel with knobby rivets covered with chipped green paint. She'd sat on the metal edge with Sam countless times, Huffy bikes abandoned in the grass nearby. They'd kick lazy circles in the sunshine while they shared a bag of half-melted M&M's they'd bought at the gas station.

Behind the merry-go-round, swings with weathered seats

made out of recycled tires dangled from thick chains, and they clinked and squeaked gently in the breeze. You had to be careful holding those chains while you pumped your legs to go higher. Sometimes, the links would pinch your palms, leaving a painful little blood blister behind.

A new play structure had been put in, painted in bright primary colors. But the old brown metal horse on his huge, rusted spring was still there. She could almost picture Justin in the shadowy morning light, yelling, "Yeehaw," as he rocked wildly, almost touching the gravel as he lunged forward and back.

Winter picked up her pace, leaving the memories behind.

The past would never change. Right now, she had to focus on what today would bring.

NOAH HAD TAKEN an instant dislike to Officer Thomas Benton the day before, and twenty-four hours hadn't improved his opinion. The guy was petulant, sloppy, out of shape, and chock-full of bad attitude. In short, he was a dick.

And, Noah thought, Officer Benton was currently bristling like a pissed off Bantam rooster, his beer gut threatening to pop a uniform button or two.

"I still don't know why the FBI had to be called in on this," Benton bitched. "We can handle this just fine at the local level. We don't even have anything back yet from the medical examiner."

Winter, her blue eyes glittering, slapped down the pitifully thin manila folder they'd been given to review. "How exactly are you handling this? By doing the bare minimum required by procedure until you can toss this in your cold case file? Have you even started checking missing persons records?"

Gary Miller, the Harrisonburg police chief, cleared his throat firmly. The man looked to be in his late sixties, with wispy gray hair that barely covered a shiny scalp, and the weary face of a man past ready for retirement.

"Tom, we've talked about this. We welcome our friends at the FBI." Chief Miller gave them a wry smile. "We're on the same team here. Play nice." He shot Winter a narrow glance, including her in the rebuke.

She nodded back, stiffly, but stood down.

It was time to smooth some feathers.

"We appreciate y'all letting us in on this," Noah said, laying his drawl down extra thick and giving both men a warm smile. "Mind if we head on out to where y'all found the bones? Seems like a nice day for a walk in the woods."

He and Winter took their own vehicle and followed the chief and Officer Benton in their squad car. "Come on now, Winter," Noah said as soon as they pulled out onto the road. "Douchebag or not, you heard what Miller said. He's going to make sure Officer Benton plays nice, and in return, you're going to hide the fact that you think he's completely incompetent."

"He is." Winter's voice was flat. She stared out the window at the fields and farms whizzing by, mountains in the distance. "You saw that file. He barely asked the guy who found the bones any questions. He literally hasn't done a single thing in the two weeks since the bones were taken for analysis."

"We're here now," Noah said patiently. "We'll figure this out. We just need to keep things copacetic in the meantime."

Twenty minutes outside of Harrisonburg and about ten northwest of Linville, the squad car in front of them pulled onto the side of the road. The land was heavily wooded and sloped sharply upward, with trees lining the west side of the road. A recent trail had been hacked through the underbrush, and it was marked with a small evidence flag that wouldn't have been noticed immediately from the road.

They parked behind the squad car and got out.

"I hope you wore sturdy shoes," Chief Miller commented, eyeing the steep path. It was clear he'd climbed it more than once and wasn't a fan.

They'd come prepared. Noah had on a battered pair of hiking boots. Winter wore a broken-in pair of cross trainers that would do just fine. They started up the side of the mountain.

"Pretty strange that someone would happen across a burial site all the way out here, isn't it?" Noah asked.

Benton, wheezing and red-faced, shook his head. "Hunter and his kid. Going after deer a little out of season, but figured it'd be more important to let us know about the bones."

Noah glanced over at Winter. He knew she had to be angsty right about now, but her face was a cool, expressionless mask, looking steadily at the dense thicket around them. Her eyes seemed to take in everything at once.

The woman had guts. It was a big reason why he liked her so much.

"Did you charge the hunter?" Noah asked, curious.

"No," Chief Miller said, skirting a big fallen branch. "I know the guy. He's laid off. Probably took the deer to feed his family. Bit of a character." The last sounded like a warning. "Kind of a conspiracy theorist. Anti-government and whatnot. He only called us because I know him from school."

The path finally leveled off, and they moved deeper into the woods. It was shadowy and quiet, the trees looming high overhead and blocking most of the sun. Mostly oak with a few pines mixed in. Probably old-growth, judging by the size of some of the oak trees.

A few minutes later, they came to a small, natural clearing

and Winter seemed to quiver beside him like a hound dog going on point. The ground was more trampled here, and he didn't need to see the gaping hole in the ground with a tarp still set up over the top of it, or the few scattered evidence flags, to know they'd come to the right spot.

"So, walk me through it," Noah said to the chief. "How'd they find the bones?"

Beside him, Winter stood silent, studying the trees, the underbrush, the patches of blue sky that showed through the canopy. Everywhere except the spot where a hole beside a freshly turned mound of earth loomed deep and dark.

Was that where her brother's remains had been all these years?

Chief Miller hitched up his pants and headed in the direction of the evidence flags. Noah glanced again at Winter. She was staring at the ground—a mixture of dead leaves and recently disturbed soil—like she could look right through it. Like she could see things he couldn't.

Benton was watching her too, the man still huffing and puffing after the exertion of the walk. Noah gave Benton a long look until the man caught him watching and moved away, and then followed the older man.

"Brian Snyder's the hunter's name. He and his oldest kid, Liam, were out with a couple of their dogs. Said they shot a doe and were tracking her when Corker, their younger mutt, went off on a wild scent. Duke, the older dog, found the deer over there." He gestured in a different direction.

"Brian followed Duke while Liam went to see what Corker was after. He came back to his dad with a femur. Brian checked out the spot where they'd found it and saw a skull, obviously human, with a hole in the back of it. He got his boy and his dogs out of there, so they didn't mess things up any further, and came straight to us."

"He stop home first to hang that deer up?"

"Of course," Chief Miller chuckled, recognizing Noah as a fellow hunter. "No call to waste good meat. The bones had been there a while. They weren't going anyplace."

"We need a cadaver dog here."

"What?" the police chief swiveled around while Tom Benton gaped at Winter. They were the first words she'd spoken since they'd gotten out of the car back on the road, and her voice was loud, clear, and decisive.

Benton curled his lip. "For what? We don't even really know how old those bones are. Could be Indian, for all we know. The forensic people just estimated. You gonna try and dig up a whole Indian burial ground?"

There it was, Noah thought, looking at her speculatively. That weird, almost eerie look Winter sometimes got, where her eyes were focused but distant too. He'd seen it before, specifically when she had a "hunch" on their first case about where their serial rapist would strike next. The rest of the team had brushed her off. She'd gone off on her own, used herself as bait, and caught the guy.

"Can I ask why?" The chief was looking at Winter oddly too. "It does make sense to get the reports back from forensics first."

Shit. Noah didn't doubt she knew something, but these guys would have no reason to believe her.

WINTER WANTED to stick her foot in her mouth. The Harrisonburg guys were looking at her like she was crazy. Noah was watching her too, his usual lazy, relaxed expression intent.

She should have learned from her last experience, but no. Instead, she blurted things out and came off like an idiot, instead of thinking out reasons and justifications ahead of time.

But she could see all around them, even when she wasn't looking at the spots directly, that the forest floor was glowing red. Not all over. In small, scattered areas. She couldn't explain it. It had happened a couple of times before, though, and she trusted…whatever it was.

The jogger in Richmond. She caught him because she'd been able to see a specific spot on a map glow red, just like someone was aiming a laser pointer at it. Instinctively, she'd known where and when to be there to take him down.

Years before that, a rash of burglaries had happened on the SUNY campus she was attending. She'd identified the guy when she saw that the watch on his wrist glowed red. She'd known it was stolen, had put together that he was the thief. But she hadn't trusted her instincts, and a friend of hers had gotten hurt.

She trusted her instincts now. There were other bodies here. Other victims.

And they *were* victims. This wasn't a Native burial site.

It was a killer's dumping ground.

3

Winter opened her mouth to defend her pronouncement, but Noah spoke first.

"Couldn't hurt. We're here. Might as well rule some things out while we're waiting for the reports from the ME. Don't worry," he told Chief Miller with an easy grin. "We'll take care of the details, and if we find anything, credit goes to you."

"Bull*shit*." Benton spit the word at the chief. His face was red, his dark eyes sunk into his fleshy face like raisins in dough. "These FBI bastards are all the same. She says jump," he snapped his fingers, "and you say how high. Next thing you know, these assholes are going to have reporters crawling all over the place, blaming the local cops for not doing their jobs 'cuz you don't have the balls to—"

"Benton," he interrupted quietly. Ominously. Gary Miller had a long fuse, it seemed, and Benton had finally burned it down to nothing. "Shut the fuck up. I need to speak to you. Privately." He barely spared a glance for Winter and Noah. "Agents, take as much time as you need. Let me know what you decide to do."

He stalked toward the trail leading back to the car. Benton tossed them one final seething glare and stomped after his boss.

"That went well," Noah deadpanned. He walked to the open pit, and Winter followed him. She didn't care about Tommy Benton's hurt feelings or the fact that the chief was probably tearing a strip off his hide right now.

She only cared about bringing the other bodies here out of the darkness.

"So." Noah glanced at her. "Care to share?"

Winter's shoulders hunched defensively. "Not particularly."

Noah let it go.

"You're going to need to check in with Max, if you haven't yet. Give him an update about what's going on here. With both of us being noobs, he wants extra reassurance that things are going well."

Winter nodded, rubbing her arms against a chill. The hole in the ground in front of them had held a child. Not her little brother, she knew now, but someone else's. It was a cold resting place for a life snuffed out before it had even had a chance to flourish. Unmarked. Maybe unmourned.

She would mourn for him or her.

"It's not Justin."

"You're sure?"

Her head dipped once. "I am."

He didn't ask questions, and he didn't ask permission. Noah just turned and pulled her into his arms. Winter stiffened at the contact but couldn't help but relax into his warmth and the comfort he offered. He rubbed a big hand against her back in a firm, soothing rhythm, and she could feel the heat of his palm through her shirt. Something that had been wound tightly inside her loosened, and she blinked back tears that seemed to be haunting her lately. She was sure now the bones didn't belong to Justin, but she felt no relief. Just an overwhelming grief for the faceless boy they did belong to.

With her forehead pressed against his shoulder, she said quietly, "There are more here. We have to find them."

He didn't even question her or hesitate for an instant. "Then let's make a trip to the medical examiner's office in Roanoke. See if we can find some kind of rationale for the cadaver dog that everyone else will accept."

FLORENCE WADE DIDN'T LOOK like a forensic pathologist. She looked like someone's grandma. She was rounded and soft under her white lab coat, and her graying hair was cut short in a messy riot of curls. A sunny, cheerful smile creased her face as they introduced themselves, and her handshake was firm and brisk. Brown eyes that shone with sharp intelligence glittered behind her horn-rimmed bifocals.

"Thanks for coming, agents."

She led them to a small conference room and set a file on the table in front of them. Opening it, she pulled out pictures and spread them across the table.

"I'm still a week or so out on my formal report, but here's what I've got so far." She pointed to the first photo with one blunt, unpainted fingernail, then the next. Pictures of the site before excavation. A small skull was clearly visible, mostly uncovered. Leaves were piled haphazardly to one side, likely from the dog digging at the site.

"The bones aren't recent. We took samples of cortical bone and tooth enamel, and through carbon dating were able to estimate time of death that we believe to be accurate within one to two years, of approximately December 1987. The remains belong to a six-year-old male, born in 1981."

She pointed to another photo, this one taken in the lab. The bones were cleaned up and arranged in their anatomical position. Winter's knuckles whitened where her hands gripped the table. They were so small.

"The remains were complete, with no elements missing and no indication they'd been buried with another body." Florence indicated the hole in the skull. "Cause of death appears to be projectile force trauma. There were no other injuries present, recent or otherwise."

"So, it wasn't an accident?" Noah asked, studying the photos.

"I believe you're looking at a potential homicide," Florence agreed, her face darkening. "Caused by a small-caliber bullet to the back of the head at close range." Noah scowled too.

To Winter, it was comforting to see their professional faces slip. She'd been questioning her own impartiality since they'd arrived in Harrisonburg. But few people were left unaffected by the violent death of a defenseless child. The rage simmering inside her was shared.

"We're still studying some abnormalities in the bones," Florence continued. "Their size and development contrast somewhat with the age of the teeth given to us by the odontologist. The subject appears to have had a congenital condition that causes delayed growth and physical deformities, but it's not one that we can immediately identify."

Winter had noted that in the arranged skeleton in the lab, the boy's legs looked bowed, his spine crooked. She pointed to the picture. "This isn't normal, right?"

"Right. Neither is this." Florence traced the arrangement of the arm bones. "The arms are shorter than they should be at this developmental stage. Additionally, the jawbone is slightly misshapen, and some of these bones haven't fused like they should by the time a child turns six. We've done some genetic testing, but we're still working to pinpoint the condition that caused this. The subject was the size of a kid a year or two younger. I'm estimating forty inches tall, probably between thirty-five and forty pounds. I also believe he would have walked with a stoop that made him look even smaller, with his head jutted forward."

"How about identification?" Noah asked. "Any idea who this kid could be?"

"Not yet. No DNA match, no dental record match. No surgical implants that would tie to any medical records. European ancestry, we know, but not much more than that at this point."

They wrapped it up, taking the copies Florence had made for them. She promised to keep them updated on anything else they uncovered.

"Find out what happened to the poor boy," she ordered them as they left. "My grandson's the same age and has Down's Syndrome. Danny's the most amazing kid you'll ever meet. I'm pretty impartial after thirty-five years at this job, but in cases like this, with the youngest and most vulnerable of us? They still make me sick."

Noah and Winter didn't talk much on the two-hour drive back to Harrisonburg from Roanoke, occupying the first half of the trip with their own thoughts. Winter thought about calling Max on speakerphone for their check-in but chickened out. Instead, she sent him a detailed and bulleted email, giving him the rundown on what they'd been doing so far.

"You know he hates email," Noah warned her.

Winter winced. "I know. I'd just as soon risk it this time, though."

Max responded within minutes, telling her he'd expect a phone call the following day. He then gave her the name and number of a Search and Rescue guy he knew of in the area who had a trained cadaver-sniffing dog.

"You want to grab something to eat?" Noah asked as they passed the exit for Pleasant Valley.

Winter wasn't hungry, but it had been a long time since their early morning pancakes. Noah, she knew, was *always* hungry. "Sure. There's a place not far from the hotel. Reggianos. They used to make a good pizza."

The place was busy for a Thursday evening, and the buzz of the customers loud. The décor hadn't changed much since Winter had been there last. Red plaid curtains at the windows. Family sized booths covered with squeaky red vinyl cushions. They found an open one at the back of the restaurant, near the jukebox.

A harried waitress came by and took their order. A meatball grinder for Winter and an extra-large pizza with every meat known to man on it for Noah. The waitress brought them their beer quickly but warned them that the kitchen was running slow because of an unexpected soccer team having a celebration party in the back room. They were giving free breadsticks to everyone who was willing to wait for their main course.

Winter took a sip of her Rolling Rock and tried to shake her heavy mood. She wasn't going to last long in the FBI if she couldn't put a case aside mentally.

"We've known each other for a while now, Dalton, and there's something I've always wondered about you."

He glanced up from the dessert menu. "What's that, darlin'?"

"How the hell do you eat like you do and not keel over dead from a heart attack?"

He laughed, a low, rich sound that made the woman at the table next to them glance over and do an appreciative double take when she saw the source. "Genetics," he declared, oblivious to the female attention. "My grandpa was a cattle farmer and used to be able to eat steak four times a day."

"Used to? What happened to him?" Noah had never said much about his family.

"Grandpa? Oh, he's still alive." He grinned and patted his trim belly with both hands. "It's just he's built up his tolerance. Now, he eats six steaks a day."

Winter rolled her eyes. "You're such a dork."

Their breadsticks came, heavily scented with garlic and dripping in hot butter. Winter's stomach growled. Turned out she was hungry, after all.

"How are your grandparents doing?" Noah asked after demolishing a breadstick in two bites. He'd met them a couple of months before, staying with Winter during their week after graduation at the FBI Academy and before starting at the Raleigh field office.

"They're doing good." Winter smiled. "I'm not far from home these days, but Grandma is still trying to teach Grampa how to Skype, so we can stay in touch when they head to Florida after the holidays. He's trying, but he acts like it's a camera. He makes faces like he's posing for a still shot."

"If your grandma was single, I'd probably ask her to marry me. She makes a bitchin' meatloaf."

"You ever been married?"

He nodded, reaching for the last breadstick. She shot a hand out, beating him to it. He gave her such a wounded look, she tore it in half. "Mary Sue Lichtenberg," Noah answered, popping half of his half into his grinning mouth. "Straight out of school."

"Let me guess. She was the head cheerleader, and you were the star quarterback. High school sweethearts."

"Nope. She was captain of the debate team, and I was a running back." He smiled, laugh lines crinkling at the corners of his green eyes, and took a sip of his beer. "After graduation, she thought it'd be fun to play house and told me she was pregnant. But I shipped off to basic training two weeks after we tied the knot at the justice of the peace. She ended up getting bored at the little apartment I'd rented for us, moved back in with her parents, and filed for a divorce."

"No baby?"

"No baby. No hard feelings, either. We were too young to get married anyway. Neither of us knew what we wanted in life yet."

"Do you ever talk to her?"

Noah grinned before licking garlic butter from his thumb. "Sure do. I was Mary Sue's best man at her second wedding two years ago. She sends me a Christmas card every year. Mary Sue and her wife, Jacinda, just adopted two baby boys from Nigeria last summer. They made me the godfather."

Their food finally arrived after Winter and Noah had finished a second round of beer and another basket of bread-sticks. The restaurant had thinned out a little while Noah kept her laughing and distracted, and Winter started to relax for the first time in what felt like weeks.

"So, this thing you do. Is it like a vision? Or hunches?"

She froze, instantly on alert. "What do you mean?"

Noah, as casually as if they'd been discussing the weather, took another bite of his pizza and chewed thoughtfully. "I imagine it's like a cop's hunch," he finally said. "But maybe stronger? I get the itch, so I can relate to that. That feeling that either tells you to watch your back or makes you sit up and take notice when you see something that looks random. Next thing you know, you've got a guy going for a gun, or see a pattern coming out of haphazard data points. Is what you do anything like that?"

Her appetite was gone, and she pushed the plate with her half-finished sub away. "Why do I feel like you've been lulling me into complacency for the last hour?"

Noah gave her an unreadable look. "We're on the same

team, you know. Right now, we're even partners. Partners watch out for each other. Share information."

"I don't know what you want me to say." Uncomfortable, she glanced around the restaurant. Anything to keep from getting pulled into that penetrating stare, covered by a veneer of affability. Noah gave the impression of an easygoing, down-home, good ol' boy, but he was gently relentless.

"The truth?"

"Fine." She could give him something. Not the whole story, but something. He deserved that much. She met his eyes, calm and green, radiating nothing but friendly concern and curiosity.

"At the crime scene, the burial site glowed red. Things do that for me sometimes, glow red when they're connected with a violent crime or the person who commits them." She scanned his face, trying to determine if he was either about to laugh or call the loony bin. When he only nodded for her to go on, she reluctantly continued, "When we were in the woods, I saw the red radiating around that hole. Then I looked around, and there were other areas glowing. I could take you back out there right now, dig up any one of those areas, and I'd bet my life there are more bodies beneath."

She held her breath, waiting for the inevitable look he'd give her. It didn't matter which one: fear, concern, disbelief, pity, scorn. They were all devastating.

Instead, he leaned back in his chair and crossed his arms, whistling softly. His look was one of admiration, and maybe a little envy. It knocked her off-balance a little.

"Hell, that's a handy knack to have in our line of work." His Texan drawl had grown thicker. "Can you teach me how to do it?"

4

The next morning, the day dawned warm and sunny again. The newscaster promised rain in the forecast and an incoming cold front, but you wouldn't know it from the sky's gorgeous shade of blue.

Winter and Noah met again for a morning run. It was easier this time, jogging past all the familiar places from her childhood. The new accord she'd found with Noah probably helped. He hadn't treated her like a freak after her confession over dinner the night before. Instead, he seemed to believe her without reservation. She was lucky to have him as a friend.

Her stomach still tightened with a vague sense of dread when they passed by Hemlock Street. Her old house was down at the end of a cul-de-sac, and she refused to even look its way. She never wanted to see the old Victorian home again.

They had breakfast at the same café they had the morning before—a giant stack of pancakes and a double side of bacon for Noah while Winter picked at an egg-white omelet. While they finished their coffee, she'd called the number for the Search and Rescue contact Max had provided for her, Jeff Dean.

He lived in Ruckersville, about an hour away, on the other side of the Shenandoah National Park. He had a day job as a contractor, only doing SAR part-time, and would be on a work site until late that afternoon. He promised to bring Caesar, his cadaver-sniffing dog, out the following morning.

"Hopefully the rain will hold off," Noah said, signaling to the waitress for their check.

"I thought about that too." Winter dug around in her bag for the expense card they'd been given. "I'm thinking we should talk to the hunter who discovered the bones today."

He nodded. "Makes sense. I got his number. I'll call him." Noah grinned. "The chief says the hunter's a little bit of a conspiracy nut, and I think your FBI vibe might scare him off."

"I don't care if he wears a literal tinfoil hat as long as he agrees to talk to us." She went to the counter to pay their bill while Noah made the call.

His mega-watt smile was back in full force when she met him by the front door. "We're all set," he said with a wink. "He was a little reluctant to have us out at his place, but I talked him around."

Winter pushed open the door. "Then let's go."

A half-hour later, Winter was ready to take back her tinfoil hat comment. The sky had clouded up pretty suddenly on their way out to Brian's place, out past Linville. The wind picked up, and the trees were whipping around when they reached the end of the unmarked drive Noah had been given directions to.

Noah slowed the FBI sedan to navigate a pothole at the end of the two-track, and Winter glancing up at the trees on either side. At least ten "No Trespassing" signs were tacked up, facing the road. A tattered yellow "Don't Tread on Me" flag fluttered in the breeze, its fanged snake coiled and hissing, mounted to a rusty flagpole just below the Stars and Stripes. Above them, wired to an overhanging tree branch, was a compact black surveillance camera pointing at the end of the drive. A small red eye glowed beside the lens. They were being monitored.

The drive was long and bumpy, probably a quarter mile through a tunnel of trees. Abruptly, it opened into a small clearing.

"Nice piece of land he's got out here." Noah slowed the car so they could look around. "I've seen compounds like this back in Texas. Mostly while busting meth labs, but a lot of the time they belong to people who just like to stay off-grid."

A couple of scraggly chickens pecked in the dirt near a floppy brown hunting dog, who snoozed in a sparse patch of grass. A faded red Ford pickup, dirty and missing a license plate, sat in front of a small, leaning garage, hood up, next to a slightly newer blue Chevy. Two trailers, circa 1960, were arranged near each other, backed up against the edge of the woods. They were painted an ugly olive green, but the trim looked fresh and white, and there were flower boxes mounted under the windows with cheerful red Gerbera daisies poking their heads out. They were still pretty and would be until the first frost.

The screen door to one trailer screeched open, and kids started piling out.

"Dad! FIBs are here!" A cute little red-haired girl, about seven, with a gap-toothed grin, skidded to a stop in front of Noah, kicking up a small cloud of dust. "Can I see your gun?"

Behind her, three more children descended on them, ranging between the ages of about four and nine. They all had hair in varying shades of red, but one of the boys looked enough like the gap-toothed girl to be her twin. While Noah laughingly fended them off, Winter noted that they were all barefoot, with dusty feet, but their clothes were clean, hair brushed, and they looked happy and well-fed.

The door squealed again, and a tall, auburn-haired man with sharp blue eyes stepped out onto the porch. He was handsome and looked fit, probably mid-forties, wearing a green t-shirt tucked neatly into faded blue jeans. Behind him was a fifth child, who looked about eleven. Brian Snyder and his son, Liam. Winter wondered where Mrs. Snyder was.

"Morning," he said. Not suspiciously, but not overly friendly either. "Go play, guys." The kids scattered as he came down the steps, heading for a tire suspended from a big oak tree a distance away.

"Mornin'," Noah said, his drawl slow and easy. "Thanks for agreeing to meet with us."

They shook hands and introduced themselves, Liam giving Winter a shy smile. Brian invited them to a picnic table nearby. In the distance, a low rumble of thunder underscored the screams and laughter of the playing kids. Winter and Noah sat down on one side of the table with Brian on the other, Liam scooted up close to him.

"Guess we'd better make it quick." Brian's tone was pointed. "You all want to know about the day we found the bones." He put a protective arm around his son's shoulders.

"The police chief in Harrisonburg gave us your account," Winter began, "but we'd like to hear your story from you directly, please."

Brian's entire body seemed stiff. "Let's get one thing out of the way first. I was hunting deer out of season. The chief talked to me about it, but I want your assurance that you're not going to call the game warden on me as soon as you leave here. Damned bloodsuckers will fine me for feeding my family, and that's just one more thing I can't deal with right now."

"No. We can see that you have quite a few mouths to feed." Noah kept his tone friendly. "Not a lot of jobs in this area. The kids probably appreciate that venison."

Winter nodded. "We're not interested in your hunting habits. We just want to know what happened to that little boy you found."

Brian relaxed a little, and taking the cue from his father, Liam did too.

"I appreciate that." He gave them a wry smile. "I've been out of a job for months now. My wife...she passed away a year ago. I'm still trying to pay off all the medical bills. Used to be a long-haul trucker, but I can't leave the kids alone now."

"That's a hard place to be," Winter agreed, feeling true sympathy for him. "Your kids look healthy and happy. From what I can tell, you're doing a wonderful job."

"'Preciate you saying so." Looking embarrassed, he looked down at his eldest son. "Go ahead, Liam. Tell the agents what you found."

Blushing at being the center of attention, the boy repeated what they already knew. They'd been hunting. Shot a doe. The animal went one way just as one of their dogs went the other, so Liam chased the dog while his dad went after the injured deer.

His voice got more excited sounding, and he wriggled a little in his seat. This was obviously the juicy part of the story, in his opinion.

"Corker was digging at something when I found him. I thought it was just an old dead deer carcass or something, and I didn't want him to roll in it and get all stinky. He does that sometimes. I pulled him away. He had a bone in his mouth and went running off again. That's when I saw the skull, kind of half-buried still. It looked like a person's, not an animal's. So, I chased down Corker and grabbed the bone out of his mouth and took it to my dad."

He looked up at his father, who tousled his hair affectionately.

"That's fine, son. You can go on, now."

Liam slid off the bench seat and ran off, probably to brag to his siblings about telling his story to the FIBs.

"You've got a good kid there." Noah nodded in the direction Liam had gone. "Was he scared at all when you guys called the police?"

"No. He's a boy. He just thought the whole thing was cool. Gave him something to talk about at school, impress his friends." His face hardened. "But I keep thinking about it. Obviously, I didn't tell my son, but that kid that was buried there was shot in the head. Some sonovabitch killed that little kid and left it there in a shallow grave."

"How long have you lived in the area?" Winter asked.

"I was born here."

"You don't remember any talk when you were young? About a missing boy?"

Thunder rumbled again, closer.

Brian hesitated, glancing around at his children. "I could tell the bones were old, and I've been trying to think back on that. There was some talk, but not about a missing kid. There was a cult that operated around here back then. The Moon People, or some shit like that."

Noah leaned forward. "Cult? What kind?"

"Nobody really knew. And it was mostly schoolkids doing the talking," Brian cautioned. "Kind of an urban legend thing."

"That's all right. Tell us what you remember." Winter didn't remember hearing anything about a cult, but she was younger than Brian, and Linville was a town away.

He shrugged, and a couple of fat raindrops spattered the table in front of them. They all ignored the wet. "Just that a bunch of weird hippie people had a place holed up in the woods around here. No one knew where, but sometimes you'd see one or two of them in town. They wore homespun dresses and stuff, and the women had long hair and the men beards. Not like the Amish, but more like Sixties throwbacks."

The rain picked up a little, and there was a quick flash of lightning. Thunder boomed, and the kids ran for the house as a pack, yelling like banshees. A frenzied bark came from inside one of the trailers. Probably the Snyder's other dog. The one that had been snoozing hopped up and loped for the house.

Brian stood up too. "They were probably pretty harmless," he added, "but that didn't stop people from making up stories."

Noah rose to his feet. "Any idea where they were located?"

"Used to be a farm, a little north of where we found the bones. The farmhouse and buildings are still there. I heard someone bought it a few years ago, raising cattle now."

The sky opened up, dumping buckets. Winter's hair almost instantly plastered flat to her head. "We'll let you get inside," she yelled over the drumming rain and shook Brian's hand.

"Thanks for talking with us," Noah shouted, doing the same.

Brian nodded, blinking against the rain. "Find the sonovabitch. Doesn't matter if it *was* years ago. He killed a kid, and that shouldn't go unpunished." He headed to the house at a jog, already soaked.

Back in the car, Winter cranked on the air, trying to defog the windows. They sat in the driveway, which had gone from a dusty road to a sloppy, muddy mess in moments.

"What do you think about Snyder?" Noah had pulled some paper towels from the glovebox and was wiping his face. He handed a couple of dry ones to Winter so she could do the same.

"If you'd have asked me when we got here, I would have doubted we were going to get any useful information out of him. But he seems credible. And the cult thing is interesting."

Noah put the car in gear and made a U-turn, hunkering down to see through the hole that had been cleared at the bottom of the windshield. "Seems like Snyder's got a grudge against the game and fishing guys and probably our government because of our shitty healthcare system. In his position, I don't blame him. But he didn't seem like the tinfoil hat type. Just a guy that likes his privacy and is doing his best with a bad hand of cards."

"Look out for that rut." Winter reached over and jerked the wheel right. The last thing they needed was to get bogged down in the mud. "Why do men always assume they should drive? It's chauvinistic."

Noah chuckled. "It's a testosterone thing, probably, but I prefer to think of it as chivalry, darlin'." The car shuddered over a set of washboard bumps, nearly bottoming out. "But you can have a turn at the wheel next time," he added.

When they made it back to the road, Noah breathed an audible sigh of relief.

"Anyway," he went on. "The cult theory seems a little farfetched to me. A bunch of hippies running around killing people? Kids? And no one ever noticed? What happened to the cult? Who was in charge? Plus, hippies are supposed to be peace-loving."

"We don't have much else to go on at this juncture," Winter pointed out. "I think we should look into it."

"Sure." Noah tapped his thumbs on the wheel. "No stone unturned and all that. But I need food first. Where do you want to eat this time?"

Winter groaned. "We're going to have to start packing a cooler to bring with us. I don't know if the FBI expense card limit is big enough to support your appetite."

5

Noah took a bite out of his burger, watching Winter. She was staring across the restaurant, as pale as if she'd seen a ghost.

He glanced around. A few families were settled in nearby booths, most with kids making messes out of their French fries or begging for quarters to feed the vintage Pac-Man game at the back of the dining area. He didn't see anything unusual.

"What is it?"

She jumped, startled at the sound of his voice. She blushed a little and dragged a fry through some ketchup. "Just thought I saw someone I knew."

"And that's what's got you looking spooked?"

"I'm not spooked." To prove it, she took a big bite of her cheeseburger. He laughed when cheese dripped down her chin and handed her a napkin.

"Harrisonburg isn't a one-horse town, but it's not exactly a metropolis, either. Makes sense you might run into someone you know. Anyone in particular you're worried about bumping into?"

She shook her head and stuffed another fry in her mouth so she didn't have to answer him, he assumed. He glanced around again. The woman behind the counter was different from the one who had been there when they came in. Shift change, maybe. This woman was staring at Winter, if he wasn't mistaken.

She was tall and slim, a dishwater blonde, about Winter's age. And she looked angry.

"Who's that at the register?"

Winter hunched her shoulders in a shrug, her full attention on her food. "I used to go to school with her."

"Why's she look like she wants to come over here and punch you in the nose? You were in, what, middle school when you left?"

"Yeah. Your guess is as good as mine."

Noah let it go, and they finished their meal. Winter took out her purse, but he held up a hand. "Let me get it this time." He winked. "I've got an expense card too."

He took their check up to the counter. "Evenin'."

The woman at the register just sniffed. She punched in the keys with quick, jabbing motions, studiously ignoring him. Hot dislike practically radiated off her in waves.

"Burgers here are good," he tried again. "Wish we had a restaurant like this back home."

She snatched the card out of his hand and swiped it through. Without looking at him, she slapped the card and the slip down on the counter with a pen.

"Thanks," he said wryly, writing in a decent tip and scrawling his name at the bottom. He made his way back to their table. Winter had been watching the one-sided exchange, and her cheeks were flushed.

"She didn't have to be rude to you."

"I've met worse. You ready?"

They'd made it out to the sidewalk when he heard the

door ding behind them. Glancing back, he groaned. The blonde was puffed up and stalking toward them, looking ready for a fight. Casually, he edged between the two women.

"You steal her lunch money or something?" He kept his voice low and directed at Winter.

"No," Winter answered, equally low. "We were best friends."

Women, he thought, giving the blonde a disarming smile. "Did we forget something?"

She ignored him. "I knew it was you," she spat at Winter.

"Nice to see you too, Sam." Winter's voice was even, but her fists were clenched, and her eyes glittered.

"Don't give me that innocent bullshit, *Agent* Black." She tried to dodge around Noah, but he kept himself firmly in the way.

"*Special* Agent, actually. I'm sorry, ma'am, but that's a federal agent you're trying to claw at. Maybe I can help you with something?"

Passersby were starting to stare. He didn't care so much about that, but Sam might when she realized how she was acting with a couple of customers out in the street in front of where she worked.

"Yeah, you can." She glared up at him, her brown eyes snapping fire. "You two can stop stomping your big federal agent boots all over my husband!"

"And who might that be?"

She scoffed, rearing back as if she'd been slapped. "As if you don't know!"

Winter nudged Noah out of the way. "You married Tommy Benton?" The surprise on her face was almost comical.

"Don't act like you didn't know. Hell, you probably used your woo-woo powers or something to figure it out." She wiggled her fingers around her ears and gave Winter a deri-

sive look. Winter stiffened, her almost imperceptible amusement at finding out Sam was Benton's wife melting away.
"Look at you. Wearing a suit, carrying a gun. Acting like
you're big shit. I can tell by looking at you, you're still a
fucking freak."

"Listen," Noah tried again. "We're here to do a job. No one
is out to stomp on your husband or anyone else. Keep your
insults to yourself. As soon as we're done here, we'll
move on."

"Don't patronize me. She's holding some childhood
grudge, and I'd bet a million dollars she's come back here for
revenge." Sam drilled her finger in Winter's direction. "If you
make my husband lose his job, so help me I'll—"

"You're going to want to stop right there." Noah's voice
hardened. Enough was enough. This woman was getting on
his nerves. "You're about to threaten an FBI agent, and that's
something you most definitely don't want to do. Go back to
work. Is that your boss?"

Sam wheeled around. Sure enough, an older woman was
standing in the doorway, wearing a flour-dusted apron, her
hands on her hips. By the look on her face, Sam was in for it.
"This isn't over," Sam hissed. She gave Winter another dirty
look and retreated.

"It was over a long time ago." Winter's voice was quiet.
Almost sad.

THEY WALKED BACK to the car in silence. Seeing Sam as an
adult was disorienting. She'd always been a tomboy, star
pitcher for her Little League team, with bruised and
scratched knees and her hair in a lopsided French braid.
She'd grown up tall and pretty, but her eyes had been dark
with dissatisfaction.

And anger.

"Woo-woo powers?" Noah broke the silence with a snort.

Winter didn't take the bait. She held her hand out for the car keys instead.

Noah handed them over, and she climbed into the driver's seat, adjusting it for her shorter legs. Noah got in next to her, the car dipping a little with his weight. He buckled his seatbelt and leaned back comfortably.

"So, you didn't steal her lunch money? Beat her up by the flagpole after school?"

"No."

Winter pulled out into traffic and headed for the hotel.

"Try and steal her boyfriend?"

He wasn't going to let it go, she knew.

"We'd been friends since preschool. I spent the night at her house the night my..." She cleared her throat. "*That* night. We fought over Tommy Benton, ironically. I told her I thought he liked me, and apparently, she'd been nursing a secret crush. Stupid kid's stuff. Our friendship could have survived that, but after I came out of the hospital, moved into a rental house with my grandparents, I went back to school. She acted supportive and sympathetic at first, but I made the mistake of confiding in her."

"Confiding what?"

The knuckles on her hands were growing white. "The weird brain stuff that was happening to me."

She felt his surprise but didn't look his way. "Things were glowing red for you, even back then?"

"No." Winter sighed, feeling beatdown and not caring that she was giving more secrets away. What did it matter, anyway? "I came out of the coma with, like, heightened senses. Everything seemed to bombard me. I'd walk into a room and notice *everything*. Scents, sounds, details. I could recall them later too. I'd be able to tell you what each student in a class was wearing, who was hiding tater tots in their desk, that Cindy Slusher had gotten new contacts, how many pimples Mark Wiessburg had on the back of his neck, the name of the song Becky Smith was tapping out with her pencil on her desk, who was cheating on their math test, and that the science teacher, Mr. Williams, had started smoking again. He had a pack of Camels in his desk, and I could smell them."

"I can't even remember who my teachers were in college, much less middle school. And you can remember all these details even now," Noah said, his voice a picture of wonder.

"I can."

"The detail thing. Is this still something you can do?"

"Yeah. I can filter things out better, but back then…it was like I was walking around in a barrage every day. I constantly felt like my head was about to explode, and I had to tell someone. My grandparents had packed up their lives and moved to Harrisonburg so I could stay in the same school, in familiar surroundings. They were taking everything else so hard, I couldn't share with them. I had a shrink, but he was always watching me like some kind of science experiment, him and the doctors, and I didn't trust any of them. Aiden…" She risked a quick glance over at him but he was studiously looking out the front window. "Maybe I would have told him, but I didn't know him well enough yet."

"Aiden? As in Aiden Parrish? Like, Aiden Parrish, SSA of the Behavioral Analysis Unit in Richmond?"

"Back then, he was just Special Agent Parrish, but yeah." She shot Noah a sidelong look. He was staring back at her blankly. She couldn't blame him. She'd dropped a lot of info on him all at once. "Parrish was working The Preacher case. He kept in touch, even after the investigation turned into a dead end."

"That explains some things."

Winter let the cryptic remark slide. "I told Sam. When you're a teenage girl, you figure you can trust your best friend with anything. Unfortunately, she told Tommy Benton, figuring rightly that his crush on me would pass quickly on finding out that I was a freak. That would have been okay, but word went around the school fast from there."

"So, your grandparents pulled you out of school and moved you to Raleigh," he finished for her.

"That's about it."

It wasn't, not really. There had been more. Kids following her around, calling her names. Knocking the lunch tray out of her hands in the cafeteria. Once, a couple of girls pushing her around in the bathroom. She'd lost her balance and hit the painted cinderblock wall. Her cheekbone had been bruised and swollen, and that's when she finally had to tell Grandma and Grampa what was going on.

Noah, thankfully, left it at that.

"You want to come over to my place and watch TV?" he asked as they pulled into the hotel parking lot. "I'd say we've earned some R&R. I popped over to the convenience store across the street last night and stocked my mini-fridge with some Rolling Rock."

Honestly, she just wanted to crawl under the covers in her bed and sleep until she forgot all about the confrontation with Sam outside the restaurant. But there was no haven in her hotel room right now. Not with the picture of Justin still tucked between the mattress and box spring.

"Yeah, TV sounds good. No *Real Housewives*, though."

To her amusement, his cheeks reddened. Noah was usually perfectly collected, affable, and laidback in any situation. Right now, he looked downright flustered. "What are you talking about?"

"Oh, Dalton," she sighed, shaking her head. "Thin walls,

and I sleep light. Does the rest of the team know about your shameful addiction?"

"No. And if they found out, I'll swear I was watching porn." His green eyes narrowed dangerously. "I'll not only deny *Real Housewives* to my dying breath...I'll know who told them."

"You've been prying secrets out of me," she pointed out as they climbed the metal stairs. "It's only fair that I get some goods on you too."

He grumbled, unlocking his door. Winter glanced over at her room. The curtains were open, the room dark within. Housekeeping had likely been through. She wondered if there were any white envelopes on the floor, waiting for her.

"I'll be over in a sec," she told Noah. "Going to change. Into *sweatpants*." She stressed the last word, forestalling any flirtatious comments.

"Not a bad idea."

She switched on the lamp as soon as she entered, opened her senses. Bed made. No envelope. Nothing felt out of the ordinary. She closed the curtains. Lifting the coverlet, she ran her fingers under the mattress to the place she'd stashed Justin's picture. It was still there. She didn't feel the need to pull it out and look at it again.

But as she stood up, a faint reddish glow caught her eye. The painting on the wall above the TV, a badly done fall scene of the Smoky Mountains, had a faint but definite red cast to it. She lifted it carefully from the wall, conscious of the thin walls she'd mentioned earlier to Noah.

There. A small camera mounted inside of a hollowed out piece of drywall. She shuddered. It pointed directly at her bed. She deliberately raised her middle finger, so anyone watching the feed would be sure to see, and mouthed the words, *Fuck you.*

Staring at its black eye, she didn't have to guess to know

who would be watching her room. The question was, how had he gotten in? Had the camera been there last night? If so, why hadn't she seen the red glow? Or was it some other perv entirely?

So many questions and not a single damn answer to be found.

Disgusted, she pulled the camera out, opened the back, and removed the battery. Tucking both the camera and the battery beneath the mattress, she gave the room another once-over, knowing she wouldn't find anything.

Unsettled now, she pulled a loose pair of sweatpants and a black t-shirt out of her bag and headed for the bathroom to change. She had a cold beer, some mindless television, and a good friend waiting for her in the room next door.

Unfortunately, Winter still didn't feel like she could trust Noah with this.

She'd always known with a deep, gut-level certainty that this had always been something she would have to finish alone. If The Preacher was going to come after her, so be it. It felt inevitable that he would.

6

Winter and Noah had no problem finding the start to the trail the following morning. A pickup truck, a Harrisonburg police SUV, and a few other county and state vehicles lined the road. It was still raining, the warm weather streak having broken, and the woods were misty-looking in the dim morning light.

"This'll be fun," Noah muttered as they got out of the car.

Winter eyed the steep trail, now a slippery slope of mud and wet leaves. "You bet."

Nerves were a tight ball in her stomach as they made the climb. Twice, she slipped and would have gone down on her face in the sloppy path, but Noah grabbed her by the back of the raincoat both times, saving her the indignity.

"You climb like a goat."

"Naturally athletic," he bragged. Seconds later, he lost his footing and slid backward a few feet. "At least I'm still upright." He grinned, gripping a slim sapling for balance.

Breathless, she finally reached the top. In the clearing ahead was a group of people, and a man with what looked like a bear on a leash. The knot in her belly tightened. If there was nothing else to be found here, she was going to look like an idiot in front of a decent-sized audience. But there were still red areas glowing around the clearing. Enough that Winter had to wonder if they'd be excavating remains for the next several months.

"Mornin'." Chief Miller had his coat collar turned up against the light rain, a clear rain cap cover over his hat. "Let me introduce you to the team."

He headed first to a woman who was directing the set-up of an awning and a table of tools. "This is Marilyn Fosner. She's our forensic archaeologist, on loan with a few of her team members to us from Roanoke."

Marilyn nodded briskly. The woman was probably in her mid-thirties, with dark skin and beautiful green eyes. She was also busy handing out orders to what looked like a ragtag bunch of interns. They were chattering and too excited about being out in the woods during a downpour looking for dead bodies to be anything but newbies.

"Robert, Jessica, Louis, Eric, and Pete. Student interns. Don't bother trying to remember their names and tell them apart." She narrowed her eyes at the grinning bunch, who apparently knew that Marilyn's bark was worse than her bite. "I'm about to send them all home to their mommas if they don't get their shit together." She waved her hand toward another group. "William Penn, Rebecca Mayfield, and Derek White, CSI."

The Crime Scene Investigation team nodded and gave them curious looks over their steaming cups of coffee. Winter smiled back but wondered if Gary Miller had told them about the freakish FBI agent who insisted on a detection dog for no apparent reason and was prepared to throw a fit if she didn't get one. She and Noah had decided to justify it to Max by pointing out that the victim had a gunshot wound to the back of the head.

Bringing in a cadaver sniffer would rule out more victims.

"And this is Jeff Dean, and the star of this particular show, Caesar. Droolius Caesar."

Jeff was a bookish-looking guy in his mid-forties and looked more suited to be an accountant than a search and rescue guy or a contractor. He had an angular face, glasses perched on the edge of a long nose, and a baseball cap to keep the rain off.

"Nice to meet you both, Agent Black, Agent Dalton." His handshake was firm, his fingers cold, and his smile friendly. "Droolius," he said to the dog, a massive Saint Bernard, "introduce yourself."

The dog plopped his butt down on the ground and grinned up at them, lifting one massive paw, and barked once. True to his name, a string of slobber hung rakishly from the corner of his mouth.

"You don't actually have to shake with him," Jeff warned. "He's pretty filthy right now and bound to get worse here pretty soon."

Noah dropped to his haunches in front of the dog anyway and held out a hand. "Pleasure to meet you, Droolius," he said, shaking the dog's paw while his tail wagged wildly. "Winter? You going to be rude and leave this guy hanging?" He wiggled his muddy hand at her before wiping it on his pant leg.

"Thanks, Noah, for pointing out my oversight." Chief Miller snorted as Winter gingerly took the dog's paw between two fingers and shook it once. He was dirty, but he was cute.

"To be honest, I was expecting a bloodhound, not a Beethoven." Noah gave the dog a scratch behind the ears that had him wiggling with joy. Well-trained, though, the leashed dog didn't get up from his sitting position.

Jeff laughed. "I don't blame you. I have mostly Labradors that I train in SAR. Droolius here was supposed to be a family dog, but he's smart and showed early aptitude, so I trained him with the rest of my SAR dogs. He's got an incredible success rate."

"Will he have a tough time with the weather?" Winter asked. "Or the fact that the remains he's looking for might be as much as thirty years old?"

"Nah. We train in all kinds of conditions. Sometimes a rotting log will throw him, but not often. And he's gotten human and animal remains mixed up a couple of times. But I once saw this dog alert in a basement where a body had been buried, dug up, and removed years before. He's good."

"Well, I was waiting on Benton, but he's late," Chief Miller said with a slight frown. "Might as well let us see what your dog can do."

"If there's anything to be found," Jeff replied with a proud look at the huge canine, "Droolius will find it."

He knelt in front of the dog. "You ready, boy? Ready to do some work?" The dog wagged his tail in what looked like doggy joy, bouncing from foot to foot. As soon as Jeff put a hand on his leash, the dog stilled.

Winter could almost sense the dog saying, *Ready.*

Jeff unsnapped the leash and ordered, "Find." The rest of the group had gathered around, and they all watched as the dog immediately put his nose to the ground.

Winter was studying the dog intently, holding her breath, and jolted as Noah put a hand on her shoulder. Her tension eased, just a bit. Noah knew she was nervous, and his silent support helped.

The dog started working in concentric circles. Small, at first, but then broadening. It was incredible to see an animal work so methodically. He came closer to the nearest red area, and she held her breath again. A second later, the dog stilled and lifted a paw, directly in the center of the spot.

"He's got something," Jeff said, going to the dog and praising him. The woman with the CSI team planted a marker while the interns chattered excitedly in quiet voices.

"Ready to go again, boy? Work?" Droolius barked once, as if in answer, and Jeff said, "Find."

The dog was off again, immediately. Within minutes, he alerted at another site. Winter's breathing came a little easier. He was finding them.

Twenty minutes later, he'd alerted at eight different sites. Eight small flags fluttered in the fitful, rainy breeze.

The interns had gone from exuberant to quiet as the implication began to sink in.

Chief Miller's face was bleak, and for a moment, there was no sound in the clearing except for the panting of the dog. Jeff, looking a little shell-shocked himself, even though he ran SAR dogs for a living, busied himself with getting Droolius a dish of water and a rawhide chew toy.

"Guess it's our turn to perform," Marilyn announced. Her strident voice sounded shaken. "CSI, go ahead and get your pictures first, and we'll be ready to go in next." She collected herself and started barking orders to her young team members again.

Chief Miller looked over at Winter, a wealth of consideration in his gaze. "How'd you know?"

"A hunch," she replied, her throat tight.

TOM BENTON SHOWED up after the CSI team had finished and the forensic excavator had begun on the first site. His eyes were bloodshot and his cheeks scruffy. Judging by the light brown mud stains on his uniform pant legs, he'd run into a spot of bad luck on his way up the trail.

He looked hungover, but the hate in his eyes was vibrant when he saw Noah and Winter in the clearing. They burned even hotter when he took in the scene around them, and the obvious evidence that more burial sites had been located.

He didn't get a chance to spill any venom, though. Chief Miller immediately cornered him and led him away from the scene. Benton's shoulders hunched, and he seemed to get smaller with every word his boss said to him.

"Wouldn't want to be in his shoes right now," Noah muttered. "The guy's on a fast track to a pink slip."

"I'm surprised the chief hasn't canned him already." Winter winced when the chief shoved a finger in Benton's face. The guy was an asshole, but the verbal beating he was getting was painful to watch. "On second thought, maybe he's doing it right now."

They turned back to watch Marilyn work. She'd marked off the first site in a grid pattern and was already two hours into her painstaking excavation. Her team was working like a well-oiled machine now, taking turns sifting dirt and debris removed from the burial site, searching for evidence, labeling anything they found, and generally making sure Marilyn could focus on her work.

"She's good. She'll have something for us soon." Chief Miller made the comment from behind them. There was no sign of Benton. Noah raised an eyebrow in silent question. "He had the flu," Miller said, sounding weary to the bone. "I sent him home."

"Guys," Marilyn called out, wiping the back of her arm over her forehead. "I've got something here."

They gathered close, careful not to get within a close radius of her work but positioned so they could see. White bone was visible, poking out of the dirt. Winter could make out an eyehole, still mostly buried. Marilyn carefully revealed more of the skull, humming thoughtfully in her throat.

"Did the handler say that dog sometimes got animal bones mixed up with human ones?"

Winter's tension came rolling back. The ground itself still looked red, almost pulsing with it, but the skull that Marilyn was uncovering wasn't human. What if, after all this, the bones that the dog had alerted to weren't human at all?

The chief evidently had the same thought. He glanced up at her, sympathy and maybe embarrassment in his eyes. He couldn't hold her gaze, though, and quickly looked back down at the site.

"Looks like a calf," Marilyn muttered, still absorbed in the removal.

"Hold on," Noah said, bending over at the waist for a closer look. "Is that a hole?"

"Hold your horses, cowboy." Marilyn painstakingly finished releasing the skull from the dirt and held it up in her gloved hands. At the back of the skull was a ragged-looking opening. "Yeah, that's probably a gunshot. Cause of death, if it matters."

"Keep digging," Noah said firmly. "The body had a similar-sized gunshot wound in the back of the skull." He looked at Chief Miller. "The killer could have used the same gun. Could be a bullet casing in the ground. We should keep going and check the other sites too. Just because we've got a baby cow here doesn't mean there couldn't be human bones anywhere else."

Winter wanted to agree with him. Back him up. He was obviously trying to lend her some legitimacy after this... misstep, and she was grateful to him. But she couldn't say anything. The words were stuck in her throat. She felt like a complete and total idiot.

Her great and wonderful talent had led her to animal bones. She knew the killer was responsible for the gunshot that had ended the life of the calf, the same as the six-year-old boy just a few feet away. But what would be in the next spot? A raccoon? How long would Noah be able to get them to humor her?

After a long moment, Chief Miller nodded. "You okay with keeping this up?" he asked Marilyn.

"Hell, it's fine," she shrugged, not looking up from her work. "I'm getting paid no matter what I uncover. Bones are bones."

CSI, though, was already packing up. One of the men grinned a little maliciously. "You don't need us anymore, right, Miller? You got this murder investigation under control?"

"Yeah, thanks, Robert. We're good here." The chief's color was high, his mouth pulled into a frown.

Winter felt worse. This felt like failure, and it wasn't just reflecting on her.

"You guys might as well head out too," Chief Miller said pointedly. "If your hunch turns up anything else, I'll be sure to let you know."

"We'll do that," Noah replied calmly. "You've got my number. We've got a few more leads to chase down."

Noah waited until they were out of earshot to elbow Winter. Hard.

"Stop it. Quit beating yourself up."

She threw an elbow right back, and he grunted. She shook her head, still unable to believe it. "They were fucking cow bones."

"That site had a dead animal in it. Doesn't mean all of the other ones do too."

Conversation stopped as they struggled down the trail, made even more treacherous by all the trips made up and down to carry equipment. Someone, probably one of the interns, had strung up a rope, so at least there was a handhold.

Back at the car, Noah offered her the keys, but Winter shook her head. She climbed in and stared out the fogged glass at the blurred shapes outside as Noah drove them back to the hotel to change clothes and regroup.

7

I t was just before four when they pulled up in the hotel lot. Noah had tried a couple of times to lift the oppressive mood that had fallen over Winter, with no luck.

As they got out of the car, he tried again. "Do me a favor. Head to the front desk and see if they've got a list of food places around here that'll deliver. I'll call Max and give him our check-in for the day. Come on over when you're done and bring your laptop. We'll do some more missing person searching."

"You and your stomach," Winter muttered, shaking her head. But she headed for the hotel office, pathetically grateful to not have to face calling their boss. She needed to shake this off and keep moving forward.

She pushed open the door, and a bell dinged overhead. The lobby was just as dingy as the rest of the place was, with worn flowered carpeting and chairs covered in cracked Naugahyde. If you sat down in one with shorts on, you'd likely regret it. She went to the deserted counter and rang the old-fashioned bell.

A short, older lady in a brightly flowered blouse came around the corner. Her eyes brightened with what looked like avaricious glee when she saw Winter standing at the counter. She patted at her gray, lacquered curls, setting her dangly parrot earrings swinging. "What can I do for you, sweetie? Or I should say, *Agent*," she added in a stage whisper.

Winter gave her a tight smile. "I was hoping you might have a list of restaurants around here that deliver."

"Oh, sure! I mean, I don't have them written out, but I can jot down a few for you." She grabbed a yellow notepad and a stub of pencil, but her attention was still on Winter. "I hope you don't mind me asking, but are you wearing a *gun?*"

Winter just kept her smile plastered on. A dull headache pounded behind her eyes. She didn't want to be rude, but she also didn't want to get drawn into a discussion with this nosy old lady.

"I'm sorry." The woman tittered. "You probably can't tell me that, can you? Top secret."

Did she think Winter was CIA? Winter just nodded soberly. "I could tell you, but I'd have to kill you. How about those restaurants? Any good Italian places nearby?"

She didn't take the hint. "You must think I'm so rude," the woman gushed. "I'm Alma. Alma Krueger. I know y'all are here looking into those bones up in Linville."

Winter raised one eyebrow. She wasn't aware that the investigation was common knowledge. "Nice to meet you, Alma."

"I just can't believe we have our very own FBI agents staying here. I watch *Law and Order* and *Criminal Minds* and *CSI* all the time, and it's just *so exciting*. My sister, Elva, she's just as jealous as can be. Have you caught the killer yet?"

Winter cleared her throat, her gaze dropping to the still empty notepad. "Well, we need to eat, you know. Keep up our strength for the investigation."

"Oh, sure, sure." Alma started to write and then stopped. She looked at Winter, her watery brown eyes wide. "Have you looked into the cult yet?"

Winter's breath stilled. Did Alma know about Brian Snyder's story? If so, how was she getting her information?

"Cult?" Winter probed.

"Well, the old Moon Disciple place is right up on the other side of where they found those bones, after all. I heard they had a burial ground up in those woods. That just gives me the heebie-jeebies, let me tell you." She shuddered delicately. "I could just imagine them killing people and hiding them in the woods. Maybe that's how they made all their money. Who knows."

Winter felt almost an internal click. The lady was a little bit of a flake, but the mention of the cult had her intuition clamoring.

"You know, Alma," Winter said, lowering her voice and stepping closer to the counter. "If you've got any ideas, I'd like to hear them. You seem like you've probably got a good knack for investigative thinking."

Alma dropped her pencil and leaned forward too, her face avid and her voice hushed. "That's what I'm *always* telling Elva."

"Tell me about this cult."

"Well…" Alma's face fell a little. "That's all I ever heard, so I don't actually know much. I moved here in the early nineties, and they were all gone by then. People just said they were creepy, keeping to themselves and living in sin on that big old farm. But," she added, her expression brightening, "I can tell you who *does* know about that cult."

Winter made her eyes go conspiratorially wide. "Who's that?"

Alma picked up the pencil again and jotted down a name

in a shaky scrawl. "You call him," Alma said decisively. "He can tell you *everything.*"

"Thanks, Alma," Winter said, taking the piece of paper and backing toward the door.

"Wait! I almost forgot! Antonio's has the best lasagna around. And if you pay an extra five bucks, he'll have one of his dishwashers drive your food over for you."

"Italian food it is. Thanks for all of your help." Winter gave her a quick wave and retreated.

"T<small>ELL</small> me you have more for me than fucking cows and some cult theory from an anti-government crackpot. Do you need me to send someone down? Violent Crimes is still strapped, but I can pull from another department."

Noah winced, but kept his voice brisk and professional. "No, sir. We're checking in to some things and will have more for you tomorrow." He quickly got off the phone and wiped his hands on the jeans he'd changed into. His palms were sweating. They were going to have to come up with something else, and soon.

Winter burst into his hotel room, still wearing her wet clothes. Her laptop was tucked under one arm, and she waved a piece of paper in the other hand. "Jeez," he joked, covering his chest with crossed arms. "Knock, why don't you? I'm not decent."

"Oh, shut up. First, we're ordering Italian. Antonio's. Second, I might have something."

He pulled on a t-shirt and went to the table where she'd opened her laptop. She told him about Alma Krueger at the front desk and how she'd mentioned the cult. "I was ready to brush it off, but something made me want to take her seriously. I went back to my room and looked up the name she gave me. Elbert Wilkins. He was a newspaperman in Harrisonburg back in the eighties. He was here at the right time, and I think we should talk to him. More importantly, though, look at this."

She turned the laptop to face him. She'd pulled up a Google map view of Linville. "Here's the farm where the cult operated from. And here's where the bones were discovered."

The farm was literally just down the road from the trail they took through the woods to reach the burial site. He sat down at the table and opened another tab to pull up a real estate site. He pasted the address of the farm in. The site listed properties, even if they weren't on the market, and as he'd hoped, they showed a satellite view marking the approximate property lines. The parcel butted up to the federal lands that Brian and his son had used for hunting.

"It looks to me like the western boundary of the farm almost lines up exactly where that clearing sits. It could even be *on* the property."

"It feels right," Winter said, her voice tight.

He looked over at her. She was shaking a little, probably from being in wet, cold clothes. He tried not to notice how the white shirt she wore under her blazer had gone nearly transparent from the rain, but hell, he was a guy. And his partner was an incredibly attractive female.

Female friend and co-worker, he reminded himself. Resolutely, he pulled his eyes up to her face where they belonged.

"It feels right," Noah agreed. "We'll call Elbert. Now go put something warm on before you catch your death of cold, like my momma always says."

Thankfully, Winter came back in a baggy sweatshirt over a pair of leggings with thick socks pulled up to her shins. They ordered lasagna and fettuccini and cannoli and tiramisu. Antonio promised to send one of his boys right over with it, and they didn't wait for dinner but got to work.

Noah started looking into property records while Winter called Elbert Wilkins.

The man, like his name indicated, sounded elderly. He also talked loudly enough that it sounded like he was on speakerphone.

"Mr. Wilkins," Winter almost shouted into the phone, holding it slightly away from her ear, "I was given your name by Alma Krueger."

"Aw, hell, I thought I got rid of that woman," Elbert roared, the words as clear to Noah as if he'd been standing in the room. "She's been trying to jump these old bones for years."

Winter almost laughed, shocked, but got herself under control. "Ah, that's actually not what I'm calling about."

"Nonsense. She's still trying to get in my pants, isn't she? Don't sugarcoat it, little girl. Tell me the truth. She and that sister of hers have been fighting over me for years."

"No, I promise. That's not what this is about." She hurried on before he could interrupt. "I'm with the FBI. I'm hoping my partner and I can speak with you about a cult that was located near Linville several years ago. Alma said you might have some information."

There was silence on the line. Winter looked at him, and Noah shrugged.

"Sir?" she yelled into the phone.

Finally, there was a heavy sigh. "Don't yell, little girl. I can hear you just fine," Elbert's voice boomed out. "I've been expecting this call for a long time." He rattled off an address, and Noah punched it into his phone. "Come see me in the morning," Elbert ordered. "Bring me coffee, a big Starbucks mocha will be just fine. Toss in a pastry, and I'll tell you everything you want to know."

There was a heavy clunk, like the sound of an old-fashioned phone receiver being thrown into its cradle. Elbert Wilkins had hung up.

"This," Winter said, staring at her phone, "has been an extremely weird day."

Noah couldn't disagree.

lbert Wilkins lived in a tidy little bungalow at the edge of Harrisonburg. The green siding was a little bit faded, but the house looked well cared for. There was no car in the drive, and Winter parked in the dappled shade provided by a huge maple tree that took up a good part of the postage stamp-sized front yard. They got out and headed to the front steps, where Noah rang the doorbell.

It was opened almost immediately by a short man in khakis and a button-down plaid short-sleeved shirt. His wispy white hair was combed carefully over an almost-bald head.

"Elbert Wilkins?" Winter asked loudly.

He pushed open the screen, staring past them with wide blue eyes. "Come on in. And don't yell at me. I may be old, but I'm not deaf. I can just never figure out how to turn up the speaker volume on my phone. Always sounds like everyone's whispering. Now give me that mocha. I can smell it."

Winter laughed and put the cup into the old man's outstretched hand.

As he led them into his house, one gnarled hand trailing

along the wall of the foyer, Winter realized he wasn't deaf. But he *was* blind.

They followed him into a living room, where a couple of old couches and an armchair that reminded Winter of her grandparents' furniture sat in front of an empty fireplace. Noah nudged her and motioned to the walls. They were lined with books. Every available surface.

"Make yourselves comfortable," Elbert offered, going to the armchair and sitting down. He smiled, showing gleaming white dentures. "Just set that pastry on the coffee table there. I'll get to it later. Might want to take separate couches. I'm afraid the big, quiet guy is going to break one if you try to share." He tipped back the Starbucks cup and slurped the mocha with greedy delight. "I don't get out much anymore. I miss these things."

"I'm Agent Black, and the big guy is Agent Dalton," Winter said, sitting down on leather cushions that had lost their squeak long ago, placing the green and white bag on the table in front of her. "Thanks for agreeing to speak with us."

"Thank you for not bringing Alma along." He chuckled, the sound raspy. "Call me Elbert."

"You can call me Noah, and that's Winter," Noah said. "I'll try not to break your furniture."

Winter leaned forward and broke up the small talk. "We were told you used to work for the local newspaper."

The smile fell away from Elbert's face, and he gazed off into the distance, his blue eyes cloudy. "I did. Right up until they downsized back in 2002. Damned internet. Wouldn't have mattered, though. I couldn't see real well by then and was totally blind by 2004. Macular degeneration."

"Are you a Harrisonburg native?" Winter asked.

"Born and raised. This is the same house my wife and I had built in 1956, too, God rest her soul. You're here about the Disciples of the Moon."

"Is that what they called themselves?"

He took another long sip of his coffee, emptying it already. "The commune up in Linville? Yeah."

"You say commune." Noah leaned forward, his elbows on his knees. "We keep hearing it called a cult. What can you tell us about the Disciples?"

"I'll tell you, if one of you will go grab me a Coke. It's a long story. Kitchen's just down the way."

Winter got to her feet. "I'll be right back."

She headed to the other side of the house. It was neat, just like the outside, but smelled a little musty, and she wondered if Elbert took care of the inside himself or hired someone to come in to help. She passed a bedroom with a double bed, covered in a white chenille spread. The next room made her stop. It was an office, as packed with filing cabinets as the living room was with books. There were corkboards covered with yellowed newspaper clippings, and a wide, dark-wood desk, its polished surface empty.

What would it be like, she wondered, to lose your sight, and with it, the ability to read and write? Something you had done all of your life, made a career of and defined yourself by?

She shivered at the implications.

Forcing her mind from that dark pathway, she continued to the kitchen and got Elbert his Coke. The fridge was sparsely stocked, and she felt a pang. Her grandparents had her, but who did Elbert have?

"Here she comes," she heard Elbert say as she headed back toward the other end of the house. There was definitely nothing wrong with his hearing.

Elbert thanked her and popped the tab on the can, taking a deep drink.

"Do you mind if I record our interview, sir?" Noah asked, taking out his phone.

"Sure. I used to record all mine," the old man replied. "Let me know when you're ready."

Noah pulled up the recording app and set it. "Go ahead when you're ready."

"Starts back during the Vietnam War," Elbert began, setting his can down on a low side table before settling back in his seat and putting his feet up on an ottoman. "A young man named Wesley Archer went off to that cursed war, figuring on being a hero. You're military, aren't you, Tex?" he asked. "I can hear it in your voice."

"Marines," Noah chuckled. "You've got a good ear."

"Well, while Wesley was there, he saw the worst of humanity. I don't need to tell you all how bad the war was. I was a correspondent back then before I settled down to write local. I traveled overseas and saw some of it firsthand. You two probably read about it in the history books or watched that old TV show, *M*A*S*H*. That'll give you an idea, but not the whole story."

Noah leaned forward, clearly drawn into the story. Winter leaned back, enjoying the rhythm of the old man's speech.

He shuddered, but that didn't stop him from going on. "I was there for two weeks. I can't imagine what it would've been like to live that hell every day. When Wesley was over there, and things started getting to him real bad, he would dream about coming back to the States. Seeing his family again. Leaving the war behind and getting back to his real life with people who weren't savages, like his fellow soldiers and those they were fighting."

"But that didn't happen," Winter murmured, unable to stop the words from coming out.

Elbert shook his head sadly. "No. It didn't happen at all like he'd imagined. Instead, anti-war protests were going full swing. He didn't come home to people who looked at him as a hero. These people had seen and heard about the atrocities committed by both sides, thanks to reporters like me. Instead of his ticker tape parade, protesters called him a baby killer. People spat on him, egged his car, his house. He ended up buying a wig to hide his military haircut until it grew out."

Elbert's voice was impassioned, and his eyes teared up. Winter could see that he probably felt some responsibility and that this story was painful for him to tell.

"While all this was going on, Wesley was dealing with a deep depression and probably some PTSD, though we didn't truly understand what that meant back then. He finally moved away from the East Coast, took some money he'd inherited and bought a farm out in Linville. He had convinced himself that this generation was doomed. We were heartless and evil, and it was just going to get worse. So, he decided to build up a kind of commune. A place where he and some like-minded folks could have a peaceful place. They could raise families, raise their kids to have only love and kindness in their hearts. Respect for their fellow man."

His voice trailed off. Winter and Noah held their silence, but Elbert didn't say any more.

Winter spoke first, hoping to nudge him along. "What happened after that?"

Elbert seemed to grapple with the question, hesitating as if he struggled with what to say next. "Wesley called himself The Bishop, and anyone who joined up with them referred to themselves as the Disciples of the Moon. More as a joke than anything, at first. They weren't running a religious cult. It was more a shared effort at making a living, back to the land, and having shared ideals. A utopian community. But outsiders saw them as scary, I guess."

"Where did he find followers?" Noah asked.

"A lot of them came from around here. Or in Linville. Maybe some were Army buddies. Who knows. They were pretty secretive." Elbert threaded his fingers together in his lap, and Winter noticed his knuckles were white. He was holding back for some reason.

"Were you one of his followers?" Winter questioned gently.

Elbert's eyes widened in surprise, and he chuckled. "Oh, no. I was too mainstream for that crowd. I liked my job reporting the news. My wife would have never agreed to make her own dresses out of burlap, or whatever they managed to weave out there at that farm."

"What was your interest then?" she asked, equally softly. "How do you know so much?"

The silence stretched, then Elbert took in a deep breath, seeming to come to a decision. Before her eyes, he shut down on them. Winter could almost visibly see it happen. His tone lightened, became more offhand. His fingers relaxed. Whatever he'd brought them here to tell them…they weren't going to get it all.

"Reporters, especially old-fashioned newspapermen, have an everlasting curiosity. We want to see what makes people tick. Why they do what they do. I've just always been interested in what they had going on out there. I collected all the info I could on the Disciples. I don't believe they were bad people. I believe that Wesley Archer thought that he was going to do his small part to make the world a better place, after going through what he did in Vietnam and after."

Noah glanced at her and shook his head. He didn't think they'd get anything more out of the old man either. "Do you have any of that information?" Noah asked. "Old interview tapes with Wesley Archer? It would really help us."

"You think those bones Brian Snyder found in the woods were put there by the Disciples." It wasn't a question. He waved a hand before Winter could speak. "Alma Krueger has her finger on the pulse of everything that happens around here. She called me yesterday and told me she heard it from her cousin Bonnie, who has a police scanner because her nephew is a deputy sheriff."

"We don't know what to think, sir. It's too early to tell what happened to the owner of those bones. We're just chasing down every angle. As a reporter, I'm sure you can respect that."

Noah's tone was respectful, bland even, but Winter was sure that Elbert would catch what Noah was implying.

"I'll give you a file of some notes I have," Elbert said after a pause, "but I just don't think Wesley would be responsible for any killing. He came back from that war thirsty for peace. Whether this country treated him as a hero or not, it doesn't change the fact that he fought for his country and came back a damaged man because of it. It just doesn't make any sense after this long to sully his memory. That cult dissolved back in the mid-eighties. Best just to leave things lie."

Elbert levered himself out of the chair slowly and headed for the hall. The interview was apparently over. Winter and Noah followed him, expecting to be led to the front door, but he went to his office. Going unerringly to the filing cabinet he wanted, Elbert went to the third drawer down and opened it. He thumbed through, his lips moving as he counted files, and pulled one out.

He held it out, and Winter, who was closest, took it.

DOTM, it read. *Wesley Archer, 1976-1980.*

"Now, if that's all…" Elbert pinned them with his unseeing gaze.

Winter bit back the stab of disappointment, and the bitter need to interrogate this poor old man further. "That'll be all. Thank you so much for your help. Can we call you with any follow-up questions?"

Elbert smiled at Winter a little sadly. "I don't think so,

little girl. I think you've gotten about all you're going to get out of me. Thanks for the mocha."

ELBERT CLOSED the door behind the two FBI agents, hearing their footsteps move farther down the sidewalk. He wondered if he'd made the right decision. Trailing his fingers along the familiar textured plaster surface of the foyer wall, he headed back to his office.

Standing there, breathing in the smell of paper and ink, he mourned his loss of sight, not for the first time and certainly not for the last. He'd made a life and a career out of digging for the truth, whatever and wherever it happened to be, big or small.

He'd been fascinated by Wesley Archer and had interviewed the reclusive man more than once. He also had his suspicions about things that went on out at that farm. But he had enough respect for Wesley, and sympathy for his moral dilemma, that he'd changed his mind and decided not to share his suspicions with the FBI.

Elbert ran his fingers over the file in the third drawer, counting. Yes, there it was. He couldn't see it, but he knew it by touch. *DOTM, Wesley Archer, 1980-1987.* It seemed like damning information, but if he was wrong, he'd be tarnishing the memory of a man who sacrificed for his country and was scorned in return.

The heavy scrape of a footstep came from behind him, and at first, he thought the big FBI agent had come back because he'd forgotten something. Or because he wanted to ask more questions. But when he smelled cologne, he knew it wasn't Agent Dalton.

"Who's there?" he demanded, clutching the file to his chest.

He heard movement, sensed someone else in the room with him. He stepped back, bumping his thighs hard against the desk behind him. The smell of cologne grew stronger. Elbert's heart thumped in his chest, pounding painfully against his ribs.

"Best just to leave things lie," a low voice said. "You probably should have taken your own advice."

The file was jerked from his grasp, and a starburst of pain exploded just above Elbert's left ear. It hurt for just one blazing moment, and he felt himself falling. Then, the pain and everything else simply disappeared.

9

"What do you think he was holding back?" Noah wished Winter had driven so he could be the one to look through the file first, but she was already nose-deep in it.

"I don't know. I definitely felt like he didn't tell us everything he'd planned on telling us before we showed up. Elbert Wilkins painted Wesley Archer as a misunderstood man and a betrayed hero, but he was definitely holding something back." Winter glanced out the window. They were heading out of Harrisonburg, toward Linville. "Where are we going? To check in on the excavation?"

"Well," Noah said smugly, "if you hadn't been so tied up with reading that stuff and keeping all the information to your little self, I would have told you that we're heading out to the farm."

She narrowed her eyes at him. "It's not vacant, as of two years ago, remember? You think we'll just be able to go up to the front door and ask to look around without some kind of warrant? See if we can find any evidence of a cult or commune or whatever that existed there some thirty-odd years ago?"

"Nope." Noah grinned. "I'm fairly certain we're going to go see if The Bishop's wife is home. Or maybe his daughter. We'll find out when we get there."

"You know, if we're supposed to be partners on this," Winter replied, poking her finger into his arm, "you'd better be a little more forthcoming with the details, got it?"

He pulled his arm away before she could dig a hole in his skin. "All right. The property search I ran last night shows that the title on the farm is now registered to a Rebekah Archer. That last name didn't mean anything to me until we talked to Elbert. Seems a bit of a coincidence now, doesn't it?"

"More than," Winter agreed. Her eyes glimmered with excitement. "I might just forgive you since you made that amazing leap of logic all by yourself. Finally, we're getting somewhere."

They passed the trail that led to the burial ground and saw an intern picking his way down the hill with what was probably evidence in a box. About three minutes later, the woods opened up, and on their left, a gravel drive led back to a pretty farmhouse, nestled at the base of a hill.

Trim white fences surrounded close-cropped fields and placid cows grazed in the sunshine. "Nice-looking Here-fords," Noah murmured.

"They're making you hungry, aren't they?"

He frowned at her. "Hush. They'll hear you."

They parked in a wide circular turnaround in front of the house, behind a newer model red pickup truck. A wide front porch ran the length of the farmhouse, and cozy-looking wicker furniture sat grouped in comfortable arrangements.

The front door opened before they reached it, and a woman stood framed behind the old-fashioned screen door.

Noah felt his mind go blank as the woman smiled. She was gorgeous.

Soft-looking sable hair fell to her shoulders in loose waves. Her eyes were hazel, her nose small, and tilted up just a little bit. He pegged her to be in her mid to late twenties, though she could easily pass as a teen. She was petite, only a couple inches over five feet tall, but she was curved in all the right places. He felt like he'd been punched in the gut.

"I'm sorry," the woman said, still smiling, "but if you're selling something, I don't have any cash. If you're pushing something, I already have religion."

Winter cleared her throat. Sharply.

Right. This was his show.

"I'm sorry, ma'am," Noah finally managed. "We were wondering if we could speak with you for a moment."

One side of her mouth lifted in one of the sexiest little smiles he'd ever seen. "Well, if you're not selling magazines or salvation, you must be law enforcement. Come on in."

She held the door for them, and Noah squeezed past her, feeling big and awkward. Winter slipped in behind him, her laser blue eyes coolly assessing the woman, smiling slightly. "Thank you. We'll try not to take up too much of your time."

"Is this about the ruckus down the street?" she asked. "I've seen police cars and other vehicles parked over there on and off for a couple of weeks now. I hope everything's okay."

"I'm Agent Dalton, and this is my partner, Agent Black."

"I'm sorry." She blushed, her porcelain cheeks going pink. "My name is Rebekah. Rebekah Archer. You're FBI?"

"We are." Thankfully, Winter took over for him. "We're actually here to ask you some questions about your father."

A shadow of sadness passed across Rebekah's face. "My father passed about ten years ago."

"I'm sorry to hear that."

"My condolences," Noah added.

"Thank you. Is this about the commune that he used to lead?"

"Yes, actually. Do you mind if we sit down and talk for a few minutes? We can go back outside to the front porch if you'd be more comfortable?"

"No, this is fine. Come on in."

The house was pretty, Noah saw, with antiques casually placed about, like an old wooden church pew that sat by the door with shoes underneath, and the big farm table in the kitchen. Rebekah gestured to the table.

After they were settled, Rebekah looked at them both expectantly. "Let me guess. You've been told by some people in town that my dad was a cult leader and he probably killed whoever they're digging up in the woods up there. Is that about right?"

"Would you consider your father's group a cult?"

Rebekah laughed at Winter's question. The sound was sweet and bubbling. "Not at all. My dad wasn't some weirdo who wore robes and chanted with incense sticks stuck up his nose. He was an amazing guy, a war veteran. He came home from the war and wanted peace. He opened up this farm to anyone who needed a place to escape from the ugliness of life."

"What was it like growing up here?" Noah asked.

Rebekah sighed. "I can't even describe it. Idyllic? Peaceful? Look around." She gestured to the view from the window behind them. This place is a little piece of heaven. Nearly a hundred acres backed right up to the George Washington National Forest? Nature was my playground. I couldn't have been happier."

"What about your mother?" Winter asked. "Did she live here too?"

"Of course. She, too, passed away several years ago, but I

was blessed with both of my parents. They were wonderful people."

"Did you have any kids to play with?"

"Oh, a few. People would come and go." Rebekah's eyes went dreamy as she thought back. "I remember a little girl named Dierdre. She was my best friend, but they moved away when I was probably seven. Before that, there were other kids, and after that too. But commune life is a transient thing. Dad would bring people here, and they'd stay for a while, and then move on when they were ready."

"And that doesn't seem strange to you? Having all kinds of people you don't know in and out of your life?"

Rebekah shook her head, looking puzzled at Winter's mildly sarcastic tone. Noah looked hard at her too. She didn't have to be rude. Rebekah wasn't a suspect.

"No, it didn't. Not really. It was what I was used to. I loved all the company. The newness and excitement of meeting different people."

Noah decided it was time for him to take over. Winter was acting prickly all of a sudden. "Do you live here by yourself now?"

Startled by the question, Rebekah's eyes widened just slightly. "Oh, yes. I've been thinking about renting out some rooms on Airbnb, but I haven't done it yet. I mean, I have a couple of guys that don't live on the property. They just come out and help me with the animals when I need it."

Noah wanted to shake his head. It was a shame. Such a pretty girl, and she had to go and ruin it with lies.

"I saw your cattle out there. I'm from Texas, and I'm not trying to be stereotypical when I say I know my cattle." This time, he smiled at her. A smile calculated to flirt and disarm.

She relaxed and smiled back, showing perfect, pretty white teeth. "I went to school for that. Animal husbandry is kind of my thing. I've been breeding Herefords for the last two years, and a couple of thoroughbreds too."

"That's great," Winter interjected with false cheerfulness. "Well, we'd better get on our way. Noah?" She shot him a pointed look.

"Things to do. Thanks for speaking with us, Mrs. Archer."

"Oh, just Ms." Her gaze fell to his lips. "Or better yet, just Rebekah."

He smiled and took a business card out of his wallet. "Hang on to that. Just in case you think of anything more about your daddy you'd like to share with us. Or, if you just need to get ahold of an FBI agent." He dropped her a wink.

"SERIOUSLY, DALTON?"

Winter didn't wait until they got to the car before lighting into him.

"What?" His face was a study in innocence, green eyes wide.

"Where's your professionalism?" she accused. "We're not here to find you a girlfriend. We're investigating a freaking murder." She wrenched the car door open and slid into the driver's seat. "You don't have time to flirt. And especially not with a potential witness."

Frustrated and irritated, she dug in her purse for the keys to the car. A jingling sound to her right had her gritting her teeth.

"You might need these if you're planning on taking us anywhere, boss."

Right. He'd driven on the way there.

She snatched the keys out of his hand and jammed them in the ignition.

"If I didn't know better, I'd say you're jealous, sweetheart."

Winter shot him one fulminating look that had the smile dropping away from his lips. "Jealous? I don't think so."

Noah shrugged and picked up the file they'd gotten from Elbert, thumbing through the contents. "If you say so. For the record, she was lying through her perfect little teeth."

"I know." Winter put the car in gear and tried to concentrate on not spitting gravel with the back tires as she headed down the driveway. She didn't know why she was so mad at him. Rebekah Archer was attractive and friendly. And if Noah wanted to bat his eyelashes at the woman, it was no skin off her nose. But he was right. Rebekah was a liar.

Winter reined in her bad mood and took a deep breath, turning out of the farm driveway and heading back toward Linville. "Why'd she say she lived there alone?" she asked, tapping her fingers on the steering wheel.

Noah shrugged. "Maybe she thought we meant to ask if there were any other adults in the house? The little pink shoes weren't exactly hidden, stuck under the bench like that."

She gave him a brief look, wondering if he was defending Rebekah's lie, but he was studying a handwritten page with a line of concentration between his brows.

"Did you see anything else weird?" she asked, frustration making her drive faster than was wise.

He still didn't look up. "No."

If she were honest with herself, Winter really hadn't been focusing as well as she should have during the interview, and that bothered her. She normally caught every little detail, but her impressions of Rebekah and her farm were a little clouded, and she could only blame her preoccupation with Noah.

That wouldn't fly.

"You want to stop by the burial site? See if there's been any progress made?"

Glad to focus on something else, Winter nodded. "Might as well. We're close."

Just down the road, they could see the hill, but the entrance to the trail was cluttered with vehicles.

"Looks like something's going on," Winter murmured, pulling up behind a county coroner van. In front of that was the chief's SUV. "I can't imagine Benton would have updated us on anything voluntarily, but Gary Miller should have at least given us a call."

They got out of the car and headed for the well-trampled trail, with its little orange marker flag now seeming superfluous. The grass was trampled down, and someone had gone through with a bushwhacker, widening the area for easier access, cutting back saplings and knocking down the underbrush.

They were only two-thirds of the way to the top when they passed one of the forensic archaeologist's ubiquitous interns. She was headed down the slope at a fast clip. "You guys are just in time." She skidded to a stop, and Winter grabbed her arm to keep her from rolling down the rest of the way, ass over teakettle.

"What's happening?" Winter asked. Her stomach tightened. *Please don't let it be more animal bones.*

"Two more bodies." The girl's pale gray eyes were wide behind her thick glasses. "You were right. It's a dumping ground."

10

The crime scene was a hive of activity.

The chief hurried over as soon as Winter and Noah entered the clearing, consternation written across his face. "I was just getting ready to call you. Two more," he said without preamble. "You're going to want to come take a look at what the forensic excavator's got."

Marilyn Fosner was also looking grim. She had her hair tied back in a bandana, and one cheek was smudged with dirt. She didn't look up from her work, painstakingly removing dirt from a shallow hole in the ground. Winter looked over the edge, which flickered a sullen red, like hot coals had been buried inside, and shuddered reflexively.

Two bodies, indeed. Tiny ones.

An almost electrical flare of rage skimmed up her spine, leaving the hair on her arms standing on end. "What kind of a monster kills children like this?" She didn't realize she'd spoken the words out loud until Marilyn answered.

"One sadistic fucker." She pointed one gloved finger toward an impossibly small skull. "Bullet wound. Same as the other two sets of bones. Back of the head." She glanced up, her green eyes glittering darkly. "I don't care how long ago this was. You find who did this. Find them and fucking fry them."

Noah nodded soberly and took Winter's elbow, leading her away. Marilyn went back to her bleak task, her shoulders hunched and her face emotionless as she wielded her excavation tools with the precise, delicate movements of a surgeon.

"No offense, but I wish you'd have been wrong," Noah said in a weary tone. "What if we have a whole graveyard of tiny bones here?"

"Maybe we do," she murmured. "But there's something else here too. I feel it."

"I think we need to go back and talk to Elbert again."

Yes...Elbert. She sighed, thinking of the blind elderly man who trailed his fingers along the walls of the house he couldn't see anymore. Filing cabinets full of information that he couldn't read.

A chilly breeze brushed a dark strand of hair against Winter's face. "I think you're right. He knows more than he's saying. Maybe if we push him a little, he'll tell us what that is."

"I'm sure you think you're even hotter shit now."

Winter turned around, not surprised to see Tom Benton behind her. His eyes were bloodshot and his face puffy. He didn't look like he'd been sleeping well. She wondered why, but let the thought go.

It was none of her business.

She was here to find a murderer. If things had been left to Benton, she had no doubt there would have been only a cursory investigation, if that. The unidentified child—children—would never have received justice.

That thought sharpened her tone when she replied.

"No, I don't think I'm hot shit. In fact, I'm not out to

prove myself to anyone. I'm just doing my job. Being a professional." The words were pointed, the implication clear.

Benton's face reddened. "Listen, bitch—"

"Enough." Noah's normally relaxed manner dropped away in an instant. Winter looked at him in surprise. His face had gone hard as granite. He took one step forward, and Benton cowered back. "Apologize."

Benton's eyes narrowed, and he opened his mouth to argue. "Look—"

"Apologize," Noah repeated. His voice didn't get any louder but instead deepened with menace. "Y'all may have known each other as kids, but we're all grown-ups here, and there's no need for name calling. Right?"

Getting a better look at Noah's face, Benton grimaced. "Sorry." He spit the word out like it tasted bad and didn't look at Winter as he said it.

Noah gave him a wide, sharp smile that didn't reach his eyes. "Now that we've got that little nastiness out of the way, can we get back to the case at hand? You grew up around here, Benton. What do you know about the Disciples of the Moon?"

Benton's eyes flared wide for a moment, but he recovered quickly and snorted, the sound wet and disgusting. "Buncha hippies back in the day? What's that have to do with anything?"

Anger sparked a fire in Winter. She hadn't missed the look on his face, even though Benton had almost immediately buried it under his customary surly glower. "I grew up in Harrisonburg, just like you. I'd never heard of them."

Benton shrugged one shoulder dismissively. "You left not long after that...bad business."

Some bad business. The murder of her parents and the disappearance of her younger brother. She bit back another surge of anger at his patronizing tone. "So, what do you know about this cult?"

"Nothing more than a kid hears. Urban legend."

"Care to elaborate?" Noah drawled.

"Look, they were just a bunch of back-to-the-land weirdos. Did some farming. They kept to themselves, so as kids we made up stories. You're grasping at straws if you want to pin this on some old commune that hasn't existed around here in decades. How you even going to prove something like that?"

They weren't going to get anything out of him, Winter saw, and Noah apparently concluded the same.

"I think Chief Miller wants to speak with you." Noah nodded toward the older man, who was looking their way, thick brows drawn together in a scowl.

Benton cursed under his breath and headed away without another word.

"Ready?" Noah's tone was smooth as he switched his focus back to Winter.

She stared at him for a moment. "I didn't need you to do that. Step in for me. Benton doesn't scare me."

Noah shrugged his broad shoulders and headed away from the clearing, leaving her to match his long-legged stride or get left behind. "Benton's a pissant."

She doubled her own stride to catch up with him, irritation bubbling. "You need to scale back this whole macho Texas-guy thing you've got going. I'm not a damsel. I don't need saving."

He snorted. "Benton's the least of your troubles." Then he gave her a sideways glance, his green eyes unreadable. "And darlin', we all need saving once in a while."

❄

JENNIE BETTS WAS RUNNING LATE.

Danny was teething, and she'd had to keep him home from daycare because he was running a fever. Then, her mother-in-law had given her a hard time about watching him. Dominic's mom always said all the right things, but she sure lacked in follow through.

Let me know if you ever need someone to watch him. Of course, Gramma would welcome time with her baby boy!

Jennie fluttered her lips in disgust.

The second she ever called her mother-in-law for anything, out came the excuses. She had a hair appointment. A slight cold. Today, it had been her cat Missy's annual checkup at the vet.

She'd had to wait until after two to drop off her fussy boy, and she was due at Mr. Wilkins' house at nine. She'd tried to call him to let him know she'd be late, but he wasn't picking up the phone.

The sky was starting to cloud up by the time she turned her beat-up station wagon into the driveway of Mr. Wilkins' house. Looked like fall was officially here. She shivered as she pulled the vacuum cleaner out of the hatchback, wishing she'd taken the time to pull on a hoodie before she left the house. The breeze was blowing straight through her thin t-shirt.

Jennie lugged the Hoover up the front walk, juggling her basket of cleaning supplies to her other hand so she could dig her keys out of her purse.

"Hey, Mr. Wilkins!" she called out cheerfully as she came through the front door, flicking on the light switch. "Sorry I'm late!"

She knew he'd probably heard her pull up in the driveway —the man had ears like a bat—but the house was quiet. Not even the radio was playing. Frowning, she set down her cleaning supplies.

"Mr. Wilkins?"

The musty smell of old paper tickled her nose like it usually did, and she rubbed the back of her hand against it. Underneath the paper odor was something else. Something that made her nose wrinkle and her belly curl. She hoped the poor old guy didn't have the flu. They'd already dealt with that in her house last week, and she'd cleaned up enough grossness to last a while.

The living room was empty, except for a green and white paper cup on the side table. Someone had brought him coffee. Maybe Alma, she chuckled. Those old people were a trip, the way they flirted.

God, she hoped the old folks weren't getting it on. She listened carefully at the door, but when she heard nothing on the other side, she opened it an inch. The bedroom was tidy, bed made.

The door to the office was mostly closed, and she tapped hesitantly. Sometimes he sat in there. She didn't know why. Maybe thinking about what was in all the books and papers that were now lost to him?

The door swung slowly open, and Jennie's eyes widened.

Then, she started to scream.

NOAH HEARD the ear-piercing shrieks the moment he opened the car door. But Winter was out and running for Elbert's house, gun drawn, nearly before the car came to a complete stop.

"Hold on," he yelled at her furiously, but she was already disappearing through the doorway.

It was getting to be a pain in the ass, working with such a spooky partner.

Inside the entryway, a young woman, curvy with dark

brown hair, was sobbing, a fist stuffed in her mouth to stifle the screams they'd heard. "Take her out of here," he growled at Winter. "Call for backup while I clear the house."

He practically dared her to argue with him, but she just gave him a level look with those cool blue eyes and led the girl outside.

The house was empty, except for the elderly man crumpled on his office floor, surrounded by spilled papers. Some of them had wicked up blood that had spread from a gaping wound on the side of Elbert Wilkins' head. The man's face was frozen into a rictus of surprise, his sightless pale gaze fixed eternally sightless now on the wall.

Noah glanced around. The filing cabinets had been emptied, papers littering the room in drifts. It was a far cry from the neat organization they'd seen just that morning. He headed outside, where he could hear the young woman's voice wailing shrilly, undercut by Winter's low, calming tone.

Winter had tucked her gun away, and the girl was hugging her like a lifeline. She looked over the brunette's head at him. Her face was priceless. A mixture of awkwardness and pleading, she obviously wanted him to take over in the comfort department.

"Ma'am, are you a relative?"

The girl finally lifted a tear-stained face from the shoulder of Winter's black blazer and sniffled noisily. "No, I clean for Mr. Wilkins twice a week. Do his laundry. Make meals. He doesn't…" she swallowed hard and corrected herself, "didn't have any family."

Before she could dissolve into tears again, Winter addressed her. "Come on, Jennie. I need you to be strong here. Tell us what happened."

She sniffled again. "Danny was teething, and I couldn't take him to daycare. I was late. Oh, God, what if I could have stopped whoever did that?" Her brown eyes welled again.

Winter stopped her firmly. "You couldn't have. If anything, you could've been hurt too. Did you try to call Mr. Wilkins? Let him know you were running behind?"

"I did. He didn't pick up. Sometimes he loses the handset to his cordless, and I'll find it in a weird place, like the fridge. I didn't think anything of it."

"Okay, you're doing good, Jennie. Did you see anyone when you got here?" Noah asked. "How about the door. Was it unlocked?"

Jennie took a deep breath and closed her eyes, thinking. "No, it was locked. I had my hands full and had a hard time opening the door. I didn't see anyone, but I was mad at my mother-in-law and thinking about that. I wasn't really paying attention. I'm sorry."

Her lip quivered, and Noah gave her a bracing pat on the shoulder. "Nothing to be sorry about," he said softly. "Go on."

"I came in the house, dropped my stuff. I called him a couple of times. His office door was mostly closed and when I knocked...I saw..." She sniffed loudly. "I saw..."

Sirens wailed in the distance, and Noah held up a hand. "It's okay. I know what you saw. Why don't you hop in your car, turn the heat on, and warm up a little? We're going to want you to stick around for a bit."

Jennie nodded miserably. "I need to call Dominic. My husband."

"You do that."

Winter waited until Jennie was ensconced in her car. The sirens were coming closer. A light misting of rain started spitting from the leaden gray sky.

"What happened to him? She came flying up on me, screaming, as soon as I came in the house."

"Someone killed him, blow to the head. Ransacked his office."

Winter winced, her face pale. "Dammit. I liked him."

"Me too." Noah watched a state trooper's SUV turn onto the street a few blocks down. "How much you want to bet we don't find anything valuable in those files?"

"Who knew we were here?"

Noah shook his head. "No telling. We'll have to check his phone. See if he called anyone after we left. Hell, that receptionist at the hotel could have been putting the word out that the FBI folks were in town and interested in the Disciples. She may have talked to someone, bragged about sending us to Elbert."

Winter gave him a hesitant look, oddly vulnerable, as the trooper's vehicle braked at the curb. "I need to go in real quick. Take a look around for...anything."

She still wasn't used to sharing her secrets. Noah nodded and gave her a half-smile. "Go do your thing. I've got this."

They could use any advantage she could offer because, now, they had not only who-knew-how-many old murders... they had a fresh one too.

11

I t smelled like her. A light vanilla smell. Girly.

I inhaled deep through my nose and grinned.

I poked around a little. Looked in her nightstand. Just a standard, hotel-issue Bible that the hell-bound sinners never looked at. The suitcase hadn't been unpacked. It looked neat and tidy, and ready to go at a moment's notice, sitting on the rickety stand at the end of the bed.

Her toiletries were neatly lined up on the sink. I resisted the urge to touch anything. Wouldn't want to invade her privacy none. I chuckled to myself. Going back out to the small bedroom area, I lifted the corner of the gaudy-patterned coverlet. Sliding my hand under the mattress, I pulled out the disabled camera and batteries. Felt around for a second more until my fingers touched smooth paper.

Pulling out the picture of her brother, I looked at it for a moment. Cute little kid, with those dimples. One to remember, for sure.

The whole Black family had been an unusual experience. Now, to have this last one become an FBI agent...I was sure she aimed to hunt me down.

She was welcome to try. Maybe I'd even let her find me, just to see what happens.

I shook my head, thinking about the way she'd stuck her middle finger up at the camera. At me. Not ladylike, at all. Just like her momma. I'd like to teach her some manners, but I couldn't help but admire her spunk.

I tucked the photo and camera into my sweatshirt pocket and slipped out of the room, making sure to lock it up tight behind me. Adjusting the toolbelt hanging low on my hips, I headed down to my truck.

I almost hoped she'd catch up to me at some point.

It'd be interesting to see the little girlie's face when she learned the truth. Right before she paid her penance too.

WINTER FELT A BRIEF CHILL, like a cold finger had traced the back of her neck. She shuddered and rubbed her arms.

"You all right?"

"I'm fine. Just ready to call it. It's been a helluva day." It was true. The rain had picked up since that afternoon, and she was cold, damp, and tired. More than ready to fall into bed for the next eight hours.

"Just about there. You good with a drive-thru dinner?" Not waiting for an answer, Noah turned into a McDonald's drive-thru near their hotel. Unsurprising, since Noah's stomach had been growling audibly for hours.

Winter ordered fries and a Coke, knowing she should eat something, but she wasn't sure she was going to be able to. It had been hard, witnessing her first victim of violent death in over ten years. Bones were one thing. The smell, the sight of murder...that was different. Elbert's vacant eyes would haunt her dreams tonight.

Noah managed to restrain himself for the five minutes it

took for them to get back to the hotel, but as soon as they turned into the parking lot, he was pulling fries out of the bag and stuffing them in his mouth.

"How do you do it?"

He maneuvered the car into an empty spot and took a sip of his Coke. "Didn't we already go over this? Fast metabolism."

"Not that." Winter looked out the rain-spattered windshield, at the parking lot light haloed with a light haze of rain. "The death."

"You did fine today. Just fine." Noah's voice was sympathetic. "Your first freshly dead person?"

"No." An image of her parents popped into her head, and she closed her eyes briefly against it. "But the first one in a long time. It was just so…abrupt. We'd just seen him. Not six hours before."

"I know. And he was a nice guy."

Winter refused to cry, but the sting of tears at the backs of her lids was unmistakable. She blinked them back, mortified. She'd just assumed, after experiencing what she had as a kid, that when it came time to make it her career, the ability to block out blood and pain would just be engrained, allowing her to just focus on the end game. It wouldn't touch her. It would just be a job.

"You need to take that emotion, make it work for you. It's all fuel for the fire that'll ultimately lead to apprehending the person that did that to him. There's no shame in having it affect you. Just shows you're human."

He put a hand on hers, where it rested on her knee. The warmth of his broad palm was comforting.

"There's bad guys out there. Our job is to find them. Feeling for a victim, sad for the loss of life, that's not going to affect your ability to do your job."

She nodded wordlessly and gave herself just another

moment to soak in the reassuring touch of his hand. She normally avoided most physical contact. It weakened her. But Noah had a gift for offering comfort.

"You'd better get that burger up to your room before it gets cold," she finally told him, easing her hand out from under his.

Noah, though, angled toward her, as much as his long legs and the cramped seat would allow. "You sure you're okay? I was going to ask you earlier if you saw anything when you went in to check things out on your own, before all the local guys got there. I figured you'd tell me when you were ready, though."

He was trying to give her space with her "gift," and she was grateful for that.

"I did, but I don't think it'll be any help to us." She closed her eyes again, ignoring the mild headache that brewed in her temples. She brought the picture of Elbert's office to mind.

The filing cabinets. Scattered papers, manila folders. Elbert, crumpled on the floor...a gaping head wound, crushed bone, a dark pool of blood. She hadn't needed to see the red glow around the crowbar on the floor to know that it was the murder weapon, and neither would the CSI team.

Instead, she'd looked around the rest of the room.

Papers had been scattered everywhere, like a windstorm had blown through. Drawers hung crazily out of their cabinets, emptied of the information that had been painstakingly collected for decades.

Elbert's life, reduced to a pile of trash in one vicious blow.

"There were prints," she finally said. "Red areas where the killer had touched things. If they were real, the CSI team will find them. But I'm sure he was wearing gloves."

"Did you get a sense of who would have done it?"

"No. It was almost dispassionate, the way the room had been wrecked."

Noah grabbed another fry and chewed thoughtfully. "Nothing of value looked like it had been taken, according to the housekeeper."

Winter nodded. "I went through the entire house. Point of entry was the back door. I didn't pick up on any other area that had been disturbed. He came in, moved through the house until he found Elbert, killed him, destroyed the office, and left the same way he came."

"Neighbors didn't see anything."

"No. The way his house backs up to that wooded area didn't help. It would have been simple to get across the yard without being seen."

"It's tied in to the bones. Elbert knew something."

"Yeah. And now he's taking whatever it was to the grave." Abruptly, the confines of the car seemed stifling. The fast food bags smelled nauseating. She grabbed the Coke. "Keep my fries. I'm going up. We'll get back to it tomorrow."

Winter opened the car door, letting in the cool, wet night breeze. The headache still threatened, and she just wanted to sleep it off.

"Bright and early for a run?" Noah asked. "Good way to burn the tension off. Keep on an even keel. Unless you're up for another kind of tension-burner." He dropped her an exaggerated wink.

It was half-fascinating, half-irritating that the thought was distracting enough to make Winter pause. She studied him in the light of the parking lot. Raindrops clung to his dark brown hair, and his green eyes were lit with amusement, his lips quirked up in a smile. He needed to shave. His angular cheeks were bristled with stubble.

"Running sounds good. Six?"

The creases of his smile deepened, like he knew what she'd been thinking. "Six, it is."

She slipped into her hotel room, locking it behind her, and froze. All warm thoughts of her partner evaporated.

She hit the light switch, bathing the room in the anemic glow of the overhead light. Nothing looked different or disturbed. Her suitcase was where she'd left it. The bathroom door was still ajar about six inches, the bedspread free of wrinkles. But someone had been in her room.

She sniffed the air. Just the slightly musty smell of the carpet.

Moving forward, her hand unconsciously on the butt of her gun, she nudged the bathroom door open. The shower stood empty, its clear plastic liner pushed back on its rings. Her things were beside the sink. Nothing glowed red.

Feeling foolish for being scared, she moved back to the main part of the room. Knelt down and lifted the dust ruffle on the bed. Beneath, there was nothing.

Running her hand between the mattress and box spring, she stopped.

The picture. The camera.

They were gone.

She told herself it didn't matter. She'd memorized the picture. She hadn't planned on doing anything with the camera. There were no prints on it. Nothing to tie either item to The Preacher.

But he'd been in her room.

The hair on her arms rose, and goose bumps pebbled her flesh.

She closed her eyes, but Elbert's vacant stare was there waiting for her. He hadn't been killed by The Preacher, but blood and death...violent death was forever going to be a trigger on any memories tied to that night.

Her breath came short and choppy. He'd been in her

room again. The hands that had so skillfully butchered her parents had touched her doorknob. Maybe other things. Shiny dots danced at the edges of her vision.

Was he watching her now?

She swung around and ripped the painting down from over the TV, gouging the wall and cracking the frame hard against the top of the television.

The empty hole where the camera had been stared back at her.

Who was he that he could get into her room so easily? Or was she crazy? The picture was gone. There was no proof her family's killer had been there. Watched her with a hidden camera. Left her a picture of her little brother.

A knock on the door had her swinging around, pulling out her weapon.

12

"Winter. What's going on?"

Noah pounded on the door. He'd heard banging coming from her room through the thin walls. It sounded like Winter was throwing furniture. But when she opened the door, she didn't look disheveled, just pale and unbelievably tired.

Noah pushed past her, his gun at his side. "What the hell was that noise?"

The painting that hung over her TV, a carbon copy of the same ugly painting that hung over his on the opposite wall, was on the bed. The frame was damaged, nearly splintered down one side. Where the painting had hung, there was a crudely gouged square cut in the drywall.

"What the hell is that from?"

He rounded on her, but she'd sunk down in one of the chairs that sat at the small table.

"There was a camera in there."

"Was? Where is it now?"

She shrugged. "He came and took it back."

"*Who* came?"

"The Preacher, I assume. Unless Alma, the nosy front desk clerk, has prurient tastes."

Fury pounded in Noah's temples as he holstered the weapon. "Dammit, I thought you'd told me everything." He grabbed the chair across from her and yanked it back, sitting down. "Spill," he bit out. "Now."

She didn't raise her eyes to him, just absently rubbed the side of her head. "He left me a picture of my brother. The first night we were here. Taken after Justin's disappearance."

"And you didn't tell me, why? You didn't report this to Max, *why?*"

Finally, she looked at him. Her eyes were dark, looking bruised almost. "It's between me and him."

He thought back to everything he knew about her teenage run-in with one of the most notorious, elusive serial killers of their time. She'd come home to find her parents murdered in their beds. Her brother gone. She'd been hit over the head with a crushing blow that had cracked her skull and been left for dead.

He knew why she'd become an FBI agent. It didn't take a genius to know she planned to leverage her new job into catching the man that had destroyed her family. She'd told him as much. What she hadn't told him was that she planned on going it alone.

"You have serious sharing problems," he bit out. "Grab your things."

"I'm not—"

"*I'm* not fucking around. Grab. Your. Things."

Her eyes sparked a little, but she did as he said. She zipped her suitcase. Grabbed a bag and headed for the bathroom, moving slowly, like an old woman.

Then, she stopped, and her shoulders tensed. Her hands flew to her head, and she moaned, hunching her shoulders. "Not *now,*" she groaned.

Noah leaped to his feet as Winter's knees seemed to crumble beneath her. She was sinking to the floor when he reached her, catching her just before she hit her head on the corner of the wall. As he reached out for her, blood splashed against his arm.

"Winter, what the hell!"

He eased her back in his arms. Blood gushed from her nose, a vivid crimson stream. Her eyes rolled back in her head, and he scrambled to balance her in one arm as he reached for his cell phone to dial 911. Her head lolled back, her long hair loose from its usual severe bun, brushed the carpet. His heart pounded. Seizure?

Before he could get hold of his phone, she gave a bone-wracking shudder, and squeezed her eyes shut, coming to with a gasp.

"She's in a cage. We have to help her."

"Hold on." He eased her to the carpet and stripped off his t-shirt. Wadding the fabric up in a ball, he dabbed it under her nose. Winter struggled to sit up, and he pushed her firmly back down.

"You don't get to scare the hell out of me and then jump up and run laps," he warned her, his voice tight. "Can I get you something to drink? Has this happened before? Is there a medication you need to take?"

Winter shook her head, taking the t-shirt from him. "I saw her. A girl. Locked in a cage. We need to help her."

"We need to help *you* first." He brushed a strand of black hair back from her cheek. Her face was damp with sweat, and her eyes looked wild, a deeper blue.

She locked eyes with him, her urgency palpable. "I'm fine. It's just another thing I can do. It's like a...vision. I can't explain it, and I'm sorry I didn't tell you. But I saw a girl at the farm. Rebekah's farm. She was locked in a cage, like an animal."

He believed her. Of course, he did. Who the hell knew why, but Noah knew to his core that Winter was telling the truth.

"Are you okay? Can you stand up?"

"Yeah." She waved away his hand and struggled to her feet. She tried to hand his t-shirt back, but the gray material was blotted with dark red. Winter grimaced. "I'm sorry about the shirt."

He didn't respond, just took the small cosmetic bag she'd dropped and retrieved her things from the bathroom. She was sitting on the edge of the bed, staring at the carpet when he came out. He hefted her suitcase. "Come on. You're bunking with me." Next door, he set her suitcase by his. "Bed. Now."

She didn't move. "We need to go out to that farm."

"We can't. I believe you about the girl, but we can't call in a search warrant based on a bloody nose and a seizure." He held up a hand to forestall her argument. "I'm not saying that's all it was. I said I believe you. But getting anyone else to buy it is more than a stretch. We need to work this through within our boundaries."

Winter stood in the center of the room, looking like she was going to fall over at any second.

Noah softened his voice. "Come on now, go to bed. You get changed. I'm going to run over and grab the blankets off your bed. I'll sleep on the floor."

He gave her a few minutes of privacy, taking his time. When he came back, she'd done as he said and was tucked in securely, her back toward the door. He made up a pallet of blankets on the floor, reminding himself that he'd slept on worse during his stint in the military.

"Tomorrow will be better," he promised Winter quietly.

She didn't answer.

❄

WINTER RELIVED the vision in her dreams.

A girl, pregnant and terrified, in a cage. The bars that imprisoned her looked meant to hold in a large animal, not a young woman. She beat at the bars, screaming soundlessly, her fists bloodied. Beneath her dirty, baggy t-shirt, a very pregnant belly strained against the fabric.

Winter slept only fitfully and woke sometime in the dark hours of the night with a new assurance that she hadn't had after her vision the night before. The girl was dead. Winter couldn't save her.

In the morning, Winter had a hard time looking Noah in the face. The alarm on his phone went off at five, and he was instantly awake, switching on the bedside lamp on the end table above him. When he sat up, his tousled hair and shoulders were backlit at the side of the bed.

"You okay?"

Instead of answering, she just nodded. His easygoing manner was as effective as a mask, giving nothing away, but he looked her over, searchingly. Finally, deciding she'd do, he stood up and stretched.

"I'll go shower next door. Then we'll be done twice as quick."

He grabbed some clothes from his suitcase and headed out without interrogating her, for which she was grateful.

She showered quickly and was just getting off the phone with Max when Noah came back. His hair still showed marks from his comb, and his black pants and gray sweater were a little rumpled, but he looked alert and ready to go.

More alert than she felt, anyway.

"How'd that go?" he asked warily.

"I brought him up to date. On everything except the obvious," she added, giving him a sideways glance. "We need to make some progress, or he's going to send someone over here to take over for us."

"Can't have that," he replied, clapping his hands together as if to punctuate the sentiment. "Let's get some coffee and hit the streets."

"We need to make a stop first."

It was early yet, but the lights were on in the motel office. The doorbell chimed cheerily as they entered the lobby, and Alma Krueger popped her head from around the door of the back office. Instead of bright flowers, today she wore black. Her eyes were bloodshot and puffy.

"I'm sorry for the loss of your friend, Ms. Krueger," Winter offered quietly.

The woman nodded her tightly permed head, her eyes welling with tears. "I just can't believe it. Elbert Wilkins." She pressed a tissue beneath a nose that was already reddened from crying and leveled an accusing look at Winter. "I never would have sent you over there if I'd have known I'd be putting that dear man in danger."

Winter had braced herself for blame, but it still stung.

"Now, Ms. Krueger, we don't know anything yet about why Elbert was killed," Noah said, surreptitiously easing himself in front of Winter. "Can you tell us anything that might help find who did this? Point us to someone who might've known about the case we're working on? I'm told you know most of the goings on in this area."

The woman visibly softened when she looked at Noah. A combination of flattery and his good looks, Winter assumed.

"Well, now, I haven't lived here long enough to know *everything.*"

He smiled at her, dimples winking, and she melted a little more. "I'll bet you're being modest. We did hear your sister is almost as well-connected as you. Might she—"

Alma waved a hand dismissively. "Elva doesn't know half

as much as she thinks she does." She grabbed a pen studded with pink rhinestones and jotted down a name. "Go see Carolyn Walton. She's worked at the library for decades and was friendly with Elbert sometime after his wife died. I daresay she'd be able to help you."

They thanked Alma and left her to her quiet sniffling.

"Don't take what Alma said personally," Noah warned Winter as they headed to the Rise N' Dine to get breakfast and wait for the library to open. "Elbert may have had a target on him from the moment those bones were discovered. His death was not our fault."

Maybe not, but it felt like they'd led a killer straight to him.

CAROLYN WALTON WAS A TALL, slim woman who looked to be in her mid-seventies. She wasn't traditionally beautiful. However, her long, waving white hair softened a somewhat hawk-like nose, and her brown eyes glittered with intelligence.

She was shelving books in the children's section when they found her. She looked afraid for a moment when Winter asked if she had a few minutes to talk, and then resigned.

"Certainly," she answered briskly. "I assume you're here about the Disciples. Please, follow me."

She led Winter and Noah to a small conference room and closed the door behind them. Gesturing for them to take a seat at a round, wooden table, she did the same.

"I heard about what happened to Elbert," she said without preamble, folding her hands on the table in front of her. "I can only imagine it has something to do with those bones being excavated out near the Archer farm."

Winter watched Carolyn's face carefully as she launched into the questioning. "Alma Krueger mentioned that you'd been friends with Mr. Wilkins. That you might have some information on the cult that would be helpful to us."

She smiled wryly. "Alma Krueger does a lot of mentioning. In this instance, she's correct. I do know a bit about the Disciples, if only because I've spent a lot of time with Elbert Wilkins. We had a personal relationship several years ago. You could say that group was a little bit of an obsession with him."

"What could he have known about them that would have put him in danger?" Noah questioned.

"I'm afraid I can't help you there. That group disbanded many years ago," Carolyn said, her brow furrowed in thought. "I know that he kept meticulous files, though. There were several people of Linville and Harrisonburg that may not have wanted it to be common knowledge that they once associated with the Disciples."

Winter's pulse quickened. "You know of former members?"

"I do," Carolyn confirmed quietly. "Many people that followed The Bishop, Wesley Archer, just sort of melted into the communities around here when the Disciples fell apart. They became doctors and lawyers and put their 'colorful' pasts behind them. It could be that someone didn't want their former connection to the group known once they started digging into the past up there in Linville."

"Why did the Bishop have so much sway with the people?" Noah asked.

"He promised a better life, and a future without violence, and that was during a so-called simpler time, decades ago. Wesley was fired up with the righteousness of a man who had witnessed the worst ways that humans could treat each other, and for better or for worse, his ideals were based in a true desire to change the world for the better. He was said to be eloquent, convincing, and impassioned. Can you honestly say that now, during times of war, increasing divisiveness in politics, school shootings, and violence becoming commonplace and sometimes even applauded, that he wouldn't have the same sway today with some people?"

"We would appreciate anything you can give us," Winter said softly, dodging the question. Indeed, Wesley Archer would have most likely had an even bigger following if social media had been available during his time.

Carolyn loosened her hands from where they clenched together on the table in front of her. Taking a deep breath, she nodded. "I've got names for you. Please be discreet in questioning these people, however. They have new lives now and may not appreciate their pasts being dredged up after all these years."

Winter jotted down the names she gave them but stopped at the last one. "Wait, David Benton? Is he any relation to Tom Benton? The Tom Benton who works for the Harrisonburg Police Department?"

Carolyn nodded. "Yes. David Benton is Tom Benton's father."

The sound of "Sweet Home Alabama" rang out in the quiet that followed. "I'm sorry," Noah said, reaching into his pocket. He pulled his phone out and read the display. "I have to take this." He stepped out of the room and was back less than a minute later. "We have to leave," he told Winter, his face unreadable. "That was Gary Miller."

They thanked Carolyn Walton for her time. She was still watching them as they left the building, her hands clasped tightly in front of her.

13

The crime scene was a study in controlled chaos.

At the center of it was the Forensic Archaeologist, Marilyn Fosner, working with laser-intense focus. At the same time, she seemed to be giving a running lecture, occasionally gesturing with a small shovel to a group of older-looking interns who were riveted to the woman's every word. Around the dig site, canvas awnings had been set up as various stations for processing evidence. Marilyn had managed to pull in additional hands, if the number of people milling about was any indicator.

"Three more." The police chief looked as if he'd aged a decade in the short time since they'd seen him last. His face was drawn, and his color wasn't good. His belly, where it sagged over his belt, even appeared to have shrunken. "What the hell are we dealing with? It's a fricking cemetery up here."

Noah cast a sideways glance at Winter. He'd bet she already knew what they had, but she played her cards close. Her smooth face was relaxed, giving away none of the inner turmoil she was probably feeling. "What's the newest?" Her voice was as calm as a lake.

The chief sighed and motioned them over to a portable picnic table that had been set up under an awning. A large, insulated beverage dispenser sat on top of it, with a tilting stack of Styrofoam cups beside it. He grabbed a cup and filled it.

"This tastes like shit," he grumbled, gesturing to them to help themselves, "but it's technically coffee."

Noah grabbed two cups and filled them with the over-cooked-smelling black liquid. He sat down beside Winter, across from the older man, and placed a cup in front of her.

"Two more infants," Chief Miller said wearily, folding his arms on the table. "And a new element to the mix. A much more recent body, still in decomp stages. Looks like a young girl. After all those bones, it sure was a helluva shock to find something like that. Not that anyone should have to get used to finding baby bones, but you know what I mean."

Noah felt Winter stiffen beside him, where their arms brushed together. "How long ago? Any estimate from Marilyn on time of death?" Her even voice was edged with pain, but only Noah heard it. He realized he was finally getting to the point where he could read Winter very well.

Miller shrugged. "She thinks the girl had been dead only a few years. They're going to need to take more time getting the remains out since the excavation process won't be as straightforward. On the other hand, there's a better chance we'll get some workable evidence. Clothing scraps, hair, things like that."

Noah cast a sour glance upward, at the distinct sound of fat raindrops pattering against the canvas over their heads. "It'd be helpful if the rain cleared up."

Miller glared at the sky. "My wife swears I'm growing mold, spending all this time out here."

"Any sign of infant remains buried near the girl?" Winter asked. "Or cause of death?"

The chief shook his head in the negative. "They haven't progressed that far. Like I said, it's a slower process. But it looks like she was alone in there."

"What about the other remains found? The infants?" Noah asked. "Any signs of birth defects? Cause of death on those?"

Chief Miller nodded. "Those, at least, are like the others. Same small-caliber hole in the back of the skull. And the medical examiner will be able to tell us more, but we're looking at misshapen heads, bone defects, like crooked legs or abnormally short arms, things like that. Florence Wade has got her hands full. I called down to Roanoke this morning. She's bringing on more hands to help so they can try and work through these as fast as they can. Priority will be on this...fresher body, once we get it out of the ground."

"What about Elbert Wilkins?"

"What about him?" Miller's face seemed to sink in even further, the lines deepening. "I've got a team on it, but no one heard or saw a thing. We've canvassed the neighborhood and haven't turned up even a nosy old lady who conveniently spends her days spying on the neighbors. Used to be, someone was always keeping one eye out the window."

Noah made a derisive sound. "Now, people don't even know who lives next door."

Chief Miller nodded. "And no one stays at home anymore. Everyone works, puts their kids in daycare." Based on the chief's expression, Noah wondered if this societal development seemed almost worse than the murder to the older man. He sighed deeply. "No prints at the scene. Nothing disturbed, aside from the room where Wilkins was found. They're working on pulling any trace evidence, but so far, we've got nada."

"You're doing the best you can with what you have," Noah told the man sympathetically. "No one expects this kind of thing to happen in their town. I had something similar a couple years back in Texas. Two bodies found, years old, seemed like no leads. Dead ends everywhere. Something will break."

Chief Miller gave him a thin smile. "Yeah, I've got more years on the job than you. I do appreciate you trying to cheer me up, though. You ever solve your cold case?"

"Yep. Took us a while, but we did it."

Winter had turned her attention away from the interchange.

She was restless, Noah could tell. She jumped up from the table to pace, her shoes squelching in the churned-up mud that blanketed everything in this area of the woods. Her head down, she narrowly missed one of Marilyn's interns, intent on carrying a heavy-looking box across the clearing. The kid dodged, bobbling the load he carried, and threw Winter a dirty look.

"Agent Black," Noah called out before she could cause more havoc in the already chaotic area. "What's on your mind?"

She made her way back to the picnic table and leaned on it, pinning Chief Miller with a look. "Do you have a man to spare to keep an eye on Carolyn Walton? A librarian in Harrisonburg?"

He looked a little surprised at her abrupt topic shift but thought about it for a moment and nodded. "I've got someone."

"Good," she replied, easing back a bit. "I don't think she'll be in any danger, but we didn't think Elbert Wilkins would be either. We got some information from her this morning, and I'd like to see her protected, just in case."

"Was she able to tell you anything useful? I never would've thought to talk to her, but she dated Wilkins a while back, didn't she?"

"She gave us a little more on the cult. Some names of people who were connected with the Disciples."

"Yeah, it's looking more and more like that's what we're dealing with up here. No missing babies in the area. A nearby group that kept mostly to themselves and didn't much mingle with people in town. Anybody belong to that group that I'd know?" Chief Miller perked up with interest. "I've only been here since 1995, when I moved up from Florida to take this job, but I know most everyone around here. I didn't figure former members would hang around in the area after the cult disbanded, but I guess it makes sense."

Winter hesitated for a moment. She reached into her bag and pulled out a small notebook, opening to the page that held the list of names Carolyn had given them.

Chief Miller took out a pair of reading glasses from his pocket and slid them on. It was a short list and didn't take him long. "David Benton?" he frowned, pointing at the last name on the page. "David's on the City Council. Nice guy. He's also Tom Benton's dad."

"Yep, that's what we were told," Noah said and looked around. "Where *is* Officer Benton today?"

Miller frowned. "I gave him a couple days of personal leave time. Wasn't the most convenient thing with all that's going on, but sounds like his wife is having some health issues. He'd used up his vacation time for the year but took family medical leave. Said they'd be out of town for a day or two. You can bet, though, that I'll touch base with him on this."

Judging by the look on his face, the experienced police chief would be more than touching base, Noah thought. He might be kicking ass. It was no secret that Benton had been very vocal about the whole cult thing being urban legend. He'd said outright that the idea that they killed a bunch of people was bullshit. That they were just a bunch of harmless hippies.

"I'll be interested in what Officer Benton has to say too," Winter said. "There's always a chance he didn't know his dad belonged." A chance, but it was doubtful.

Noah stood up. "In the meantime, we'll make ourselves useful, look through some missing persons reports. See if we can start narrowing the field a bit on the most recent body found while we wait for the ME to take a look."

Chief Miller nodded, still looking pensive. "Let me know if you find anything out. I'll get an officer to keep an eye on Ms. Walton. The CSI team should be done over at Wilkins' place later today, and I'll give you a call when they're finished."

"I'd appreciate that," Noah replied. "We'd like to take a look through his files, or what's left of them, and see if anything might've been overlooked when they were tossed."

Winter had pulled herself out of her thoughts and thanked the chief for meeting them, giving him a small smile. That was good. Noah had been meaning to tactfully bring up her way of interacting with other people. He understood that she had an intense focus and tended to block everyone out at odd moments, but to others, she might come off as a bitch.

To him, she was an ever-changing, fascinating puzzle.

"Did you need to go over there? Check things out where Marilyn's working?" Noah asked her in a low voice when they'd gotten out of the chief's hearing distance.

"No," she answered, not looking in the direction of the dig. "I've seen all I need to. I can give a description of the victim. That should help us with the missing person's reports."

Watching the tight set of her shoulders under the black blazer as she preceded him down the path to the trail, Noah decided he wasn't really jealous of Winter's abilities at all. She looked like she was carrying the weight of the world.

THEY WERE SITTING in a small hipster-haven coffeeshop with their laptops when Winter found her.

Kayla Bennett.

The girl was pretty and smiling in the high school picture they'd used for her missing person flier. She had long, silky-looking brown hair that hung past her shoulders, partially obscuring the school sweatshirt she wore for the photo. Light blue eyes that crinkled at the corners when she smiled. A sweet, rounded face with a stubborn chin.

According to the information her parents had given in the police report, Kayla was an honor student in tenth grade at a private school in upstate New York, near Saratoga Springs. She was athletic and popular and had never given them any trouble. When her parents had gone through a divorce, Kayla had withdrawn from both of them. She started staying out late and acting out, smoking pot, though she'd always been a well-behaved kid.

One night, after a particularly bad fight about infidelity between the parents, she'd taken off, running away from home. An avid hiker and nature-lover, she'd taken only her car—a silver Ford Focus she'd gotten for her sixteenth birthday—and all of her hiking and camping gear.

Her car had never shown up, stolen or otherwise. And except for a couple of early sightings of the girl by hikers on the Appalachian Trail, Kayla hadn't been seen either.

But Winter knew that face. She'd seen it just the night before.

Conversations buzzed around them in the coffee shop, and Noah hummed the chorus of a country song, at counterpoint to the folksy-sounding music piped in overhead, while he looked through his own search results.

Winter studied Kayla.

Her vision came back to her with crystal clarity.

A cavernous-feeling, dark room. A cage, open at the top, but with thick, closely set metal bars, padlocked from the outside. A cot with a couple of blankets and a flat-looking pillow. Kayla, her long hair tangled and matted on one side, as if she hadn't had access to a brush in a while. Her face, not as round, streaked with dirt and tears.

She wore a t-shirt that was ripped and stained. The front of it read "WSSS Basketball." Waldorf School of Saratoga Springs. Beneath the t-shirt, Kayla's pregnant belly strained with her efforts to escape the cage that held her.

Who had taken her? Was her pregnancy and fear of her parents' reaction to it the reason she'd run away? Had she been kidnapped while she was hiking the AT? If that was the case, why hadn't her car been found at a trailhead somewhere? What was the connection with the dumping ground and the farm?

However she'd gotten there, Kayla had ended up in Harrisonburg, Virginia, more than five hundred miles away from home.

Winter turned her computer to face Noah, who looked up from his own laptop. "This is her."

His eyes darkened as he looked over the face of the innocent young girl on her laptop screen. "She looks like a sweet kid. You're sure?"

"I am. The timeline fits. It's her. She was wearing a t-shirt with the logo of her private school on it, so if enough of it is left, they'll be able to identify her pretty quickly. She was sixteen."

Noah's face hardened. "Email that to Miller." He rattled off the chief's email address. "Tell him you'll send more as you find them. We probably should send over a few, just so it won't look strange to hit the nail on the head the first time. Once the ME is done, though, it'll be clear that this is our girl."

Noah had a very deeply ingrained sense of right and wrong. Black and white. Crime and justice. It felt strange and wrong to provide their colleagues in law enforcement with even a couple of additional photos that they knew wouldn't identify the correct girls, but Noah decided that Winter was on shaky enough ground already. She knew too much about the case that she shouldn't know, and Chief Miller wasn't stupid.

If she was right—and she hadn't been wrong yet—the t-shirt Kayla Bennett wore would identify her as the runaway from Saratoga Springs. If not, there were dental records available and DNA. Meanwhile, they'd work with the extra knowledge they had. It made his head hurt a little, thinking about the logistics of running a parallel investigation, but he had to believe that everything would even out eventually.

"You ready to blow this popsicle stand?"

Winter closed her laptop almost gratefully, the smiling face of Kayla Bennett disappearing from view. "Going to do some rounds? Interview some former Disciples?"

"Actually, I think it's time to head back to the Archer farm."

"We don't have a search warrant," Winter reminded him, raising one dark, finely arched eyebrow. "Are we just going to walk up to the door and ask Rebekah if we can take a look around the farm for a rusty cage that may or may not have been used a couple of years ago to house a runaway whose body has been uncovered just south of her property?"

He gave her a half-smile. "No warrant, and my weak male brain hadn't come up with that straightforward of a reason to go back. I was thinking instead that maybe I could flirt with the owner, get her to give us a tour." He bobbed his eyebrows. "If you think you can control your jealousy this time."

Her eyes glittered at him for a moment. "I'll try to restrain myself from starting any catfights," Winter deadpanned. "Are you sure you're up to the task, Casanova?"

"I think so. I might need a little extra fortification first. Are you going to finish that blueberry scone?"

14

"I'm getting tired of restaurant food," Noah complained from the passenger seat. "I'd even settle for my own cooking at this point. Do you know how to cook?"

"No," Winter replied, keeping her eyes on the road ahead of her. The back of her neck was tingling. She had to consciously keep her focus on maintaining the speed limit. She had a feeling they were going to find something at the farm. Intuition or whatever it was that was prodding at her, it didn't matter. She wanted to get there, and in a hurry.

"Didn't your grandma teach you how to cook?"

She shook her head. "You ate literally twenty minutes ago. I don't know how you're still even thinking about food."

"Hey, just making casual conversation. What about her meatloaf recipe? Did she give you that?"

"She's shown me how to make some things, but I don't have her creative talent. As far as the meatloaf recipe goes, she promised she was taking that one to the grave with her."

"Beg her to leave it to you in her will," Noah advised. "How are your grandparents doing, anyway?"

After his week-long stay with them, it seemed he thought

of them as extended family. Which was fine because they'd certainly adored him. It appeared the feeling was mutual. "They're doing well. Spending some time at their condo in Florida. Kind of a week-long test run to get them excited for when they go down for the winter. Grampa has gotten the hang of Skype, for the most part."

"You'll have to let me know next time you're giving them a call. I wouldn't mind saying hi."

And he *wouldn't* mind, either, she thought, glancing over at him. Noah was sprawled carelessly in the seat, the back lowered, his fingers laced across his flat belly and his eyes closed. Probably fantasizing about her grandma's meatloaf.

They'd adored him, all right. Noah had charmed Grandpa Jack by cheerfully losing at poker, and Grandma Beth was a sucker for servicemen with dimples. They'd hinted strongly over the past several months about how nice "that Noah" was, as they called him. Her grandma had even stopped trying to set her up on blind dates with friends' grandsons, probably pinning all her hopes on "that Noah."

If she were looking for a relationship, Winter admitted, he'd be the best candidate. He brought her out of her dark shell with his bright charisma. He made her remember to laugh. He got along with everyone effortlessly and was a natural leader. Plus, he was hot. She hadn't been so out of it the night before that she didn't notice how incredible he looked without a shirt on.

No fraternizing, she told herself, letting her lips curl into a grin.

She turned into the driveway of Rebekah Archer's farm, and Noah's eyes flew open as soon as the car started bumping over the rutted driveway. "Cool it, Don Juan," she murmured as they came closer to the house. "It doesn't look like the lady is home."

The truck that had been parked outside of the house when they'd last visited wasn't there.

He shrugged. "Might as well knock anyway."

Winter let Noah take the lead. He headed up the steps ahead of her, the wooden stairs creaking under his weight. He knocked and waited a minute, then rang the doorbell. There was no response. "No shoes under the bench," he noted, looking through the stained-glass style window into the foyer.

"Better luck tomorrow, I guess," Winter said, tucking one of their cards in the frame of the screen door.

"I wasn't exaggerating," Noah said, checking out a couple of cows that had come up to the fence to watch them curiously. "Ms. Archer does have some nice cattle."

"Yes." Winter tucked her tongue firmly in cheek. "I noticed you checking out the heifer. I mean, heifers."

He shot her an unrepentant grin and moved toward the fence. One of the cows—Winter really didn't know a heifer from a Hereford—let out a low bawl when she saw him coming. "You have a way with *all* the ladies."

"This one's a gentleman." He scratched the cow's snout and the bovine drooled. "Technically. He's a steer. Castrated," he clarified in a helpful voice.

Casually glancing around, Noah started walking toward one of the barns at the back of the house.

"What are you doing?" She hurried to keep up with his long strides in the tall grass.

"Just being nosy."

"Pretty sure that's not okay as it pertains to warrantless searches of private property."

He'd already reached the barn doors and was glancing inside. "I'm not going in," he pointed out. "Just taking a quick look at her setup."

Winter looked too. No large cages, just open pens. Still,

electric tension raised the fine hairs on her arms. "Great. You looked. Satisfied your curiosity. Let's go."

"You see that?" Noah asked, pointing farther out into the field. A yurt-like structure squatted in the wide open space. It was round and low, with what looked like a tented top. "Wonder what's in there?" He headed off in that direction.

"Seriously, Noah, come on. We're already on the edge with Max. What's it going to look like when we're caught trespassing? We'll get pulled off the case." His response was to whistle a couple of bars of the old Kenny Rogers song, "The Gambler."

Up close, the yurt looked old. The cream-colored walls were mottled with mildew on the outside. Grass had grown deep on all sides, and the semi-permanent decking that sat outside the front door was warped and weathered a grayish green. The door itself was made of thick wood and sounded securely locked when Noah jiggled the handle. He stepped down off the creaking deck and waded through the deep weeds to one of the windows set into the side of the canvas wall. The plastic was murky, yellowed with age, but he peeked in.

"Check it out," he told her.

Winter had to go up on tiptoes, and the musty smell of the canvas tickled her nose, but she could make out a round room with benches ringing the walls, sitting on flooring made of the same decking material as the tiny front porch. In the center of the room sat a kind of podium, or altar, with a cross sitting on top. It was flanked by two tall candles.

"I wish we could get in and see how fresh that candlewax is. It's hard to tell, but the place doesn't look like it's sat empty since old Wesley's time."

The sound of rapidly swishing grass behind them caught their attention at the same time someone yelled, "Hey! This is private property!"

Rebekah Archer was struggling toward them through the field with a small child on her hip. Her face was red with exertion and fury.

"She looks like she'd be immune to your charms right about now," Winter whispered.

Noah lifted a welcoming hand to the irate woman. "Just smile, and try not to look jealous, darlin'."

When he plastered a big, nonthreatening grin on his face, Winter had to admit, if he turned that wattage on her, she'd be inclined to forgive a little casual trespassing.

"What are you doing here?" Rebekah demanded, her voice hard. "I saw your card in the door. It's illegal for you two to be running around on my private property without my express permission."

"I'm sorry," Noah said, his voice as smooth as fresh-churned butter. "Agent Black, Winter, told me the same thing." He shrugged, looking almost boyish. "I'm afraid when I saw your cattle out there, it got me homesick, and I wanted to get out here and take a look at your spread. From a purely curious perspective, of course."

Rebekah's eyes narrowed, and she set down the child she held, holding the little girl's hand tightly. "Don't feed me any of that down-home bullsh—"

Noah cleared his throat, drowning out the last word. He hunkered down into a crouch and gave one of his winning smiles to the little girl beside Rebekah. Winter didn't know much about children. She avoided them, usually, as painful reminders of the brother she'd lost. But this one was gorgeous.

She looked to be about three years old, plump and sturdy. She had long, dark brown hair pulled up into a ponytail at the back of her head, held in place with a little red bow that matched her red and white checkered dress. Her face was like a porcelain doll, smooth and perfect, with rosebud lips and large blue eyes ringed with dark lashes.

"Mama," she whispered, tugging on Rebekah's hand. "That man ith pretty."

Noah chuckled. "You're pretty, too, sweetheart."

"But you hath denth in your cheekth," she lisped seriously. "Right here." She pointed one finger to the side of her mouth.

Rebekah's face softened as she looked down at the little girl. "Jenna, it's time to go up to the house now. Remember? We were going to make cookies this afternoon."

"Can tha pretty man come with uth, Mama?"

"He'll walk back with us, kiddo, but he has to leave now. Right?" She gave them both a pointed look, her eyes still dark with anger.

Jenna tugged free of Rebekah's hold and walked to Noah. She held out one hand, as regally as a tiny princess, and he straightened and took it with due deference. Jenna pulled him to where Winter stood and held another hand out for her, looking up. "You can come with uth too."

"Thank you," Winter replied with the same level of seriousness. She took the little girl's other hand. It was warm, and Jenna squeezed her fingers tightly.

"You're pretty too. Like Thnow White." Jenna blinked up at her owlishly. "Don't eat applth, jutht in case."

That startled a laugh out of Winter. Even Rebekah smiled a little. The kid was unquestionably adorable. They made their way through the long grass, Noah carrying on an animated conversation with Jenna about fairy tale characters.

"Your daughter is charming," Winter said to Rebekah, who walked silently beside her, watching Jenna like the two of them were going to steal her away.

"So's your partner," Rebekah answered wryly, looking at Winter squarely. "Did he honestly think I was going to fall for that good ol' boy act and ignore the fact that you were both searching my property without a warrant?"

Instead of angry, Rebekah just looked exasperated now. Winter still didn't like her or trust her, but she gave her a small smile. "He didn't lie. He started out by petting one of your cows. It mooed at him."

Rebekah just shook her head and rolled her eyes. "Next time, make him wait until I'm home to go poking around. It's an invasion of privacy."

Winter studied her closely, but Rebekah's face gave nothing away except irritation. Either she was a good actress, or she really had nothing to hide. She didn't want to push her luck, but the other woman seemed resigned to the fact that she'd caught them snooping. "I don't suppose we could get a real tour?" she asked lightly. "I promise not to bat my eyelashes at you."

Rebekah made a snorting sound. "I don't peg you as the eyelash-batting type. But today won't work. Jenna's got an art class later, and I promised her we'd bake cookies first. It's her instructor's birthday today."

"Art?" Winter asked, genuinely curious about this woman and little girl.

"Painting." Maternal pride shone in Rebekah's grin. "She's incredibly gifted."

"You're a lucky woman." She looked down at Jenna. The girl was still gripping Winter's hand tightly, but she was absorbed in an outlandish story Noah was telling about the time he met a dragon at a grocery store. In the produce section. It was a vegetarian dragon.

"I know," Rebekah murmured, also looking at her daughter. "I'm thankful for Jenna every single day."

"How about tomorrow?"

"Tomorrow?"

"For the tour." Winter batted her eyelashes exaggeratedly.

She was rewarded by a quirking of Rebekah's lips. "You're persistent. And you're really bad at that. You look like a gnat just flew into your eye."

Winter laughed, and Noah glanced over at them in surprise.

Rebekah finally shrugged. "If it'll convince you that my dad and this place had nothing to do with the bones on the hill, fine. Come back the day *after* tomorrow. Noon. Jenna goes down for her nap, and you guys can roam the place then and poke your nosy noses into all the corners you want. I'll even give you a key to the dungeons." She batted her lashes at Winter in return.

"Mama, we don't have dungeonth," the little girl pointed out.

"Thank you, Jenna. My mistake. Our old, spiderwebby basement, then. Now say goodbye to the FBI agents."

They'd reached the front of the house.

Noah made Jenna giggle when he bowed formally. "It was a pleasure, Princess Jenna."

She dropped a pretty impressive curtsy in return, and then turned around and gave Winter a tight hug around her thighs. The kid couldn't reach her waist. Taken by surprise by the show of affection and the unexpectedly warm glow that came with it, Winter patted the girl's silky hair awkwardly.

Jenna stepped back and looked up at her. "Thmile more," she whispered soberly, her china-blue eyes shining in what looked like sympathy. "Your mama and daddy wouldn't want you to be tho thad."

Winter's breath froze in her chest as she watched Jenna spin around, sending her checkered skirt swirling around pudgy knees clad in white tights, speckled with grass seed from her walk through the field. Jenna grabbed Rebekah's hand and led her up the stairs, crowing, "Cookieth!" like a normal kid.

"Winter? You all right?"

Noah was watching her, concerned. He was probably worried that she was about to have another one of her spells and crumple on the driveway of the Archer farm. But it was the bang of the screen door slapping shut behind Rebekah and her daughter that shook her out of her daze. Digging in her purse for the keys, she tossed them to him with hands that felt weak.

"I'm fine. It's your turn to drive."

He gave her a last, searching look. She climbed into the passenger's seat to avoid answering his unspoken questions.

15

"Tommy, you've had enough."

Tom Benton gripped the whiskey tumbler tighter in his right hand and scowled. "Don't call me Tommy. I'm not a kid." Even to him, his voice sounded whiny. That just pissed him off more.

"You need to go back to work tomorrow, and you don't need to be hungover, either. The last thing we need right now is for you to lose your job." Samantha moved around the den, picking up dirty plates and cups, and he wanted to yell at her to just go away.

He rubbed at his gut, the pony keg that used to be a six-pack. His ulcer was acting up again.

He sighed. Pitifully.

"It's not my fault. It's those stupid fucking Feebs."

Getting Sam fired up right now wasn't a good idea, but he couldn't seem to help himself. He'd rather have her mad at Winter and Agent Dalton than seeing him for the pitiful excuse for a man he was feeling like right now.

It worked.

Sam straightened up, anger in her brown eyes. "Have they

been giving you trouble? Talking to the chief about you behind your back?"

"Now, hon," he placated, secretly enjoying her defense of him. "Don't go getting all mad. You know you almost lost *your* job when you went after Agent Black at the restaurant the other day."

"That wasn't even my fault." She dropped the plates back down on the coffee table with a loud clatter. "She was just so high and mighty, parading around with her badge and gun, pretending she was better than me."

"She could never be better than you. She's a freak," he reminded her.

"Damned right." Like she did whenever she was anxious, she took out the elastic from her hair and shook it out around her shoulders. He wished she'd dye it again. When they were dating in high school, it had been a pretty, brassy blonde. Now, it was faded, mostly back to its natural darker blonde color that more closely resembled dishwater. She grabbed it all up again and dragged it back into its usual ponytail, chewing on her bottom lip as she snapped the elastic.

"I'm going to talk to Chief Miller. She can't throw her weight around like this and get away with it. Hell, she's probably using that woo-woo shit on him."

"No. No, you're not going to talk to my boss." He sat up too fast and slopped some of the amber liquid out of his glass. It dripped off the back of his hand and stained the flowered arm of the chair. Oops. "Hon, you can't go off on anyone in the condition you're in."

Frowning, she put a hand to her belly. She was still skinny as a pole, and if he hadn't seen the positive pregnancy test for himself, he'd never believed she was actually pregnant this time. It was early days yet, though, he reminded himself. He couldn't get excited yet. They'd had their hopes crushed too many times before.

"Sweetie," Tom cajoled, setting the glass on the table. It would leave a ring on the glass and Sam would complain later, but he didn't care. He stood up, a little unsteady on his feet, and made his way over to her. "C'mere." He pulled her into his arms.

She wrapped her thin arms around him. Or as far around as she could get, he thought in disgust. He had to lose some weight.

"I just want her to go away," Sam said, her voice muffled against his shoulder. "I don't like her being back here."

"She'll go away," he promised. "Winter will be heading back to Richmond before you know it. Poof. Gone like she was never here."

A sick feeling swam in his stomach, and it wasn't from the alcohol he'd consumed. He wished the high and mighty FBI agents *would* just up and disappear. They were stirring things up that should stay buried, and there was nothing he could do about it.

"YOU WANT to try to talk to Benton Junior before we corner his dad?" Winter made a face, and Noah laughed. "Did you know you do that every time his name is mentioned? You wrinkle up your nose. It's kind of cute."

"Can it, Dalton. I'll call Chief Miller and see if Benton made it into the office today."

He was glad to see that she was back to her normal self. Or, as normal as Winter usually got. She was so damned secretive, it drove him nuts. Something had spooked her at the farm, but she wasn't spilling about it.

Not yet.

He listened to her side of the conversation, letting the car idle in the parking lot of the hotel. Finally, it looked like the chief was going to get his wish. The clouds and rain had disappeared, and for the first time in a few days, the sky was vivid blue. The morning breeze was pretty crisp, and he eyed Winter as she talked to the chief. She had her fingers tucked into the sleeves of her coat.

He shook his head and turned on the heat. His eyeballs would be sweating in about two minutes, but Winter was skinny. She got cold easily.

"Benton's there. He said he'll let us talk to him together, find out why he didn't mention anything about his dad being a former Disciple before now. Hopefully, Benton's got his story straight, because he's going to feel like he's walking into an ambush."

She stared out the window as they made the drive to the station.

He was going to give her another thirty seconds before he started pushing her about her reaction in the driveway of Rebekah Archer's farm the day before. Before he finished counting to twenty, she turned to him.

"There's something weird about Jenna."

"Yeah? I thought she was a pretty cute kid."

"Absolutely. And I don't really even like kids. But she said something to me before I left yesterday."

Bingo. Hallelujah, she was sharing. He tried to control his grin. "The Snow White comment? I thought that was pretty funny. With that black hair and white skin, she wasn't too far off, y'know."

Winter folded her arms, hugging herself. Even though he felt like his face was on fire, he clicked the heater up another notch.

"Seriously, Dalton. She hugged me and told me to smile. That my mom and dad would want me to be happy."

He glanced away from the road for a moment. "Kids are weird sometimes. Even the cute ones. I've got nieces and nephews, so I know this from personal experience. Hell, one of my little cousins had an imaginary friend he named Baba Jane. Later, when he got old enough to talk about her, he described how she looked in detail. Scared the hell out of my grandpa. Bobby's description matched Grandpa's deceased mother-in-law perfectly, right down to the scraggly mink shawl she always wore."

Winter didn't look reassured. "I don't know," she muttered, looking back out the window as they passed a playground. "Her eyes. She just looked sad for me when she said it. I don't know how to explain it."

Noah flicked on the turn signal and made the turn into the station parking lot. "Well, since you finagled us another shot at looking around the Archer place tomorrow, maybe you'll figure out what makes the little princess tick then."

Inside the station, Benton was already at his desk. He did a double-take when he saw them come in, his face reddening to match the bloom of visible blood vessels in his eyes. Noah felt his lip curl a little in distaste. Even from four feet away, he could smell booze sweat. The guy had been on a bender the night before.

Benton shot an ugly look at Winter as they passed him on their way to the conference room next to Chief Miller's office. She didn't appear to notice, focused on their destination. Noah bared his teeth in a rictus of a smile at the slimy officer as they passed, and it was gratifying to watch the asshole shrink back in his chair.

Winter might not like confrontations, but Noah was looking forward to this particular one.

"Morning." Miller gestured for them to take a seat at the oblong table. He poked his head out the door, into the hall. "Tom, come on in here for a sec, will you?"

With dragging steps, Benton shuffled in. There was a mustard stain on his uniform shirt.

"Sit down, Tom. Status meeting." Coffee in hand, Chief Miller sat down at the head of the table. "Agents, would you like to start us off?"

"Sure." Noah pulled out his notebook. "So, what we've got so far is a clearing full of bodies."

Benton snorted. "Tell us something we don't know."

The chief sent Benton a warning glance, and Noah went on as if he hadn't spoken. "The first body, a boy of approximately six years of age. Severe birth defects, congenital abnormalities in the skeletal structure. Cause of death at this point believed to be a bullet wound to the back of the skull. Time of death is estimated around 1987. Remains were found by Brian Snyder and his son while hunting in the area."

He flipped a page. "We called in a cadaver dog because of the nature of the cause of death. The dog alerted to several other areas. Second burial site contained bones of an animal. Relevant because of the similar wound believed to have killed it. Third site, two victims, possibly siblings. Evidence of entry wound from a small-caliber bullet at the backs of both skulls. Both victims, children under the age of five. Visible bone defects. Fourth site, an infant. Same story, cause of death bullet wound, believed to have had skeletal deformities."

Noah looked around the table. The chief was going over his own notes, his brow furrowed. Winter was waiting calmly for him to continue. Benton was scowling, staring out the window like his thoughts were a thousand miles away.

"Then we have the anomaly. Body of a female uncovered at site five, approximately sixteen years old. Cause of death appears the same as the older remains, pending forensic investigation. However, the victim was killed within the last three or so years."

Benton leaned forward in his seat, now intent. Before he could speak, Chief Miller cleared his throat. "Recent discovery. You were out of the office."

"Proximity," Noah went on as Benton shrank back in his chair. "We learned of the existence of a group operating out of the area during the approximate era in which the earlier victims were believed to be killed, which led to an interview with Elbert Wilkins. Wilkins shared information with us about the leader of the Disciples of the Moon, Wesley Archer. Also known as The Bishop. Wilkins was murdered in his home within hours of his interview. His office and files were ransacked."

Benton had gone a sickly shade of paste-white. "Why didn't anyone call me about this?"

The chief folded his arms and leaned back, his chair creaking. "Check your voicemails, son."

Winter picked up the thread. Her voice was cool and detached, and inwardly, Noah rubbed his hands together in anticipation. Her very calmness was guaranteed to piss Benton off.

"We received a list of names from another individual, of people who were active in the Disciples during the time of the murders. Tom, your dad is on the list. Can you tell us why this information wasn't disclosed sooner?"

Benton shot upright, his chair wheeling back to bang into the wall. "What the hell is this? An ambush?"

Winter held up a hand to forestall any comment from the others. "We're going to go speak to your dad. He's not a suspect at this point. We're just gathering information. If there's anything else you can tell us, now would be the time to do it."

"You fucking bitch," Benton hissed, glaring at Winter. His

fists clenched and unclenched spasmodically. "This is all some kind of revenge for a little teasing in middle school. What kind of freak carries a grudge for that long?"

She smiled. Just a stretching of the lips, really. "I was assigned to this case by my supervisor. I'm just doing my job. Believe me, if there were a way to do it without having to encounter you, you'd never have even known I was here."

"Tom," Chief Miller snapped. "Sit down. Act like an adult and not a hotheaded idiot. The only reason I haven't canned you is that this behavior is so unusual for you, and I have to wonder why. Tell us now, like you should have before. Was your dad involved in this Moon cult?"

The guy looked like he was about to stroke out, but he sat back down. "My dad's a respected member of this community. He's been on the City Council for years. He's a card-carrying *Republican*. He wouldn't have had anything to do with a bunch of crackpots like that, much less anything to do with the murder of a bunch of kids."

His boss stared him down for a long moment, until Benton squirmed in his seat.

"Fine. If that's all you have to tell us, you can go back to your desk. You're relieved from this case. I'll give you your new assignment this afternoon."

Benton's jaw dropped, and hectic color rushed into his face. "You can't do that! Just because these federal assholes step in and—"

"Enough." Chief Miller slapped his hands down on the table in front of him, and the sound echoed through the small room like a gunshot. He levered himself up, his face hard and unrelenting. "You're officially on desk duty. Your conduct is unprofessional and unbecoming an officer. If you can't get your shit together, you can start looking for another job."

SAMANTHA CURSED the transmission on her Camry as she pulled into the lot of the police station. Every time the car shifted, it shuddered like it was going to shake loose a part and leave it in the street. She wished her husband would just ask his dad for a loan. They were barely making ends meet, and pretty soon, money was going to get even tighter. As it was, the chief let Tom drive his squad car home. But if the Camry died, they'd literally be without their own transportation.

She pulled up next to a black sedan and flipped down her visor. She fixed her lipstick and fluffed her hair out around her shoulders. Tom might be mad that she came down here, but he needed a kick in the ass.

It was bad enough that Chief Miller hadn't promoted Tom yet, like Tom said he'd been hinting around for the last eight months. It was even worse that he was letting Winter and her muscle-headed partner push Tommy around. If Tom wasn't going to say something, she would.

She opened the Camry door with a hard shot of her shoulder since there was a dent in the side that made it difficult to open. As she stepped out, the front door of the station opened at the same time, and Winter stepped into the late morning sunshine.

Sam couldn't help it. Her blood boiled.

Winter had grown up from a spooky kid into a stunning woman. Her hair was thick and black, even though she wore it scraped back, and she didn't look like she had any problem with the zits that had plagued Sam since she was sixteen. And those big blue eyes made her look all sweet and innocent. She wasn't. She was a freak.

Sam's voice came out so shrill, it surprised even herself. "You did it, didn't you? You got Tommy fired."

Winter squared her shoulders and walked down the two steps that separated them. The fact that the move shoved Winter's perky C-cups forward under the tailored, expensive-looking blue shirt the same shade as her eyes just made Sam angrier.

She'd never admit to herself she was jealous.

"I'm going to say this one last time. I don't have a grudge against you and Tom. I grew up. I moved away from here and put the past behind me. We were all kids. I'm here to do a job, and then I'm moving on. Moving on is healthy. You should try it sometime." Her butter-wouldn't-melt expression slipped at that, and Winter scowled.

"Your high-paying, fancy-ass job," Sam sneered. She'd googled just last night how much an FBI agent made, and it was a helluva lot more than a waitress at a shitty small-town café.

"Are we done here?"

Winter looked at Sam like Sam was something to be scraped off the bottom of her shoe, and she snapped. Sam lunged forward and pushed Winter, hard.

She stumbled back, but recovered quickly, her eyes narrowed. "You don't want to do this, Sam. Your husband's on shaky ground here, and this isn't helping."

"Shaky ground because of *you*," Sam screamed. "Why couldn't you have just died that night too?"

Winter's face lost all color, like Sam's words had drained her of every drop of blood. She looked younger. Hurt. For a second, Sam remembered how they used to sit on the merry-go-round at the park, sharing candy from the corner store.

"I'm sorry," Sam gasped. Tears burned her eyes. "I didn't mean that. I'm such a bitch." The tears overflowed, scalding her cheeks. "I'm pregnant," she blurted, putting a protective hand over her stomach. "We can't afford to lose Tom's job. It's high-risk, and I've had so many miscarriages and I—"

Abruptly, she shut her mouth as Winter's partner, the big handsome guy, stepped out.

Sam backed up a couple of steps. "Please," she finally said in a low voice. "Please don't get Tom fired. We just couldn't survive that right now."

She'd gone too far. She despised herself for losing it like a crazy person and *begging* on top of that. It had to be hormones.

Retreating like a coward, she slid into the passenger seat and blindly cranked the ignition. As she backed out, the car jerking into reverse, Winter just watched her go.

16

"Well, this has been a fun morning so far."

Winter hardly heard Noah. She was thinking about what she'd said to Sam. *I'm here to do a job. And then I'm moving on.* It wasn't true. She could solve these murders. Go back to Richmond. Get assigned to another job. Become an FBI lifer and retire out at the mandatory age of fifty-seven. Even catch The Preacher and see him locked in a cage. But she still wouldn't have moved on. She'd still be stuck here in Harrisonburg.

"I need you to drive me past my old house."

"Sure," Noah readily agreed. He flicked on the turn signal and made a right.

"I don't even have to tell you where it is?" Goose bumps pebbled her skin, and the skin at the back of her neck felt tight.

"I'm a cop, sweetheart. It's my job to know where stuff is. You sure you're ready for this?"

"After so many years? I'd better be."

"Hey, I heard what Benton's wife said. Don't let it get to

you. She's one of those small, petty people that never got over high school and will never be satisfied with what she has."

"Yeah, Sam doesn't bother me." It was true. She'd been shocked by the other woman's malevolence, but she could see for herself that Sam was lashing out because she was unhappy. Winter didn't wish her ill. She hoped Sam's pregnancy went to term with no problems. She obviously badly wanted a baby and miscarriages had to be heartbreaking.

And speaking of heartbreaking…the streets around them became more familiar.

She wondered if the old guy who had lived on the corner was still alive. He'd always grouched at her brother for cutting through his yard on his BMX. He'd literally sit on his porch and yell, "Get off my lawn!"

Mrs. Beverly had lived in the blue house in the middle of the next block. Her roses were always gorgeous, but now they looked overgrown, sprawling out in all directions and climbing haphazardly against the side of the porch.

Memories came faster the closer they came.

The place in the sidewalk where a huge oak had pushed up the concrete. She'd hit that ledge and gone over her bike handlebars at nine years old. The scar was still a faint line under her chin, but the oak tree was now a stump.

Dan Riley's house. She'd had a crush on him at twelve and use to rollerblade back and forth in front of his house daily in hopes of seeing him. She'd been heartbroken when he'd gone off to college.

Mr. and Mrs. Bleeker. Full-sized candy bars on Halloween.

Little Betsy Tanis' house. She'd babysat there twice. Betsy bit her the second time, and she'd refused to go back, despite the lure of three dollars an hour.

She realized she was narrating her memories out loud to Noah when he chuckled. She decided to keep talking. She could share this with him. He'd proven himself to her over and over.

The car slowed, and then cruised to a stop.

She could smell the dead leaves she'd crunched through, huffing her way home from Sam's house in the middle of the night. Feel the cold breeze against her face that carried the smell of woodsmoke from someone burning leaves earlier in the day.

The house sat big, dark, and silent. Sharply shadowed in the bright moonlight. The image in her mind was superimposed now over the run-down reality. Grass grew thick in patches in the yard, and a crooked "For Sale" sign sat drunkenly near the cracked sidewalk. The wood siding was a sickish faded green now. Her dad had painted it that summer, and it had looked crisp and grassy-colored, paired with immaculate white trim.

She'd stomped up the front walk, wrenching open the front door with its heavy brass knob. Her parents never locked up, especially when she was out for the night. It was a safe neighborhood.

She'd kicked off her Nikes in the hallway and made her way up the stairs in her stockinged feet. A smell had caught her attention. It was almost like hamburger. Coppery and heavy in the upstairs hallway, where the bedrooms were.

Her stomach lurched at the memory, and she took a steadying breath. It wasn't real. It was a memory. The light, masculine smell of Noah's aftershave grounded her as much as his silence did.

She'd walked past her parents' door, slightly ajar. Her brother's bedroom door was closed, and the faint, bluish glow from his SpongeBob nightlight showed under the door.

She had her hand on her doorknob when something made her stop. A slight scrape.

She'd shivered, turning around.

The hallway was empty. Moonlight streamed through the window at the end. On the carpet in front of her parent's door, she noticed clumps of mud. The carpet had been flattened in places, as if by heavy boots.

Which was strange. Mom never let anyone wear shoes in the house. She said the carpet would last longer that way.

She backtracked, slowly, looking down at the clumps of mud as if they'd speak up and tell her how they got there. In front of her parents' door, a flash of movement beyond it caught her eye. She put her face up to the crack and didn't understand what she was looking at for a moment.

Someone had written all over the walls. Crosses. Letters. Numbers. Big splatters that went almost all the way to the ceiling and ran down the light blue plaster walls in streams, only to trickle over the wide wainscoting and puddle on the wood floor.

From where she stood, she could see her dad's hand, hanging over the side of the bed, like it usually did when he slept. As she watched, a drop of paint slid off the end of his index finger to land in a small pool at the side of the bed.

She drew in a breath to scream almost before the scene had fully registered in her brain. She pushed the door open wide and took three steps into the room, her sock-clad foot stepping in paint, still wet, making her slip a little.

She locked eyes with her mom. Mom's were opened wide, as wide as it was possible for them to be open, and she had paint all over her face, even in her mouth. Behind her, Justin called her name. She spun around to tell him to stop, to go back to his room, but something slammed into her head.

There was an explosion of pain.

Starbursts of white lit behind her eyes, and she didn't feel herself hit the floor.

Faintly, for the first time, before the white sharply faded to black, she heard a voice echo through her mind.

"Sorry, girlie. I don't want you. Just him."

NOAH FELT SHAKEN to his core.

She'd walked him through it in third person. Calm and detached. Just like she'd been reading to him from a Stephen King book. He'd been quiet, understanding it was something she needed to relive. Something she hadn't done yet.

He felt like he'd seen the horror of that night through the eyes of a thirteen-year-old child. Relived it right along with her. It was enough to ice his guts. Even her voice had sounded younger somehow. Like she was possessed by the soul of some other kid who had gone through that bloody experience.

Now, she looked as wrung out as a dishrag. Her shoulders were slumped with fatigue as she stared at the house she'd grown up in. But her eyes, when she turned to look at him, were sharp with discovery. Dark with pain, but energized somehow.

"He'd intended to take Justin. I never knew for sure. I've never remembered that before."

"Are you finished here?" His voice sounded like he had something caught in his throat.

"Yeah." She lay her head back against the seat and looked at the house again. "Thank you."

"Don't thank me," he burst out angrily. "Son of a bitch, Winter. If I'd had any idea..."

She shook her head and gave him a small smile. "You

couldn't have had any idea. No one does. Honestly, though, it had to be done. Thanks for hearing it through."

He shoved the car into drive and pulled away from the curb so quickly, the tires squeaked. "I need some fucking coffee."

"That sounds good."

How did she sound normal? How did she go through every day like a normal person? He was beginning to think he'd wrapped his head around her abilities. Those were just like weird personality quirks, and he liked quirky people.

But that…?

How could anyone go through something like that and hang on to their sanity afterward? It was devastating. Damaging. And that was just to hear it.

They drove in silence to the same hipstery coffee shop they'd stopped at before. The Mumford and Sons song playing, usually one that made him tap his fingers, grated on his ears. "A large coffee, double shot of espresso," he told the girl behind the counter curtly.

The college-aged girl, huge holes gauged in her earlobes, her nose and lip pierced, blonde hair—judging by her almost invisible eyebrows—dyed a dark purple, raised an eyebrow and turned her back to get his coffee.

Winter stood beside him, silent as a wraith, studying the menu.

The barista slapped his to-go cup on the counter hard enough to slop coffee over the side. "And you?"

"Large mocha. Decaf, no whip, please." Winter gave the girl an apologetic smile and nudged Noah hard in the ribs. "Ignore Oscar here."

The girl sniffed and fired up the grinder with a loud roar.

Winter paid with the company card and left a generous tip.

They picked a couple of battered-looking armchairs by the front window, near a half-dead ivy plant.

"Stop looking at me like that." Winter sipped her coffee, steam wreathing her face.

"Like what?"

"Like I'm going to crack and fall into a million pieces. I feel better. Really."

"Maybe I'm the one that's going to crack."

"Trust me. It helped."

He took a swallow of his coffee and relished the burn that scalded his throat. "I'm sorry," he told her gruffly. "I didn't get it before."

"Don't apologize." Fire came into her eyes. "And definitely don't start pitying me or treating me any differently just because you 'get it' now. That's exactly what happened right after."

"Tell me. I need to know it all."

She sipped her mocha again and plucked a dead leaf off the ivy plant, setting it down carefully beside her cup on the table in front of them.

"I was in a coma. You knew that."

He nodded.

"When I came out of it, it was scary. Everything was bright, too bright, and so loud. I had these headaches. And everything, every detail, just about jumped out and punched me in the face. I remember this one nurse, I could tell what she'd had for lunch, right down to the Dijon mustard on her sandwich. It was awful."

She pulled off another brittle brown leaf and twisted it between her finger and thumb for a moment. Then, she set it down next to the other one. Two dead leaves. He stared at them, unable to look at Winter for the moment.

"No one would tell me about my family. I'd missed their funeral. My grandparents came to the hospital as soon as I woke up...but for an hour or so, I had no idea what had happened. When they got there, they explained most everything. That was probably the hardest part."

She plucked a third leaf. This one was still partly alive, the green and white pattern faded into crinkly brown edges. That leaf was dead. It just didn't know it yet. It went in the line on the coffee table.

"My grandparents moved everything to Harrisonburg. We didn't live in the same house. Instead, they rented one near the middle school. We couldn't just pretend everything was different but normal. Kids at school looked at me weird. Started calling me Lizzie Borden, like the murders were my fault."

Noah swore. *Lord of the Flies*, in real life. Adolescence was a cruel age to be an outsider.

"Ironically, I have Samantha and Tom to thank for getting me out of that situation," Winter said with a half-smile. "Along with dealing with all the crap at school, I was struggling with the new things my brain could do. Like I told you before... Sam didn't react like a BFF should. It got around school almost immediately, and the harassment got worse. Then, the media labeled the killer as The Preacher because of the crosses, so kids taunted me with things like Bibles. My grandparents finally pulled me out of school when an eighth grader knocked me into a wall hard enough to almost break my cheekbone. We moved out of Harrisonburg, to my grandparent's house, and started over. Things got better."

Noah glanced over at the barista. She was scowling into her phone, texting like there was no tomorrow. If Winter had a normal life, she might've still rebelled and remade herself like goth girl over there.

Instead, she had faced trauma that no child should ever have to endure, the abuse that followed, and came out ahead.

Noah felt like he'd been coldcocked. Looking at her

across from him, face serene and composed, a strand of black hair fallen loose from her bun, tickling her collarbone, he realized he had a problem. Flirting was one thing. He bantered as easily as he breathed. But what he felt for Winter was something else altogether.

He could very easily find himself in deep—treacherously deep—waters.

avid Benton's address was listed in a posher part of town. He'd apparently done well for himself over the years, since Tom had grown up near Winter, in a smaller, middle-class area. A sprawling two-story with an attached four-car garage sat placidly behind a black iron fence that enclosed a perfectly manicured yard. A gardener puttered in the beds out front, clipping things back for the winter. The gate stood open, since Noah had called Benton Senior to let him know they were coming.

Winter thought she caught a glimpse of a figure standing in front of the bay window at the front of the house, but the curtain dropped back into place, and the outline disappeared. "So, how are we going to approach this?" she asked, breaking the silence that hung in the car.

She was glad to be getting back to the matter at hand. Noah had been staring at her oddly since she'd taken her trip down memory lane. She couldn't tell what he was thinking, and it bothered her. She wanted to get back to their easier, friendly, working relationship.

"You want to take the lead?" he asked. "You know the guy, right?"

"Only in passing. I'm told he went to the funeral, but I don't remember seeing him other than at school events and things like that. But yeah, I'll take it."

The sidewalk that led to the front door was made of weather-aged brick. Winter noticed that not even a spare blade of grass had been allowed to poke through between the bricks.

Their knock was answered by a housekeeper wearing a traditional black dress and white apron. It seemed pretentious, but the woman gave them a professional-looking, welcoming smile and opened the door wider.

"Come in. Mr. Benton is in the library. He's expecting you."

The foyer of the house was discreetly elaborate, with gray marble floors and skillfully painted landscapes framed in gilt on the walls. The housekeeper led them down a short hallway that opened into a high-ceilinged room.

David Benton stood up from where he'd been seated at a large mahogany desk, a brandy snifter in front of him, though it was barely after noon. He gave them a politician's smile, wide and toothy. She wouldn't have recognized him if they'd passed on the sidewalk. Instead of his son's portly build, he was tall and lean. Black hair, faded to distinguished white at the temples, was brushed neatly back from his narrow face.

"Little Winter Black," he said warmly, holding out a hand. His nails were groomed neatly, and an expensive watch gleamed at his wrist, beneath the sleeve of his white dress shirt. "It's very nice to see you again. I always wondered what happened to you after you moved away. It seems that you've done well for yourself. The FBI, of all things."

Winter forced herself to smile. "It's nice to see you too."

He gave an avuncular chuckle and turned to Noah. "And you must be Agent Dalton. We spoke on the phone. I must say I was surprised to get your phone call. How can I help you?"

"I'll defer to my partner." Noah's smile was remote. "Special Agent Black is the case agent, and therefore my superior."

Winter shot him an amused look. Humble Noah was a new persona for him.

"Certainly." David Benton laughed again and addressed Winter instead. "Still seems like you're playing pretend to me, like you used to when you were a kid, running around in my yard. But *Agent Black*, please have a seat. Maria, will you bring coffee for our guests?"

The maid, who had been standing quietly attentive at the door, murmured her agreement and hurried off, her low black heels tapping on the marble tile.

"I'm sure you've heard about the human remains that have been found just north of here, in Linville," Winter began, pulling out her notebook and pen.

"Yes, of course. My son is an investigator on that case."

Noah cleared his throat but didn't say anything. She saw him lean back in his seat from the corner of her eye and cross his ankles.

"We're hoping you can give us more information about the...um, religious group that operated near there, back in the eighties."

David arched one smooth black brow. "I'm afraid I wouldn't be much help with that."

Maria came back with coffee, and set the tray with three cups, a pitcher of cream and sugar on his desk. "That'll be all, Maria." His tone was cutting, and she looked at him in surprise. "Please close the door behind you and make sure we're not disturbed." Another pointed look from David and she scurried out much faster than she'd entered.

"We're told that you were a member of Wesley Archer's group, the Disciples of the Moon."

Small spots of color showed high on David's cheekbones. Seemed he did share some tendencies with his son, namely, a short fuse.

"That's ridiculous. Who told you that?" He was trying to stay cool, but Winter could see the skin around his white collar was darkening as well. "Was it that old newspaper writer? Wilkes?"

"Wilkins," Noah put in.

"Whatever. He's been around for years. Digging into government conspiracy theories and such. Writers have such wild imaginations. He had files on everything from aliens to chemtrails. If he said anything, he can't be believed."

Interesting. David Benton was the first person who had cast any doubt on Elbert as a reliable source of information.

"Actually," Winter said, watching Benton closely. "Elbert Wilkins was murdered. His files were destroyed." It was a stretch, since they hadn't actually been destroyed, just rifled and possibly stolen.

A look of relief passed so quickly over Benton's face that it would have been unnoticeable for someone not paying such close attention. The smooth, urbane mask dropped back into place, and David smiled sadly. "I'm very sorry to hear of his death. Maybe one of his government conspiracies finally got him in the end."

"That seems a little insensitive," Noah put in.

"It wasn't Wilkins that told us." Winter nudged Noah's foot discreetly. Noah nudged back. "And there is no source," Winter lied smoothly. "We discovered some old documents, and you were listed. You and your wife."

David's face paled. "That's impossible."

Her bluff had paid off.

Before she could push him further, there was a mechanical whirring sound outside of the closed double doors, and a rubbery squeak. David fumbled for his phone and stabbed at a button, his knuckles gripping the edge of the handset until they whitened.

"Daaard." There was a thump, and the door rattled.

"Maria. I said we were not to be disturbed." He was angry but also afraid. Blazingly so.

Before he could protest, Noah had jumped to his feet. "I've got it. No problem," he offered cheerfully. He'd hardly opened the doors before an electric wheelchair buzzed into the room. Noah stepped back, barely saving his toes.

"Daard." The word was accusing.

The man in the wheelchair had David's dark hair and lean face. He was very thin, strapped into the chair so he didn't topple out sideways, counterbalancing the odd curvature of his spine. He looked to be in his twenties, but his face was scruffy with a day's worth of beard, threaded with silver strands. His eyes were wide and almost childlike in their silent accusation. His hands, where they curled over the arms of his chair, were misshapen, the knuckles knotted, tendons standing out thick. The green plaid shirt he wore with rumpled khakis was loose on his painfully thin frame.

David looked at the newcomer in silent horror, and Winter didn't miss the calculating glance that he threw their way in the next moment.

Maria bustled in quickly. "Jake!" she exclaimed. "I thought you were watching your movie. I'm so sorry, Mr. Benton." She took the handles of the chair and flicked the switch to manual operation. "Come on, sweetheart," she murmured, casting a nervous look at Winter and Noah. "I've got cookies. Peanut butter."

The offer of cookies didn't placate Jake. "Daard!" His

voice echoed in the hallway, abruptly cut off by the swift click of the doors closing again.

"My nephew," David said bluntly. "When my sister passed away, God bless her, I took Jake in."

"Sounded like he was saying 'Dad,'" Noah pointed out unnecessarily.

"He's nonverbal." David's voice was hard, matching the cold glitter in his eyes. "He could have been saying anything. And he thinks of me as a father. I've been raising him for a long time now."

"Without your wife's help?"

A muscle popped in his jaw. "My wife's been dead for twelve years. Cancer. Now, if that's all," he stood, not waiting for a reply. "I'll see you both out."

"I'm afraid we have more questions for you, Mr. Benton," Winter said when he rose.

"I'm afraid I have a meeting." He tossed a cursory look at his watch. "In ten minutes. You'll have to call back and schedule an appointment, but there's nothing more I can tell you. By the way, my son would have told me if my name had been found on any 'paperwork.' I wasn't a member of that cult."

They weren't going to get any more out of him. Winter and Noah were ushered out so quickly that there was no time to say anything else. Noah stood on the doorstep, worked in a beautiful circular brick design, looking at the door that had slammed behind them.

The gardener stopped deadheading black-eyed susans to give them a curious look.

"Something tells me that getting another appointment with the estimable David Benton won't be as easy next time," he commented wryly.

"Excuse me," Winter asked the man with the basket tucked over his arm. "Could I ask you a quick question?"

"*Lo siento. Yo no hablo Ingles.*" He shrugged his stooped shoulders apologetically.

"*Esta bien. ¿Quién es el hombre en silla de ruedas que vive aqui?*"

The gardener looked surprised for a moment. Not that she spoke Spanish, but that she didn't know who the man in the wheelchair was. "*El hijo de jefe.*" His face creased in an affectionate smile. "*El es un buen chico. Fuerte a veces pero muy dulce.*"

She smiled back. "*Si. Pude ver eso. Gracias. Tenga un buen dia.*"

He gave her a polite nod and went back to his flowers.

"What was that about?" Noah asked on their way back to the car.

"The gardener was just telling me what a nice boy his boss' son is. Loud sometimes, but very sweet."

THINGS WENT EXACTLY NOWHERE the remainder of the afternoon. Noah had called two other names on the list Carolyn Walton had given them. Tony Collier, a retired schoolteacher, was very brief with them.

Unlike David Benton, he lived in a modest house in a run-down neighborhood. Like David Benton, he also lied through his teeth. No, he didn't know anything about the Disciples or Wesley Archer. His wife had died of cancer a few years before, or they could ask her themselves, he'd said, a little desperately.

Neither of them had ever been a part of a cult.

"Do you live here alone?" Noah asked, deceptively casual.

Absolutely, was the answer. A widower. No kids.

Back in the car, on their way to the next stop, they hashed out the evidence they'd both seen that there was definitely another person living in the home. Framed artwork on the walls, beautiful, melting watercolors, signed "Alison" in shaky black ink. Well-worn American Girl books and volumes of fairy tales on the shelves next to novels by John Grisham, Shakespeare, and Peter Straub. The wheelchair ramp that led to the front door.

"It never ceases to amaze me," Winter sighed. "Why do people lie about such easily proven things? The man has a wheelchair lift on his van."

At the third stop, Darin Bowman wouldn't even open the door. They knocked for a good five minutes. Darin lived just down the road from Tony, in a neatly maintained ranch house. He had been friendly enough and had promised he'd be home that afternoon when Noah spoke with him that morning. An older Nissan sat in the driveway, but there was no sign of movement inside the house.

"They're closing ranks."

Winter agreed. "Did a call from David Benton do it, do you think?"

"Could be. Knocking on doors makes me hungry. Where are we having dinner, since I can't get at your grandma's meatloaf anytime soon?"

They ate at a steakhouse that evening where Noah put away a massive T-bone steak, salad, baked potato, and side dish of macaroni and cheese. Winter settled for a petite filet with thick French fries and treated herself to a glass of red wine. Despite the drama of the day and the dead ends they'd seemed to run into at every turn, they'd made progress. She was actually looking forward to calling Max for their regular update.

"How soon until we try to shake Tommy Benton down again?"

Noah buttered his fourth biscuit thoughtfully. "As much as I'd like to take this particular bull by the horns right now, things could get volatile if we go to his place, especially if he starts drinking as soon as he gets home from work like I suspect. We could do it in the morning?"

"Before we head out to your girlfriend's farm?" Winter teased, glad things seemed to be settling back to normal between them.

Instead of retorting that she was just jealous, or making some off-color response, Noah looked up at her with an uncharacteristically serious expression in his green eyes. She was cutting a bite of steak, and the intense look on his face made her hands go still.

"Trust me, sweetheart. If I could pick any woman in the world out for myself right now, it wouldn't be Rebekah Archer."

18

Tom Benton woke up with a headache. It was nothing new. He knew he'd been drinking too much lately, but dammit, a man had the right to unwind at night when he got home from work. Especially a man with as many worries as Tom had.

He rolled out of bed, careful not to wake Sam up. Her back was to him, her long hair spread out on the pillow, tangled like it usually was in the morning. Sam wasn't a restful sleeper. She tossed and turned and gritted her teeth. He knew she was stressed, and almost getting let go from her restaurant job hadn't helped matters any. Money was tight and what had turned into an endless battle of getting pregnant—and staying that way—was taking a toll on both of them.

This time would be different, she'd promised him. The lady doctor Sam went to had told them that Sam likely wouldn't be able to carry a baby to term. She didn't have a strong enough uterus for it, or something. But Sam was almost painfully hopeful, promising that she just knew it would work out this time. They'd have the perfect baby boy, just like they'd always wanted, in about eight months. He couldn't bring himself to get his hopes up, and he wasn't looking forward to the inevitable heartbreak.

Nothing was going his way lately. He felt like he was wearing a shit magnet around his neck. Deep in his heart, he knew this pregnancy wouldn't be any different.

His mood already sour, Tom left the bedroom and padded down the hall, barefoot and only in his jockey shorts. In the bathroom mirror, his face looked puffy, his eyes bloodshot as hell. He took a piss and then brushed his teeth. He wasn't looking forward to work this morning. He thought about showering, but after a quick sniff at his pits, decided he'd be fine for another day. It just seemed like too much effort.

He pulled on the uniform pants Sam had hung up for him like she always did and swiped on some deodorant. Dragging a white t-shirt over his head, he was about to reach for his polyester shirt when the doorbell rang.

Shit. It was only six-thirty.

He hurried out before whoever it was could ring again and almost groaned when he saw two shapes on the other side of the wavy, clouded glass of the front door. It was Winter Black and her meathead sidekick. Anger bubbled as he yanked open the door.

"What the hell are you doing here?"

The meathead gave him a friendly smile, and Tom wanted to slug him.

"Morning, Officer Benton. We were wondering if you had a moment to speak with us. Sorry about the early hour." The asshole grinned, showing a toothpaste-commercial smile, looking as harmless as a Jehovah's Witness. "Just wanted to catch you before you left for work."

Winter watched him steadily with those spooky blue eyes, unsmiling.

"No, I don't have time to talk. You can catch me at the station."

"Well…" the meathead drawled. "We didn't figure you'd want to talk at the station. Being that this is about your dad and all."

His dad. He'd known it was coming, but dammit, he still wasn't ready to deal with this.

Rage spiked, and Tom opened his mouth to blast them when he heard Sam's sleepy voice from the bedroom. "Hon, who is it?"

Sam. She couldn't overhear this.

He lowered his voice, looking daggers at the unwelcome visitors. "I'll meet you at the McDonald's up the street. We will not do this in my house."

Shutting the door in their faces, he swallowed back his anger and went to the kitchen to make his wife a cup of the expensive herbal tea she bought down at the hippie food co-op. She swore it was good for expecting mothers. The FBI assholes could just wait.

"Nothing to worry about, sweetie," he called to Sam. "Forgot to pay the paperboy again."

"Think he'll show?" Noah asked, glancing at his watch again. It had been nearly a half-hour since they'd left Tom Benton's house.

"He's here." Winter had her eyes trained on the parking lot.

He polished off the last of his spongy pancake and washed the syrupy-sweet mouthful down with overcooked coffee. They both watched as Benton got out of his cruiser and stalked toward the restaurant.

"Good cop/bad cop won't work. He's a cop, too, and he doesn't like either of us particularly well."

Winter looked at him with that unusual depth that sometimes showed in her blue eyes. When she got that look, he knew whatever she said would turn out to be right. "He'll tell us what he knows today. He's done dodging. Look at him." She inclined her head slightly to where Benton stood at the counter, placing an order. "He's tired."

It was true.

Benton's usual belligerent stance had softened into what looked like defeat. His shoulders slumped a little, and he looked like a man who didn't have any hope left in the world. The guy was an ass, but Noah couldn't help feeling a little sorry for him.

Benton's bluster wasn't up to its usual setting as he slid into the chair across from them. "Can we do this fast? I need to be to work on time."

Noah bit back a comment on the fact that Benton was the one who had kept them waiting. He also wanted to bristle at the way Benton addressed only him, pretending Winter didn't exist. He nodded instead. "We'd like that as much as you. Winter and I stopped by your dad's house yesterday. We met your brother."

Despite the circumstances, Benton quirked a smile. "How's Jake doing? Did he chase you with his chair? That thing does like twenty miles an hour. I always tell him I'm going to clock him one of these days for speeding."

Noah was surprised that the man across from him hadn't acted like his brother didn't exist. It must not be a family secret...just one that Benton's father didn't want tied to the investigation.

Winter, though, wasn't fazed. "So, he's your brother?"

"Of course." Benton scowled, narrowing his bloodshot

eyes. "You think I have a problem having a brother with disabilities? What kind of asshole do you think I am?"

Her mouth pressed into a line, like she was holding back answering that last question. Instead, she went with a different one. "Why didn't I know you had a brother?"

"You probably forgot." Benton shrugged. "Or just never met him. My mom homeschooled him. She was pretty protective. Both my parents were."

"Why'd your dad tell us Jake was his nonexistent dead sister's son?" Winter's voice was sharp. "And that he never had anything to do with the Disciples of the Moon?"

Benton looked at them both, his expression shuttered. "My father didn't have anything to do with the murders. I just want to put that right up front."

"Sure," Noah lied, his voice smooth. "We never thought he did. We're just a little curious as to why you claimed no knowledge of all this from the beginning, and your dad appears to be doing the same."

Benton took the lid off his coffee and laid it aside. The eating area was thankfully empty, except for the three of them. Noah and Winter patiently watched Benton study the murky brew like it held the answers to the infinite problems of the universe.

"They were a couple of the original members," he finally said. "Joined up with The Bishop early on. Former hippies. They left after my brother was born."

"Why did they leave?" Winter asked.

Benton looked up at them, silently pleading. "I don't know a lot, okay? Nothing that would be helpful to the case. Hell, if it had been, I would have brought it all up sooner. I just didn't see any need to. My father's got political aspirations and my mom..." He winced. "My mom passed. I don't see any reason for tarnishing her memory in any way. She was an amazing person."

Noah took a drink of his own lukewarm coffee. He wanted to tell Benton that he could have compromised the entire investigation by holding back. He didn't deserve to wear a badge. He wanted to tell him that he was a spineless coward and should have not only given the chief any information he had up-front, but recused himself from the investigation in the beginning, given his family ties to the cult.

Instead, he nodded with what he hoped looked like encouragement while Winter sat in attentive silence next to him, studying Benton intently.

Benton took a steadying breath. "Like I said, my parents were early members. They didn't talk a lot about their time there, but from what I pieced together over the years, everything started great. It was a happy place. Wesley Archer was a visionary. Had this vision of a new generation being raised up smarter and kinder than the current generation. He fired up his whole congregation. They were going to raise their kids to save the world."

"What went wrong?" Noah asked as Benton trailed off.

"I don't know. They never talked about it, like I said. But I got the feeling things weren't as utopia-like as they should have been. My mom got pregnant with Jake. Gave birth to him there. But something went wrong. He was born with severe disabilities, as you saw."

"Does he have a specific diagnosis?" Winter asked in a quiet, sympathetic-sounding voice.

Benton seemed to relax a little.

"No. He's got a lot of things…some, the doctors weren't even able to stick a label on. Spinal issues. Bone density stuff. Cognitive disabilities. You met him. He doesn't talk. I could always understand what he wanted, though." Benton smiled a little. "Disabilities or not, he's my big brother. We still managed to get into some shit when we were younger."

"Were you born there too? At the commune?"

Benton shook his head at Noah. "They left when Jake was a baby. There's six years between us. I don't know why, but I kind of wondered if it was because Jake needed more medical care than they had access to out at that farm. My parents were always really protective of Jake."

"I can see that," Noah offered. "If I had a kid who had some health troubles, I'd want to be close to town."

"It was more than that, though." Benton turned his coffee cup between his hands, deep in thought. "They were afraid for him, I think."

"What were they afraid of?" The question came from Winter.

"I don't know," Benton said again, frustrated. "I just know that I got to run around and pretty much get into anything I wanted to. Jake couldn't run around the same way, obviously, but it still seemed like my mom...hovered. Jake has always spent a lot of time in the house. Or right out in the yard. She homeschooled him like I said, but she didn't even want to take him out for his doctor's appointments. She seemed paranoid or something. I remember hearing them argue about moving away. Mom wanted to pack up and start someplace else. Dad vetoed it. It was one of the only times I ever heard my mom stand up to him."

"What about you? You tell us all of this like you were on the outside looking in. Was it hard to have a brother who took more time and attention?" Winter's question seemed to surprise Benton. He looked up at her quickly.

"I always understood. Jake is special." The statement was made without an ounce of resentment. "Mom took care of him. Watched over him until she passed. She died of cancer when I was in high school."

"What kind of cancer, if you don't mind me asking?" The number of mothers that seemed to have contracted cancer after their time with the Disciples was more than a coincidence, Noah had noticed. Could it have been something environmental?

"She had a rare, aggressive form of uterine cancer. It only took a few months from the time her doctor diagnosed her. And then..." his voice almost broke, and he cleared his throat, "she was just gone." Judging by Benton's face, he still grieved.

Noah felt an unwelcome pang of sympathy.

He was painting a picture of Tom Benton's childhood, and it was a lonely one. A brother with disabilities who, by necessity, got the lion's share of the attention and focus. A father, who by his very lack of mention, didn't sound very involved. A mom, gone too soon to a vicious disease. The guy was still a jackass, but dammit, he was a relatable one now.

"Any idea why your father would lie to us about Jake not being his son?"

Even Benton looked troubled by the question. "Honestly, that bugs me. He's always been there for Jake. Not real hands-on, but that's just how he is. The provider. I don't know why he wouldn't have wanted you to know." His expression darkened. "He'd better not have done it out of embarrassment or some stupid shit. Jake doesn't deserve that."

Their luck at having an empty eating area abruptly came to an end when a harassed-looking mother and her four noisy kids sat down nearby. The echo of whining and bickering siblings put an end to any further questions Noah had planned on asking.

"You know, don't you," Winter cautioned, as they stood up to leave. "You have to tell Chief Miller all this."

Benton nodded, resigned. "I should have done it sooner." He dropped his untouched coffee in the trash. "Listen, I'm sorry I've been a dick." His eyes met Winter's for the first time, and he looked uncomfortable. "Back then and now. You didn't deserve it."

Winter flinched, in surprise or remembered pain, Noah couldn't tell. It was only a brief moment. She recovered almost instantly and shrugged, like it didn't matter. "It's all in the past."

"You guys haven't been as obnoxious as I figured you'd be." He smiled a little.

"Wish we could say the same," Noah said, but grinned back at him. He still didn't like the guy and couldn't wait until they'd wrapped this case up and didn't have to deal with him anymore. He'd finally come through with something, though, and it wouldn't hurt to play nice until they left.

Benton had probably gotten himself in a crapload of trouble so far. It'd be interesting to see if his belated confessions would leave him with a job when his boss found out.

19

Winter was glad when Noah suggested they set up shop for the morning at what was becoming their usual coffee shop. She didn't want to be at the police station when Benton finally talked to Gary Miller. She also didn't want to be back at the hotel.

Noah continued to sleep on the floor of his room while she slept in his bed. He insisted that he'd rather have her where he could keep an eye on her. He even regularly swept the room for bugs or hidden cameras. The close quarters were getting to her, though.

She was uncomfortably aware of him, especially in the middle of the night. She could hear every rustle of the blankets when he shifted. It was too intimate. She'd seen the way he'd been watching her lately. And if Winter was being honest, she'd been watching him back. They were co-workers. Friends, too, but she couldn't let it go any further than that.

The coffee shop was mostly empty of hipsters that morning, and they had their corner with the comfortable chairs to themselves. The coffee, too, was better, and there were fresh-baked scones.

"So, we've got a definite pattern forming," Noah said, settling back with his laptop open, his fingers already moving rapidly over the keys. "We'll have to check out cause of death for the other former female cult members on the list, but it's looking like cancer."

"Disabled children," Winter added. "Buried near the property. At least two surviving kids. Jake Benton and probably Alison Collier. Pregnancy is a recurring theme here." She opened up her file of notes and began to type up a transcript of their conversation with Tom Benton.

"I'm going to check into environmental concerns in the area. PFAS is a thing now. They're discovering it in water sources all over the country. Has some health concerns, and cancer's one of them. So are birth defects. CDC records should show if there's a higher level of cancer rates in this area of Virginia."

"David Benton needs a closer look too," Winter said. She had done some reading on Perfluoroalkyl Substances and agreed that PFAS was concerning. "He sure acted like a guy with a lot to hide, and I didn't like the way he talked about Elbert Wilkins. We need to dig there and see if there's any reason he might have either killed Elbert or paid to have it done."

They worked for a couple of hours, Winter finally switching to decaf. It had to be the caffeine that had her so restless. They'd be meeting with Rebekah Archer, but she couldn't get the face of the girl from her vision out of her mind.

Noah's phone rang at about a quarter past ten. Since they were the only customers in the coffee shop and the barista was rocking out on headphones behind the counter, he put it on speakerphone and kept the volume low.

Florence Wade, the medical examiner out of Roanoke was on the line. Her voice sounded harried, which was no surprise since they'd sent her a steady stream of work. "I'm still knee-deep in all this," she said darkly. "But I wanted you all to know that I took a look at the older female victim. The female, approximately sixteen or seventeen years old, based on her teeth, had given birth. I can't tell how long it was before she was killed, but there's evidence of ligament tears on the inside of the pelvic bones. They show up as shotgun pellet-sized pockmarks and are unmistakable."

Winter's pulse sped up, and her palms went damp. She leaned forward to catch every word, and Noah did the same.

"Jane Doe was an anomaly, since we've otherwise been dealing with remains of children, decades old. From initial tests, I'd say that she's only been in the ground two, two and a half years."

Noah asked her a couple more questions. He finally thanked her and disconnected the call, but Winter barely noticed. Her mind was spinning with possibilities.

"We need a warrant," she told Noah. She was already dialing Chief Miller's cell.

Understanding flared in Noah's eyes as he quickly made the connection. "You're thinking Jenna isn't Rebekah's daughter at all."

"Start digging on her," Winter said, impatiently listening to the phone ring on the other end of the line. "We should have focused more on her to begin with. See if you can find out if Jenna is really hers."

She closed her eyes briefly and could see the little girl's face clearly.

Winter knew Noah wouldn't find any birth records for Jenna Archer and she had a feeling it wouldn't matter. They were going to be too late.

❋

THEY COULD SEE smoke in the distance almost as soon as they turned off the highway in Linville. It was Noah's turn to drive, and he had to pull over for a fire truck at one point. Grimly, his hands gripping the steering wheel so hard his knuckles whitened, he followed it, keeping just a few car lengths behind and passing other vehicles in its wake.

"I'm sorry." Winter felt Noah glance at her, but she didn't want to look at him. "I should have known. I should have been able to figure it out sooner."

"Knock it off," Noah replied. He eased the sedan around a curve, hardly slacking in speed. "You're not some mind-reading superhero. I'm just as capable at putting two and two together. We had no reason to think that Jenna wasn't Rebekah's daughter. Even now, we can't be a hundred percent sure she's not."

"She's not." Winter knew it to her bones. That sweet, uncannily smart kid was the daughter of a teenager who had been locked in a cage somewhere on Rebekah Archer's property before she was murdered.

How did this all tie in with the old murders? Rebekah was too young to have been involved. She'd have been little more than a child herself. Were they dealing with two completely different things? Or was Rebekah beginning...*something* where her father had left off?

Winter rubbed her forehead. An ache was beginning to throb behind her eyes. Not the vision kind, she could tell, disgusted with her fickle "gift." The tension headache kind. Jenna, the adorable little girl who had held her hand and told her not to be sad. And Rebekah had seemed like a devoted, proud, protective mother. Would she hurt the child?

They didn't speak as they passed the trail to the crime scene on the hill. They could see smoke billowing above the treetops, and smell it, even though the car windows were up. There was no doubt about where it was coming from. The fire truck ahead of them switched off the sirens and slowed, turning left into the driveway of the Archer farm.

The house was in flames. It was a completely involved structure fire, and there were already several trucks and dozens of firefighters moving around in coordinated chaos, trying to get it under control. Noah parked out of the way, in the long grass in front of the low hill that sloped down to the road.

They got out of the car and took in the flaming destruction. The air was choking and thick, reeking like woodsmoke, electrical components, and burning plastic. Underlying it all was a heavy, charred meat scent.

It wasn't just the house on fire. The barns, too, were in flames.

"The cattle," Noah murmured, horror spreading over his face.

There weren't any animals in the fields, Winter realized with a jolt. They were all locked into the burning outbuildings. She felt sick at the realization.

She and Noah walked farther to the south, and through the heavy smoke, could see that the yurt, the little canvas-sided chapel, was already gone. It was amazing that the long grass around it hadn't caught like tinder. The rain they'd gotten lately had appeared to at least keep the fire from spreading. They could have been dealing with a wildfire at this point.

"Did Rebekah burn all this down? Tell us to come back for a tour to buy herself some time, and then set fire to everything?"

Noah was still staring toward the biggest barn, where firefighters in heavy gear were attempting to knock back the worst of the flames, but it looked like a futile effort. "I don't know. She could just as easily be a victim. I can't imagine anyone who works with animals doing something as cruel as locking them in and sentencing them to death like this."

She was going to make a snarky comment about his rose-colored glasses when it came to Rebekah Archer, but the words wouldn't come. She remembered instead the way she'd gone back and forth with the woman the day they'd been caught on the property.

Rebekah had actually seemed like someone she'd like under different circumstances, with her obvious devotion to her daughter and her quick sense of humor when they'd negotiated about the tour.

She found herself hoping the woman wasn't capable of what they were seeing here. But more, she hoped that someone else was responsible and that Jenna and Rebekah weren't next on their growing list of homicide victims.

"Let's go see if we can find someone who can tell us more."

They found the incident commander easily. He was outside of his red SUV, a phone between his cheek and shoulder, yelling into it and giving orders to the people who swarmed around him at the same time. They waited for him to get off the phone before approaching him.

Noah briefly introduced himself and Winter, and they held out their identifications. The chief wore a beleaguered frown but shook their hands.

"A woman and her child lived here," Winter said without preamble. "Were you able to get anyone in for a preliminary search? See if there were occupants inside?"

Kurt Leggitt shook his head in the negative. He was in his forties, with the weathered look of a man who spent a lot of time in the sun and wind. At the mention of occupants, he appeared stricken. "God, I hope no one was in there. By the time we got here, things were raging. I wasn't willing to risk a man, sending him in to look around."

Winter nodded. "It's okay. There likely wasn't anyone inside. Were there any cars here when you arrived?"

Kurt shook his head but was obviously still troubled. "I just took over when the last chief retired. I was a volunteer fireman for fifteen years, so I'm not inexperienced, but I haven't had to oversee anything bigger than a brushfire until this."

"You're doing fine," Noah assured him. And they were. Smoke still billowed up sullenly from the roof of the farmhouse, but already, the flames had been beaten back to a large degree. Both the house and barns would be a total loss, but enough would remain to investigate.

"Who called this in? Was it someone who lived nearby and saw the smoke?" Winter asked the question, suddenly intent.

"That one I can answer." A young woman in full gear came up in a hurry, her face streaked with soot. "A woman named Becky Fletcher talked to our dispatcher. She claimed she was driving by and saw flames." She gave a little salute and headed back to the structure.

Winter could tell that Kurt was itching to get back to work, so she stuck out a hand. "Great, thanks. Go ahead. You've got your hands full." The fire chief turned away and Winter looked at Noah, relief washing through her. "Becky Fletcher? Rebekah Archer? Isn't that a little obvious?"

"Archer. Fletcher. Someone who shoots arrows and a person that makes arrows? I guess I can see it." Some of the tension left Noah's shoulders and Winter knew he was just as concerned about little Jenna's welfare as she was. They now had a possible suspect, at least in the teenager's killing, but at least there was no reason to believe that Jenna might be in immediate danger.

Noah's phone rang, and he pulled it out and checked the display, raising one eyebrow. "It's Tom Benton. I hope he doesn't want to invite us bowling after work, now that we're copacetic and all."

He answered and listened briefly. Winter could hear yelling on the other end of the line, but by the look of concern on Noah's face, she didn't think Tom was angry. A chill shivered through her that had nothing to do with the cool breeze that fluttered the leaves of the oak tree above them.

Noah hung up the phone. "Samantha's gone."

20

"What do you mean, she's gone?"

Noah didn't get visions or see things, but his gut was telling him right now that this was not a coincidental development. Winter stared up at him, waiting for a response. She already looked like she had the same feeling.

"Benton says that he was suspended from the department. Two weeks without pay, and he's on probation when he gets back. Apparently, the conversation with his wife afterward didn't go well. Come on."

He headed for the car, Winter close on his heels.

"My turn to drive," she said, and he handed her the keys without argument. "Did he check with her family? Mom? Sisters?" She slid into the car and adjusted the front seat, cranking the ignition almost before he even opened the door.

His foot had barely left the ground before she had the car in gear. "Yeah, they haven't seen her. Benton said that tempers were running high. Sam got on him about his drinking. He snapped on her for losing another job because of her attitude, and she started saying she was having cramps. She locked herself in the bathroom, and he went nuts, convinced she was starting to miscarry again. He heard her talking to someone on the phone, then she came out and threw some stuff in a bag and left."

She pulled a U-turn in the front yard of the farm and headed down the driveway. "Could she have been calling her doctor?"

"Benton said no. That was the first call he made after she took off, but the receptionist said she hadn't even been into the office in months. Sam claimed she'd confirmed the pregnancy and her doctor would be watching her closely, but that apparently wasn't the case, after all. He checked the emergency room, too, and they didn't have her registered."

Winter usually kept to the speed limit, but right now, she was pushing eighty in a fifty-five mile per hour zone.

"What are you thinking?" Noah asked.

"We need to find out more about Rebekah. Former friends, classmates, hell, even her college transcripts."

"We'll be lucky not to get kicked out of the coffee shop," Noah commented, cracking the window. "We smell like a bonfire."

He knew she'd been avoiding the hotel room, and he couldn't blame her. It was getting harder and harder to pretend he was okay with sleeping on the floor next to her bed like a guard dog. He'd rather be on top of the bed. On top of her.

"It's fine. We'll go back, hit the laptops and take showers. We don't want to give David Benton any excuse not to talk with us."

"You think we'll get anything out of him?"

"I know we will."

Noah didn't miss the steely glint in her eye and didn't doubt her for a second.

❄

FOR THE FIRST TIME, Winter wished she could bring on her visions at will. She'd take a raging headache right now if it meant somehow seeing the connections in all these seemingly random occurrences.

Babies buried in the woods decades before, murdered in cold blood.

The Bishop: disillusioned by war, bent on molding a new generation in the name of peace.

A teenager killed in the last few years, but not before giving birth.

Rebekah Archer, Wesley Archer's daughter. Either a victim or murderer.

A retired reporter killed supposedly at random, his files ransacked.

A prominent member of the community, lying through his teeth.

Women, dead of reproductive cancers.

Disabled children.

She half-heard the shower shut off as she crossed items off a list. She'd checked before, but looked again, unable to find a record of Jenna's birth, either in or around Harrisonburg. She did find Rebekah's college transcripts, and as she'd told them, Rebekah's college major had been in animal husbandry. She had a Facebook page, but didn't appear to have updated it in a long time.

She scrolled through the friends list and past posts, looking for leads. There was one possibility that caught her eye—a former boyfriend. His profile was public and when she went back a few years, he'd listed himself as in a relationship with her. She scribbled down his name and began a records search for a current phone number.

"Winter. Take a break."

Noah's voice startled her, and she jolted, nearly dropping her pen.

"Take a break," he repeated. He'd changed out of his earlier jeans, pulling on a white button-down shirt and black slacks. He smelled like some kind of woodsy aftershave. "Shower." He pointed in the direction of the bathroom. "I'll pick up where you left off. I'm starting to be able to read that chicken scratch you call handwriting."

When she slid toward the edge of the bed, Winter realized she likely hadn't moved or changed positions since she'd sat down. Her legs were stiff, and her shoulders ached. "There's a name there—"

"Go. I've got it." Noah had already stretched out on the bed, barefoot. His hair was still darkened and wet, curling a little at his neck. He was reading her notes, notebook in one hand, his phone in the other. "I'll check in with Benton. See if Sam's turned up yet."

"You need a haircut."

Winter felt like an idiot when he quirked a smile at her and lifted the phone to his ear. His green eyes crinkled a little at the corners when he grinned like that. She hadn't meant to comment on his hair at all. She grabbed her last clean outfit and retreated to the bathroom, pulling the door closed behind her with more force than necessary.

She showered and changed quickly, braiding her towel-dried hair. It had only taken about fifteen minutes, but by the time she came out, Noah had his shoes and coat on and was ready to roll.

"No Sam updates. Benton's close to pulling his hair out. I also added a few names to your list of possible acquaintances. Double checked a couple of other databases and didn't find any Jenna Archers born to any Rebekah Archers... or Becky Fletchers, for that matter."

He picked up the black bag that held his laptop and slung it over his shoulder. She slipped into a pair of flats and pulled on the jacket that she usually wore to cover up her service weapon.

"It's a good thing you don't take as long as most females to get ready." Noah eyed her from hair to feet. "We've got an appointment with David Benton. I'd hate to keep the guy waiting after he went to all the trouble to fit us into his cramped schedule."

"He agreed to meet with us?" Winter asked in surprise. "I thought we'd just drop in on him and demand he talk. How did you manage another interview?"

Noah smiled, but there was no humor in it. "Since we couldn't turn up any dirt on such a vaunted pillar of the community, I had to resort to veiled threats. I as much as promised I'd leak the whole story as we know it right now to the press. Put it under the guise of enlisting the public's help in breaking a cold case. I also implied that as one of the few former cult members we know of, I couldn't guarantee his name wouldn't come up. As you can imagine, Mr. Benton has suddenly become very cooperative."

DAVID BENTON FINISHED his brandy and lit another of his short cigars. He'd asked Maria to take Jake out to a movie and dinner for the rest of the afternoon, to avoid any more unexpected interruptions.

He paced in front of the bay window of his study, his heels clicking restlessly on the marble tile. How to play this? The asshole FBI agent had to be bluffing. There was no way he'd compromise his investigation by bringing in the press at this point. And he had no way of knowing that it was only because of David's intervention that reporters hadn't been camped out at the spot in the woods since the beginning.

It was a small town, but few people knew what was going

on up there. He'd had to grease a few palms to keep it that way. There was no guarantee how long that would last.

David felt like his world was crumbling apart, brick by brick. He was only keeping everything together by strength of will, and even that was starting to fail him.

He cursed himself again for losing control. He was famous for his self-command, but when Jake had rolled into the office, he'd panicked. He should have known that they'd check out his story. He didn't have a sister. They were probably just as aware of that as he was at this point.

He flicked back the curtain and felt his armpits dampen with sweat as the black unmarked sedan pulled into his driveway.

He stubbed out the cigar in an ashtray and grabbed a couple of mints from the tin in his desk. When the doorbell rang, he had himself pulled together again, greeting his visitors in Maria's absence with his usual cool composure.

"Agents, it's a pleasure to see you again." Another lie.

Agent Dalton gave him a hard handshake that carried a challenge. Winter just looked at him, her eyes icy.

"Come into my office," he urged them with a smile that he hoped was welcoming. "You know the way by now, of course."

"Of course." Agent Dalton gave him a look that bordered on smug, and David wanted to punch him. He set his back teeth and followed them into the room, still hazed in blue cigar smoke.

When everyone was settled, drinks offered and denied, Winter wasted no time in coming to the point. "Is your son here today?" Her voice was hard. She didn't look anything like the scared, skinny little girl he remembered from so many years before. This Winter was smart and cold.

He schooled his expression into blandness, trying one more bluff. "I'm afraid Tom's not here."

"We know. Tom is busy with his own concerns right now. My partner was probably referring to Jake, the son you denied was yours." Noah sat back in his chair and crossed a leg, his face looked carved from stone.

David hated being on the defensive. "I'm sure you understand, I'm very protective of Jake."

"Sure." Noah's expression didn't change. "Any good father would be. As long as you understand that it's generally a bad idea to lie to the FBI."

Winter's nostrils flared, the only hint of emotion she provided. "We need your cooperation this time. No bullshit. Your daughter-in-law and future grandchild's lives could depend on it."

David felt his hands go cold. "What are you talking about?"

"Tell us about the Disciples." Her face was set. Implacable. But in her eyes, he saw something. Worry?

"What does this have to do with my son's wife?"

"She's missing," Winter replied, her blue eyes like lasers in his skin. "Since earlier today."

His heart was pounding. "Again, what does that have to do with the Disciples? Wesley Archer's been dead for years."

A few more carefully placed bricks were coming loose. David's stomach clenched. He wasn't going to be able to salvage this situation.

"We've got reason to believe there's a connection," Agent Dalton put in. "Maybe you can start at the beginning. Tell us about the Disciples of the Moon."

"I will," he promised, sweat beading on his forehead. He could feel it. They could see it. "Just tell me what's going on with Tom and Samantha, or I'm not saying another word." He reached for his phone, lifted it from the cradle. "Forget it. I'll call Tom myself."

"Samantha's pregnant again. She's also missing." Winter

leaned over and locked eyes with him. She reached out and pressed the disconnect button on the base. "I believe the events that began up near Linville decades ago have started up again."

After the initial stab of fear he felt at her flat statement, a calmness settled over him.

David set the phone gently back in its cradle and sat back in his chair. He looked at the framed photo of Nancy sitting on his desk. It was taken the year before she got sick. She was standing next to Jake's wheelchair, her hand on his shoulder and her other arm around a teenaged Tom.

It was taken on one of their vacations to Florida. She was so gorgeous. Tanned, long-legged and windblown, wearing a bikini top, cutoff shorts, and a huge smile. She only ever had that carefree look when they were away. Away from Harrisonburg. Away from Virginia.

Otherwise, she was watchful. Cautious. Scared.

He wondered if the cancer had been growing inside her, even then.

Agent Dalton cleared his throat, and David reached into his bottom desk drawer for a bottle. He poured another brandy. He always needed a brandy when he thought about the past. And he thought about it a lot.

"We were so young," he finally said, still looking at the picture of his wife. "Nancy and I. We got married in 1978. Nancy wasn't born at the right time to be a flower child, but she didn't let that stop her. It was her idea to move to the Archer farm."

David expected them to interrupt or to at least look victorious as he spilled his truth, but the agents sat in stony silence while memories flooded him.

"I had my doubts, being raised in a conservative family. But the farm, the people. I took to it. Nancy loved it there. Wesley Archer wasn't some crazy-eyed Manson type. He was quiet and soft-spoken, kind and gentle. His vision was of peace. Love. The only oddity about him was that he was obsessed with the next generation."

"Babies?" Noah prompted.

David nodded and took another drink. Remembering the next part was painful.

"There was a religious aspect to everything. It wasn't too far out and woo-woo. I was raised Catholic, and that would have weirded me out. Sent up red flags. Instead, we met on Sundays and prayed for peace. But it always ended with a prayer for the next generation and the future of humankind. And the fertility and good health of our wives. Nancy was one of the first to get pregnant. It was just a couple of months after we moved to the farm."

He closed his eyes on the memory of her telling him that joyous news. The celebration. The lovemaking that followed. The first time he felt the baby move under her skin.

Swallowing hard, he took another sip of his drink before he was able to continue.

"She was almost a celebrity among the couples that lived there. There were about five couples at that point, young and idealistic, married or not, starting lives together. We'd become almost like a family. The women banded around Nancy, and everyone watched her progress. Researched ways to combat morning sickness. Shared in the first movements, the first kicks. Our baby was added to the Sunday prayers, praised as the first of many to come. And then, finally, Jake was born."

He raised his eyes, pleading with them to understand. Dalton was watching him patiently. Winter's hands were folded in her lap, fingers laced tightly.

"I was never ashamed of my boy. As soon as I saw him, held him, even though I knew something wasn't right, I never once regretted him being born."

"What about the rest of the group? Your wife?" Winter asked. "Archer? He put a lot of emphasis on perfection."

"Nancy loved Jake instantly and completely. She was made for motherhood. The women, including Wesley's wife, Claire, had already formed a strong bond, and shared in the raising of Jake as if he were their own. Then another baby was born with severe birth defects." David scrubbed his face with his hands. "And another after that."

David shuddered, remembering the broken little bodies.

"What happened then?" Noah prompted.

David sighed. "Sunday prayers became a little more fiery. Wesley became a little less kind, less gentle. We had to pray harder. Believe in our purpose. Two years in, we had three babies. Three babies with severe health issues. Three more women were pregnant. Things were less happy, there was more tension. Another woman gave birth. There was talk about God's anger. Purity. Perseverance. Then, a baby disappeared."

21

D avid Benton looked haunted.

The longer he talked, the older he looked, until even his wrinkles deepened. He was a man dealing with remorse. Regret. Long-buried secrets.

"By this time, you have to understand that these people were our friends. Our family. We worked together, prayed together. Lived together. When the first baby went missing, we grieved. But it was thought to be an act of God."

Noah raised an eyebrow. "God kidnapped a disabled baby?"

David's face reddened. Not in anger, but in guilt.

"You don't understand. You'd have to have been a part of this group to get it. We all believed in what we were doing at that point. We were faithful servants, living in a peaceful community, but for whatever reason, we were being tested. The mother became pregnant again almost immediately. We thought it was a sign."

"Whose baby was it?" Winter asked.

"Andy and Catherine Kinney," he answered with no hesitation. "They moved on before the second baby was born. I never knew where they ended up."

Winter scooted to the very edge of her seat. "Who else?"

"Betty Talbot's babies were next." He scrubbed his face again. "She had twins. She and her husband went to bed one night, and the twins just disappeared. They were gone in the morning. No one heard or saw a thing. Wesley preached divine intervention, and they stayed for a month or two more, but ended up leaving. Betty died a few years later, and Jerry remarried. I heard he moved out somewhere in Montana during the mid-nineties."

Winter wrote notes as David talked, feeling like he'd be more comfortable if he felt like he wasn't being scrutinized. Her hand trembled a little. She was having a hard time understanding how a group of people could just accept that their children were going missing and not *do* anything about it. Move away? Why didn't they call the police? What kind of sway did The Bishop hold over them?

"People continued to come and go over the years. Some families with small children of their own. The population of the farm became more diversified, not as many of the original members. Then, an older child, the baby born after Jake…a boy named Patrick. He was just gone one morning. Nancy was close to his mother, Joanna Bowman, and they were both devastated. Our kids played together. By that time, Jake was six, and Nancy and I decided to get out."

"Joanna Bowman?" Winter asked. "Darin Bowman's wife?" She couldn't believe they had found the key in David Benton. He was spelling out the names of the victims, one by one, and giving them a hell of a reason to suspect Wesley Archer was behind the murders.

Patrick Bowman. Their first victim now had a name.

"Joanna died a year before Nancy. Darin never remarried. Never got over the loss of his wife and child."

"What about Tony Collier? Are Jake and Alison still friends?"

If David was surprised she knew about Tony's daughter, he didn't show it. "Alison was a little younger than Jake. She was the third baby born at the farm. They weren't close, and I haven't seen Tony in years."

His eyes darted down and to the left. He was lying about that.

Noah didn't miss it. "Except for when you told him we were coming to talk to him and to close ranks," he put in pointedly.

David sighed, his body deflating as the air hissed out from between his lips. He nodded. "Except for then."

"Why was your wife so paranoid, even after you left the farm?" Winter had wondered about that ever since Tom had mentioned it to them. If you were afraid of your child disappearing, why would you still be afraid after you removed them from the situation you feared?

"Nancy wanted to leave Harrisonburg altogether, but my father passed away, and I inherited his car sales business. It was the only way I could see at the time to support the family. I threw myself into work and what I saw as real life, pretending our time there had never happened. But after the babies started going missing, Nancy would have nightmares. They didn't end when we left Archer's place. She was convinced someone was going to come for Jake. I never managed to assure her that it would all be fine. Even after Wesley killed himself, she'd still wake up in the middle of the night, screaming for Jake."

David looked up at them suddenly, his eyes blazing with anger, grief, and unshed tears. His face had turned a mottled red, and Winter feared he might be having a heart attack. "What, David? Tell us what you need to say."

A vein popped out across his forehead and the glass

tumbler cracked in his hands. "I don't regret Jake. Not at all. But I do regret ever hearing Wesley Archer's name."

THEY MANAGED to extract a promise from David to meet again, but it was obvious the man had shut down, and they wouldn't get any more out of him that day. He'd lost the control over himself that he'd exhibited in their previous meeting. When they left, he looked like a broken man.

"I can't help but feel a little sorry for him," Winter admitted. It was her turn to drive, and she hit the turn signal to make a left onto the tree-lined road that led from the enclave of wealthy homes back to Harrisonburg. "He obviously loved his wife, and whether or not he treats Tom fairly, he cares about his family."

"And now we have a name for at least one of the victims. We need to speak to Tony Collier and Darin Bowman." Noah sounded distracted, and Winter glanced at him.

"What's wrong?"

"Just thinking. I'm trying to decide how everything ties together with Rebekah."

A deer darted out in the road, and Winter automatically tapped the brakes. It wasn't a close call, but it was nearing dusk and a reminder to pay attention.

She relaxed her grip on the steering wheel, missing her little car. She was getting used to its quirks, but the bigger sedan handled differently than she was used to. "All those women at the farm, it can't be a coincidence that they later died of cancer. We haven't come across a single female former Disciple. Did you find anything on the PFAS thing?"

Noah didn't immediately answer. He was watching his side mirror intently.

"What is it?" She glanced in the rearview and frowned to see a black truck with its headlights off rapidly approaching.

"Careful," Noah warned. "There's that wide bend up ahead. This asshole might try to pass."

On the left side of the road, a wooded hill sloped upward. The bend Noah was talking about curved to the right. She'd noticed it when they'd driven out to meet with David Benton before. The hill sloped more sharply on the other side of the hill, and downward into a gully.

Within a few seconds, the truck was hard on their tail, and she tapped her brakes to flash her lights at him. He didn't back off.

Over the low hum of the radio, the truck's engine roared even louder as the driver stomped on the gas, pushing the large vehicle faster. Winter gripped the steering wheel tighter as the front bumper kissed the back fender of the sedan, causing the car to swerve a little.

"What the hell?" she muttered, accelerating. The truck dropped back, and she stared hard in the mirror to get a glimpse of the driver. She couldn't see the occupants since the evening sunlight glared off their windshield.

"Shit, get down!" Noah's big hand came down on top of her head just as a loud crack reverberated all around them. The next thing Winter knew, she was looking out the front window through the steering wheel. There was a crunching sound, and reaching up quickly to adjust the mirror, her fear was confirmed. Someone in the truck was firing at them. The back windshield was webbed with cracks.

She mashed down on the gas pedal, going into the widest part of the curve. To her right, the tops of the trees caught the setting sun, making their leaves look orange and red.

She'd been at the top of the class at Quantico in their defensive driving training, and the knowledge was there.

Winter could almost hear her trainer's voice in her ear, calmly listing off instructions.

"Don't worry about swerving. Your attacker's going to have a hard time hitting you from a moving vehicle anyway. He's gotta worry about line of sight, lateral movement...you just worry about keeping control."

Noah was already on the phone with Gary Miller, giving the chief their location and situation.

Thudding sounds came from the back of the car as bullets hit the trunk. Winter felt her shoulders stiffen, sure that hot lead would tear through her body at any second. She had to force herself to relax her arms.

Noah cursed.

Even as a second curse left his lips, one of the back tires blew. The car whipped hard to the left, and Winter could see the reflection of the car's right headlight on the guardrail as they went nearly sideways.

Again, her driving instructor's voice was in her head. *"Even though it sounds counterintuitive, accelerate to straighten out the car."*

She pressed the gas pedal down hard, nearly flooding the throttle. The car maintained speed while she worked on getting it under control without going into a spin.

"Don't yank the wheel..."

The force of heavy impact interrupted her thoughts as the car swung farther, into a complete one-eighty. They'd been rammed. She had just enough time to realize that they were facing the direction they'd come, when the sedan slammed into the guardrail hard enough to knock her head against the window. Metal on metal screeched as they ground along it as the big truck blasted past them.

Noah unhooked his seatbelt and twisted to follow its path. "Brake lights. They're slowing down too." Gun in hand, he waited, tense.

From the corner of her eye, Winter could see the tops of the tall trees, still painted in evening sunlight.

Another truck came into the curve—a semi—and Winter stomped harder on the brakes, laying on the horn. The driver reacted quickly, turning on his flashers and switching on his Jake brake with a shuddering helicopter sound. He moved to the center lane, and she could hear the vibration of his tires on the rumble strips as he slowed.

"The truck's taking off," Noah shouted. "Dammit, I can't make out the license plate."

Winter realized he was still on the phone with Gary Miller when he began rattling off the make and model.

Finally, the Ford vibrated to a stop. The semi driver jumped out of his cab and ran toward their car. She let her hands loosen from the wheel, taking a shaky breath, her head falling back against the headrest.

"Holy shit," the older man yelled, his eyes wild under the green John Deere cap he wore pushed back on his head. The windows were up, muffling his voice, but she could still hear him shouting. "What the hell you folks trying to do? Get yourselves killed?"

No, but someone else was obviously trying to do the job.

"HOLD STILL."

"Will you just leave it? It's fine."

"You've got blood all over the side of your head. It's not fine. Pull your hair back up out of the way."

Noah watched as Winter winced. Strands of her dark hair had come loose from the braid she'd twined them into and were stuck in the dark blood that had dried on the side of her face. He resisted the urge to help her. Instead, he turned and ran the water in the hotel sink until it was warm.

"I still think you should get checked out. You could have a concussion." He held the washcloth under the weak stream of water.

"I told you," she said slowly, sounding like she was gritting her teeth. "I'm fine. Trust me. I'm familiar with head trauma."

He turned her chin to one side and carefully dabbed at the cut on the side of her head. It was a shallow slice near her ear, about two inches long. Her fair skin was darkening into a bruise already around it. It wouldn't need stitches, but it probably hurt.

Noah quickly finished, rinsing the washcloth. He handed Winter a bottle of ibuprofen and a glass of water as the phone rang in the other room.

"Call and order us a pizza, will you?" She slipped around him and grabbed her purse from the bed. He didn't miss her grimace at the name on the caller ID.

"Agent Black speaking." Whoever was on the other end started talking loudly, and she fished a couple of pills out of the bottle and washed them down quickly. "Yes, sir. You're right, sir. I had just picked up the phone to call you."

Max Osbourne. Winter hadn't checked in in two days, and he probably wanted to know why. Grimly amused and irritated at her stubbornness, Noah pulled up a chair and propped his feet up to watch her try to talk her way out of trouble with the Special Agent in Charge of the Richmond Violent Crimes Task Force.

She kept her calm, he saw, even though she glared at him for eavesdropping. She ran through recent developments as concisely as if she was reading a report off a piece of paper in front of her. The benefits of having an uncanny memory, he figured. When she got to the part about them being almost run down into a ravine that evening, she glossed over the finer points.

And then, her face whitened as she listened to whatever Max had to say. Her eyes narrowed, and she opened her mouth several times to argue, but Osbourne just barreled right over. The conversation was over two minutes later, and Winter looked ready to spit nails.

"Care to share?" Noah looked down at his phone to avoid her ocular daggers, checking for the closest pizza delivery joint.

"Max is sending out another agent."

"The more, the merrier." Noah shrugged. "We could use an extra pair of eyes."

He tapped the screen to pull up the number for Pizza Express. It got good ratings on Yelp, and he was hungry.

"He's sending Aiden Parrish."

His thumb hovered over the call button. "*The* Aiden Parrish? Head of the Behavioral Analysis Unit. What'd we do to deserve the honor?"

Winter looked furious. Her cheeks were flushed, and she jumped off the bed to pace the short width of the room. "Yes. *The* Aiden Parrish." March, march, march, turn. Repeat. He quit watching her, looking back down at his phone.

"What's wrong with Aiden Parrish? Besides the fact that sending us a bigwig to help seems like overkill."

"He volunteered to come here," she spat. "He's been hovering over me for as long as I can remember."

Noah knew a little about Parrish's backstory. He'd been the agent in charge of The Preacher investigation and had met Winter when she was thirteen, after her family was murdered. He'd kept in touch over the years, followed Winter's progress through college, and ultimately, was the reason she'd been assigned to the Richmond office.

He'd also tried to poach Winter from their unit, just a few months after they'd joined up. She'd threatened to quit, and he'd rescinded the transfer order.

Noah was good at observing. He'd seen the way the man had looked at her. Winter wasn't a kid who needed help and guidance anymore. She was a sharply intelligent agent with seriously good looks, who'd graduated at the top of her class at Quantico.

Well, tied for top place, he reminded himself a little smugly.

"Why's he coming here? Doesn't he have his own department to run?"

March, march, march, turn. Repeat.

"Apparently, he's taken an interest in the case. Violent Crimes is still booked up and can't spare any agents. Max thinks we're in over our head as newbies, and Aiden just happened to pop up this evening and offer to help. I wouldn't be surprised to find out he's got somebody spying on me. The man is the most interfering, infuriating—"

She broke off, apparently out of adjectives and Noah looked at her narrowly.

She was protesting an awful lot. The guy was brilliant, serious, and experienced, and they could use his help. Different departments, same team: they were all federal agents. There was no reason for her to be this worked up, except maybe pride.

But her fury went beyond ego. It looked personal. Maybe, he'd have to keep an eye on Parrish, after all. Not that he was suddenly feeling a little possessive or anything.

Winter propped the pillows up behind her and punched the power button on the remote. The TV came on, and she stared sightlessly at the evening news. She was obviously still pissed and trying to distract herself.

Noah wasn't as hungry as he had been, but he dialed the number to order the pizza anyway.

22

Winter was in a bitchy mood. She freely acknowledged that fact. She hadn't gotten much sleep, and when she did get out of bed, the small wound on the side of her head throbbed uncomfortably. Noah's usual good mood just made her feel grumpier.

She needed coffee.

She was sitting on the bed, brushing her wet hair, when someone knocked.

It wasn't even seven. Too early for housekeeping. The shower was still running—she and Noah were comfortable enough with their shared room arrangement now that they just used the same bathroom—and she moved to the door quietly.

Her hand on her weapon, she looked out the peephole and hissed out a breath. Staring back, his icy blue eyes unblinking as if he could see her, was Aiden Parrish.

Winter undid the chain lock and opened the door.

He gave her a cool smile and a nod, his eyes immediately going to the room behind her. "I thought you were in the next room over."

"I thought you'd call when you got to town."

He shrugged carelessly, his tailored jacket barely shifting over his shoulders, and held up a cardboard cup carrier. She could smell chocolate and espresso and reluctantly stepped back so he could enter the cramped room.

She didn't miss the way he took in the rumpled bedcovers and the blankets on the floor next to the bed. He raised one eyebrow in a sardonic expression, and when she just glared back, set the coffee at the small table and sat down.

Winter had always liked Aiden. He'd been there for her during the most difficult time of her life. She'd even thought she was in love with him when she was a senior in high school and he had shown up to see her graduate. He'd been so sophisticated with those tailored suits, well-shined shoes, the expensive cologne. The man literally never seemed to have one single hair out of place. To her teenage eyes, he was perfect.

Now, it was more complicated. She was too old for crushes. She was also too old to have someone protectively watching her every move, trying to control her career out of a misguided sense of responsibility.

"Where's Dalton?" Aiden asked, taking one of the coffee cups out of the holder and sitting back in his chair.

"Use those powers of observation you're so famous for," she retorted, feeling immature and not caring what conclusions he cared to draw. "You can hear the shower running." As if on cue, the water shut off with a clunk.

Aiden had a leaner build, but he was tall—just an inch or so shorter than Noah. If Noah was a lion, Aiden was a sleek panther. The room was about to get uncomfortably crowded.

She turned her back on him, using the mirror over the TV to finish brushing her hair. She deftly braided it, studiously ignoring him. That didn't stop her from seeing his mocking smile out of the corner of her eye.

The bathroom door opened, and Noah stepped out, a too-small hotel towel wrapped around his hips. He didn't look surprised or embarrassed to see Aiden, just grinned and saluted with one hand, the other holding the towel together. "Forgot to get my clothes," he explained. He grabbed some out of his suitcase and disappeared back into the bathroom.

"Can I ask why you're sharing a room when the FBI is paying for two?" Aiden's voice was cool. Almost indifferent.

"You could," Winter replied, mimicking his tone. She snapped an elastic band around the end of her braid. "But I'd just tell you it's none of your business."

"I'm afraid of the dark," Noah called out from the other side of the door. Winter snorted. Hotel doors were thin.

Aiden's smile disappeared.

Oddly, she felt *her* mood improve.

AIDEN LOOKED as out of place in their coffee shop as Noah would at a black-tie charity function. He seemed comfortable enough, leaned back in one of the vintage-looking chairs near the window, but he didn't so much as loosen his tie.

Noah had to admit, though, the guy was as sharp as a scalpel. He already seemed to know every detail about the case and came prepared with questions and theories. And it was nice to have a third set of eyes, with all the research they had ahead of them.

"I've been thinking." Winter leaned forward and tapped a rhythm on the coffee table absently with a ballpoint pen. Aiden watched her without speaking, his eyes focused on the fist-sized smudge of purple on the side of her head where she'd whacked it against the window. The cut in the middle was inflamed a little, but already healing.

"From everything David Benton was telling us yesterday,

it sounds like the women of the Disciples were given some sort of fertility drug. Something that worked like it was supposed to—increased fertility rates—but caused birth defects, and later, cancer."

"It would have had to have been in the water or something," Noah said, already tossing around possibilities. "Some way without their knowledge. Benton would have mentioned if his wife was getting injections."

Aiden just nodded. "It fits. Call the ME and have them test the remains for unfamiliar chemical compounds. This was more than thirty years ago. Who knows what kind of side effects an undeveloped drug might have had. Or, maybe it was something herbal. The ME should be able to test for that."

Winter scribbled notes as he talked. "Noah, if you can call Florence Wade, I'll keep looking at Wesley Archer's background. Friends, former military connections. I want to do a property search, see if he's got any other hideaways around that Rebekah may have taken off to."

"I'll check in with Benton, too, and see if he's heard from his wife yet," Noah offered. "And the chief. He put out an APB for a black Chevy Silverado with some front-end damage. I want to find out if they've made any headway on the Wilkins murder too. I'm sure he'd have let us know, but the guy's got his hands full."

"If you can send me that list you started, Winter," Aiden said, his fingers already flying over the keys of his laptop, "I'll start following up on some of Rebekah Archer's classmates and acquaintances."

Noah squashed the urge to pull out his own laptop, just to show Aiden what fast typing really looked like. Shaking his head at his own stupidity, he dialed Officer Tom Benton instead. As he feared, Samantha Benton and her unborn child were still missing.

He called Gary Miller next, and since the chief's department wasn't large, Noah didn't hold out hope that any progress had been made. He was right. There were no new developments in the Wilkins case. He also learned that no black trucks with matching front-end damage had been found lying around in conspicuous locations.

But after a couple hours of silent work, except for the tapping of keys, they ended up with a lot to go on.

"Joe Meier," Winter said. "Boyfriend of Rebekah Archer. Lives in St. Louis with his wife."

"Do we have a number?" Noah asked. Winter rattled it off, and he entered it into his phone.

Joe picked up on the third ring. From the picture on Winter's laptop, Meier looked like a skinny, bookish type. He had Buddy Holly glasses and a prominent Adam's apple. On the phone, though, his voice was quiet and deep.

"Mr. Meier? My name's Special Agent Noah Dalton. I'm with the FBI. I'd like to ask you about a former friend of yours from Iowa State. Rebekah Archer."

"Rebekah?" He sounded surprised. "Hold on a sec." There was a rustling sound and murmuring voices. He came back on the line a moment later. "Sorry," Joe explained. "My wife. I'll tell her about this call, of course, but I've gone into another room. Go ahead. What's Rebekah done?"

"What's she *done*?" Noah asked. "Not what's *happened* to her?"

"I'm sorry." Joe sounded flustered. "It's just that Rebekah's always been the type that seems capable of looking out for herself. What's this about? I haven't seen her for years."

"Ms. Archer is connected to an investigation I'm working on. I'm wondering if you can tell me anything about her. The two of you were in a relationship?"

Joe laughed a little. "I guess you could say that. We dated for a little while. She wanted to move things along faster than I was ready for. Seven months in, she was talking about marriage and kids. We were sophomores in college."

"But you're married now," Noah pointed out.

"Well, yeah. But this was four years ago. I've got my career now, a house..." He coughed, the sound spearing into Noah's ear. "Back then, we were living in a crappy rental near campus, eating ramen noodles. It just weirded me out. She was obsessed with starting a family."

"Obsessed how?"

Silence stretched out for several seconds before Joe admitted, "I don't know. I joked with her, wondering if her fixation on kids was because of the classes she was taking. Breeding, biology, genetics, stuff like that. She was going for a double major in Animal Science and Genetics. But once she got the idea in her head, she wouldn't let it go. She wanted a kid. Nothing about love, just how we were both so smart that we'd be sure to have a little brainchild."

"And you ended the relationship?"

Joe laughed again, a little bitterly this time. "Actually, no. When I refused to marry her. Well, refused to participate in her breeding experiment, since it was about offspring and she didn't actually even care about marriage, she left me. We'd been living together for a few months by that point, and she just packed her things and moved out."

"Can I ask you what you majored in?"

"Chemical Engineering."

"Did Rebekah ever talk about fertility drugs? Creating them or working on an existing one?"

"Jeez, no. She was brilliant, kind of intense, but that would have wigged me out completely. Especially once she started making noises about ovulation and fertile windows."

"Did she ever mention her father? Or a group called the Disciples of the Moon?"

"No." Joe sounded genuinely baffled. "But I'm thinking from this conversation, I dodged a bullet with that one."

"You just might have," Noah replied wryly. "Thanks for the information. Save my number, will you, in case you think of anything else we should know?"

Joe agreed and disconnected, probably to go tell his wife about his weird ex-girlfriend.

When Noah hung up, Winter was practically bouncing in her seat. He raised an eyebrow at her. "All right, what've you got? It's obviously something better than I turned up."

Aiden, too, closed his laptop and looked at her expectantly. Almost like a proud teacher would look at a pupil, Noah thought in disgust.

"Scott Kennedy," she nearly shouted. "Super rich guy who lives just outside of Washington, D.C. His family owned a pharmaceutical company, started it in the fifties. They made a name for themselves manufacturing an early fertility drug during the Baby Boom, similar to Clomid. After Kennedy's dad died, he inherited everything and sold the company to a big pharma corporation. Made a boatload of money, retired fairly young."

She paused, looking at them both expectantly, a half-smile on her lips.

"I'll bite," Aiden said in that cool voice that made Noah want to grab him by the collar and shake. Hard. "What's the connection?"

"He served with Wesley Archer in Vietnam." She turned her laptop so they could see the picture she'd pulled up on her screen.

Two guys, dressed in fatigues—the picture was obviously taken in a war zone—one with his arm around the other. Both had short, military haircuts. One man was smiling—a cocky, shit-eating grin on his face, leaning on a rifle. The other man, one Noah recognized as Wesley Archer, wasn't smiling. Though the picture was in grainy black and white, there was a darkness in the other man's face that was clearly visible.

On a sudden thought, Noah leaned forward. Right clicking the cropped photo, one Winter had found on Google images, he did a reverse image search. The first link directed to an old newspaper article.

"Another connection. Check out the byline. Elbert Wilkins." He pointed at the screen. "Anyone up for a trip to Washington, D. C.?"

Scott Kennedy lived in a posh community in Bethesda, Maryland, about a half-hour outside of Washington, D.C. The houses were massive and imposing, closed in by iron gates and stone walls. Rather than the newer-constructed gated communities full of medium-sized mansions, Kennedy lived in an older part of Bethesda, where the homes had more character, but also carried price tags in the multiple millions.

From what Winter could uncover in the two-and-a-half-hour drive from Harrisonburg, Scott Kennedy inherited half of his father's fortune when the old man passed away in the 1970s. On paper, it looked like both brothers invested their money into building up the company, but Scott, after acquiring a majority share in the company under shady means, sold out to a larger pharmaceutical corporation and hung his little brother out to dry.

He had no children, but had been married three times and divorced twice, each wife younger than the last. His third wife, only twenty-eight years old to Kennedy's sixty-one at the time of his marriage, had died in an avalanche while skiing in Switzerland in 2012. So far, there was no Mrs. Scott Kennedy number four.

Kennedy had been a big-time political donor in the nineties, so there was plenty about him in the newspapers. He'd run for Congress at one point, but failing to get elected, had spent most of his recent years out of the spotlight.

In a photo from 2015, Kennedy looked like a man much younger than his age, either from healthy-living or more likely, cosmetic surgery. He had dark hair, with distinguished white wings sweeping dramatically back from a craggy, still-handsome face. The snapping dark eyes were the same as the younger Kennedy in the decades-old newspaper photo, as was the wide, smug grin he wore. If she hadn't known he was nearing seventy, she'd have guessed he was in his fifties.

"Home sweet home," Noah muttered as Aiden slowed the car. He pulled into a long drive, blocked with an eight-foot tall wrought-iron gate. Aiden lowered the window and pressed a button on an intercom mounted near the road.

"May I help you?"

"FBI Agents Black, Parrish, and Dalton to see Mr. Kennedy."

There was a pause, and the black gate swung inward. No house could be seen from the road, just manicured foliage and glossy ivy crowded into what looked like a mercilessly well-maintained wilderness. Winter caught a glimpse of a fountain through the trees. A moss-covered concrete woman in Grecian robes stared off into the distance, pouring water endlessly from a narrow pitcher.

After several hundred feet, the trees gave way to an upward-sloping lawn. A huge brick house sat at the crest. It had to be at least ten thousand square feet. Windows lined the front, looking out onto a brick turnaround drive with another fountain in the center. Immaculate gardens still bloomed with color in the late evening sunlight—asters and purplish grasses and spikes of bright red celosia—even though it was nearly October. A six-car garage sat at an angle to the house, and behind it, part of a tennis court was visible.

Winter wondered what kind of house Scott Kennedy's brother lived in, since Scott appeared to have claimed the lion's share of the family fortune.

Aiden parked his black SUV under the front portico, and a butler opened the door before they could all get out of the car. "Welcome," the older man said, his voice sounding anything but. His shoulders were rounded with age under his immaculate black uniform. His seamed face was drawn into deep, disapproving lines. "If you'll follow me, Mr. Kennedy will see you in his study."

As he turned to follow, Noah's shoes squeaked and echoed in the marbled foyer, where twin, curving staircases led to the second floor. The décor was tasteful and screamed old money, from the antique furniture pieces artfully scattered about to the dreamy impressionist paintings on the walls and Turkish carpets on the floor.

Aiden seemed distracted, tapping the screen of his phone. Noah gave a soundless whistle when they passed what looked like an original Monet and nodded at it, raising his eyebrows at Winter. She hardly noticed. She was focused on her senses, tingling with a vague warning that she couldn't interpret.

The butler stopped at a heavy mahogany door and tapped lightly.

"Come in," boomed a voice from inside.

The butler soundlessly pushed open the door and stood back to let the three of them enter. The room was obviously a rich man's idea of a man cave. The walls were lined with floor-to-ceiling bookshelves of dark wood, and what wasn't covered with wood had been painted a dark forest green that contrasted nicely with the thick carpets of burgundy and gold. The windows looked out on a swimming pool. Hunting scenes in oil paint were hung on the walls, and the fixtures in the room were gleaming brass. A small fire crackled in a fireplace at the other end of the room.

Scott Kennedy stood behind a mahogany desk, smiling as they entered. "Welcome." His voice was rich and deep, like one of the politicians he'd aspired to be. His dark eyes were lit with intelligence and apparent good humor. Despite the lateness of the day, he was dressed in a dark suit that was expensive-looking and well-tailored.

He grinned at all of them in turn, but his eyes lingered on Winter. She had to stifle an automatic shudder as he gave her a once-over, his eyes lingering on her breasts. *Perv*, she thought, keeping an impersonal smile pinned to her lips.

"Please, sit down." He gestured magnanimously to the three chairs in front of the desk. Covered in plush, padded burgundy velvet, they were all low, she noted. Seated in front of him, they left Kennedy in the power position.

"What can I do for you, Agents?" he asked after brief introductions. His hand had lingered longest on hers, and although he addressed all of them, Kennedy only had eyes for Winter.

She could feel Noah bristling next to her, and even Aiden's posture was stiff. Winter felt like she might possibly drown in the testosterone flooding the room, but since Kennedy was responding to her, she was obviously going to have to take the lead.

"Thank you for seeing us on such short notice, Mr. Kennedy," she began.

"Scott," he interrupted, smiling warmly. His eyes crinkled at the corners. "Mr. Kennedy was my father."

"Scott," she corrected, nodding in acknowledgment. "We're investigating a case that involves an old acquaintance of yours."

"Wesley Archer." He nodded and settled back in his chair, arms crossed. "We served in Vietnam together. I was sorry to hear of his passing a few years back, but unfortunately, suicide is common amongst veterans."

She was surprised he seemed so forthcoming. More surprised that he knew why they were there. Noah beat her to the punch on the next question. "How did you know we were here to speak about Wesley?"

Kennedy smiled briefly at Noah, but it didn't reach his eyes. "I have many friends. Law enforcement...FBI. I know a lot of things. Unfortunately, nothing that would help you solve those unfortunate cold cases down in Harrisonburg."

"Could you tell us how long it's been since you spoke with Wesley Archer?" Aiden fixed his cool, blue stare on Kennedy. Winter watched as Kennedy shifted a little in his chair. She knew what the power of one of Aiden's stares felt like. A rock would shift in its chair.

"Oh, it's been years and years ago." He waved a hand negligently, regaining his composure. "We were very different people. War...it brings you close. Forges a bond. Sometimes, if that's all you have in common, the bond dissolves when you're stateside. Every day isn't a life and death struggle anymore, and you don't have to depend on your friends to watch your back in the same way."

"That's an interesting perspective," Noah said, his tone casual. "I served in the military too. Active combat. 'Brothers in arms' is an old term for a reason. I would instantly be able to pick out any of my unit members in a crowded room fifty years from now, and I'd still feel as close to him as a brother. In my experience, those bonds don't 'dissolve.'"

Kennedy gave him a patronizing smile. "You're young. I'm...less young. You may feel that way now, but—"

"How long did you keep in touch with Archer after you

served?" Noah gave Kennedy no time for his condescending attitude.

Kennedy's polished smile slipped a bit. "You're talking about decades ago. I couldn't give you a date."

Aiden spoke next, but Winter didn't hear him. Her eye was caught by a faint, reddish glow. It was coming from near the floor, behind Kennedy's desk. From the position, it was likely originating inside a drawer of the mahogany desk. She glanced around, looking for any other visual clues she might have missed. On one wall, coming from a vent near the floor, red light leaked sullenly through the old-fashioned metal grating.

Her stomach tensed.

There was something here. Something that Kennedy was hiding.

Kennedy's raised voice caught her attention again. "What are you implying?" he blustered. "That I had something to do with a bunch of bones buried in the woods in some podunk town?"

Aiden gazed back at him coolly. "I don't believe I implied anything of the sort. I merely asked about the nature of your relationship with Wesley Archer and how much you knew about the Disciples of the Moon."

"What a stupid name," Kennedy scoffed, curling his lip. "A bunch of weirdos running around worshipping nature? Hell, maybe they were making human sacrifices to the moon. Do I look like the type of person who would participate in that kind of bullshit?" He held his arms out, as if his snappy dressing and trim appearance should absolve him of involvement.

"No, sir, you don't," Noah drawled. "Anyone can tell you're a businessman, through and through, just by looking at you. Money is the bottom line, am I right?"

Kennedy gave him an approving nod, like Noah was a

dumb student who'd managed to hit upon the right answer. "I came back from the war to find my father in declining health. I didn't have time for anything except turning around a lagging family business."

"And how did you intend to go about that?" From the tone of Aiden's question, he already knew the answer. Again, Kennedy scowled.

"The usual way. Trimming expenses, streamlining operations. The company structure was outdated."

"And you knew this as a young guy in your twenties, fresh out of the military?" Noah's voice was admiring, and Winter realized they'd picked up the questioning thread while she was distracted.

The good cop/bad cop routine seemed to be working. Scott Kennedy preened a little. "I've always had a good head for business. I increased the family fortune substantially while the company was under my leadership."

"Could you tell us about a patent you pursued in 1981? For a drug called…" Aiden slowly flipped a page in a small leather-bound notebook. "Ah, here it is. Progesteraline Six?"

Winter glanced over at Aiden, surprised. Noah just looked disgruntled. Aiden didn't seem like the showboating type, but he should have shared any information he'd uncovered *before* they met with Kennedy.

Kennedy's tan face paled in shock. His eyes darkened further in anger, but he seemed to get himself under control. A grim smile on his lips, he shook his head. "Sorry, that's not ringing any bells for me."

Aiden raised one eyebrow. "No? Your signature was on the paperwork."

Kennedy shrugged. "As well as on a hundred other patent applications. I'm just a businessman. My pharmaceutical scientists, research and development people…they would put things on my desk, and I'd sign them."

Aiden made a noncommittal noise, jotting something down.

"What about Elbert Wilkins?" Winter asked. Kennedy's eyes flicked to her, and again, she wanted to shudder. They were flat black. Opaque.

He lifted a shoulder. "The name sounds familiar, but I can't place it."

She took out her phone and pulled up the picture she'd found of Kennedy and Archer. "He was a photojournalist. Took this picture of you and Wesley Archer."

Kennedy sat back and rubbed his chin thoughtfully. A thick gold ring glinted on his pinkie. "Come to think of it, I do remember him. Weedy guy, skinny. Balding prematurely. He thought he'd write some Pulitzer-winning anti-war piece, but he puked like a kid the first time he saw a dead body. So what?"

"He was murdered." Aiden's voice was flat. "His office ransacked."

"Sorry. I don't know anything about that. I'm not sure why you think I would. Now, if that's all…"

He rose to his feet, their cue to leave. Winter wished there was some way she could get into his desk. He had information. And it was obvious, he wasn't willing to share any of it. She glanced over at the vent. It, too, still glowed.

"Thanks for your time, Mr. Kennedy," Noah said, holding out a hand. "We're sorry to have interrupted your evening." Winter recognized Noah's smile as obviously false, but it was no worse than the one Kennedy flashed back at them. He looked like a well-fed shark.

"It was my pleasure." Again, he caught Winter's eye. His smile turned almost predatory, and she felt her teeth clench in response. "Harrison will see you out." He pressed a button beneath the desk, and the butler appeared as quickly as if he'd been hovering right outside.

Silently, he ushered them to the front door.

The heavy wooden panel had barely closed behind them when Noah burst out, "What the fuck was that, Agent Parrish?"

Aiden didn't bat an eyelash. "I didn't have time to brief you. I sent for the information before we left Harrisonburg and my contact didn't email me with a copy of the patent application until just before we got here."

"Not the time and not the place," Winter put in. Noah looked like he wanted to take Aiden apart right there on the brick driveway. Both men ignored her.

"And Agent Dalton," Aiden added mockingly, "that's SSA Parrish to you. You do understand that I outrank you in both seniority and job title, right? I'd suggest you cool off, rookie."

Aiden wasn't built on the same broad lines as Noah, but something about him had always told her he'd be lethal in a fight. And he wasn't backing down from the menacing look on Noah's face. In fact, he looked like he'd welcome an excuse to rip into the younger man.

Winter's irritation bubbled over, and she stepped between the two bristling males, giving each of them a fulminating glare. "Get your shit together. Both of you. You're acting like assholes."

Tensions didn't ease, but Winter headed to the SUV. They could have a dick-measuring contest if they wanted, but she didn't need to see it. Besides, Noah could fold himself into the back seat for the drive back. She was taking shotgun.

After a long moment, both men climbed in the car and Aiden cranked the ignition and flicked on the headlights. His mouth set in a hard line, he roughly jerked the car into drive. They'd nearly reached the road, the wrought iron gates open wide to let them out, when a muffled sound came from outside of the car.

"What the hell?" Noah demanded, twisting in his seat to look behind them. "Shit. Turn around."

"I can't," Aiden muttered tersely. "The drive's too narrow. Hang on."

He reversed quickly, the engine whining. Winter turned around as well, straining to look out the back window. The driveway was dark, the trees on either side crowding out the moonlight. As soon as they broke out of the trees, though, she could see the house, backlit with an orange glow.

24

I n a strange parody of the first time they'd pulled up, the butler again pulled the front door open as if he were waiting for them. This time, however, the man was distraught, cradling his right hand. He wore an expression of someone dangerously close to shock.

He ran unsteadily down the steps, his hair mussed, and glasses crooked. "Thank God you're still here. I don't know what happened. Something exploded."

"Kennedy," Aiden demanded. "Is he still in the house?"

The butler let out a half-gasp, half-sob, sagging a little. If Noah hadn't stepped forward to brace him, he would have collapsed.

The old man's eyes filled with tears. "I tried to get into his office." He held out his hand. The skin on his palm was already badly blistered. "The door was locked. Only Mr. Kennedy has the key. Please, please help him."

Winter was through the front door before Noah or Aiden could stop her.

Dimly, in the back of her mind, she wondered what kind of explosion could cause such a quick, intense heat. The butler shouldn't have been able to burn himself on the door-knob so quickly. Even if someone launched an incendiary device through the office window, causing a violent explosion, it should take time to build up enough heat for the metal doorknob to get hot enough to burn.

Already, the house was hazed with a thick layer of black smoke. She pulled her shirt up over her nose, knowing it was a futile gesture, and tried not to breathe.

She went straight to Kennedy's office. Smoke leaked out from beneath the heavy, solid wood door. She'd be dealing with a backdraft situation if she tried to kick it in. The sudden inrush of oxygen would feed the fire, and she'd be lucky to survive the flames that would burst from the room.

If Kennedy was still in there, there wasn't anything she could do for him from this side of the door.

She went to the next room instead.

It looked like a large parlor, with furniture arranged in conversational groupings. The smoke was lighter, and she had no problem locating a reddish-orange glow on the left-hand side of the room. There was no vent, as there had been in the other room, but a square of color showed up against the flat paneled wall anyway.

Whatever was hidden in there, she wanted it.

Already feeling the tightness in her chest from the smoke, she looked around the room for something she could use to make a hole in the wall. There was a fireplace on the other side of the parlor, and she grabbed a heavy black poker from the tool stand beside it.

Holding it in both hands, she swung at the wall. Again and again, until she'd made a small hole in the plaster and paneling. The smoke in the room was getting thicker, and she kicked at the hole to widen it. More red light spilled out. Some from the firelight shining through on the other side and some from the object hidden within the cubby.

Finally, when she cleared an area about the size of a shoe-box, she reached in.

Winter hissed out a breath as her questing fingers touched hot metal. She pulled her sleeve down over her hand, using it to protect her palm from the worst of the heat. Thick, dark smoke poured through the opening she'd made, and she felt dizzy with the effort it took to hold her breath.

Wrenching against the object, ignoring the pain that blossomed in the palm of her hand, she maneuvered a small lockbox until a corner of it stuck out of the ruined paneling. She yanked on it in frustration. Her throat ached with the effort of not taking a deep breath, and she caught her breath on a choking cough.

Picking up the poker again, she went back to work widening the opening in the wall.

"I'll get her," Noah barked.

"No, you stay out here with him." Aiden nodded at the man Noah had helped to the ground. "Call 911." When Noah opened his mouth to argue, he cut him off with a hard look. "I'm pulling rank, Dalton. Do as I say."

He took the front stairs two at a time. The foyer was dark, and the smoke was rank, heavy with a chemical odor he couldn't immediately identify. He didn't know what it was, but he didn't want to breathe any more of it than was necessary. The office was to the left, but before he could head that way, he caught a flicker of movement at the top of the stairs.

Cursing silently at Winter for being so headstrong, he hesitated a moment but headed up one side of the curving staircase at a run. He had his doubts that this explosion was an accident, so conveniently timed with their departure. Kennedy was deep in whatever this situation was.

The hallway at the top of the stairs led off in two directions. He turned toward the right, where he'd spotted the movement.

The hall was lined with doors on both sides, all closed. He pushed them open as he went, scanning rooms. Sumptuous guest bedrooms alternated with luxurious bathrooms, all vacant. Urgency ate at him. Winter was in the house somewhere, doing who the hell knew what, and he was chasing shadows.

The last door on the left opened on a huge master bedroom. There was a fireplace on one wall big enough to park a small car in. Like the office downstairs, the room was lined with bookshelves, a sleek flat-screen mounted on one wall. There were two doors. Weapon drawn, he pulled one open.

Aside from a walk-in closet the size of most people's living rooms and racks full of clothes, there was nothing else in the room. The other door led to a bathroom. Wherever the shadow had gone, it wasn't in there.

He headed out of the bedroom, frustrated.

The smoke was already thicker on the lower floor, and he headed for the office. Movement caught his eye in the room before it. He swung around in time to see Winter pull something free, low on the wall. She fell back to the floor when it came loose and went into a spasm of coughing.

Narrowing his eyes, he swept into the room. She squinted up at him, the whites of her eyes already bloodshot. Not bothering to speak—she'd hear about this later—he tucked his gun back in its holster and scooped her up.

"The case," she rasped, struggling in his grip. "Be careful."

Shifting Winter's weight in his arms, he grabbed a handkerchief from the inside pocket of his coat. He wadded it up to protect his hand and grabbed the box by the handle. Even through the crumpled linen barrier, the heat radiating from the box was intense.

The crackle of fire eating at the other side of the wall beside them was audible. He shifted her again, ignoring her protests, and headed out of the room. By the time they got to the front door, he could hear sirens approaching.

Noah had moved the butler farther away from the house. He was crouched over the man on the ground, the First-Aid kit from the storage area of Aiden's Acura open on the ground beside him. When they came through the door, he looked up at them swiftly. Aiden could read the hot fury in his face, even from the distance.

Aiden didn't care. Making friends on the job wasn't his priority and never had been.

He deposited Winter on the ground next to the injured man and moved his SUV as the first firetruck roared up the drive. Paramedics followed shortly as the evening was broken by the sound of diesel engines, the blast of air brakes, and the shriek of sirens.

As soon as Winter had been handed over to the paramedics, who quickly snapped an oxygen mask over her face and started treatment for the mild burn on her palm, he jerked his head to Noah, silently telling him to join him.

The bigger man followed Aiden a short distance away, resentment clear in every step he took. "Look," Aiden snapped out, as soon as they were out of Winter's earshot. "We don't have time for your wounded ego. I saw Kennedy in the house."

"Why didn't you go after him?"

Aiden shook his head in disgust. "I did. He was upstairs. Disappeared into the master bedroom." He turned his back on Noah and headed for the back of the house. "I searched it, but he was gone."

Noah followed, his footsteps surprisingly soundless for a

guy his size. "You think he staged that little fire to make it look like he was a target."

"Maybe briefly. More of a distraction and a way to get rid of whatever was in his desk."

"How do you know he had anything in his desk?" Noah stopped beside Aiden and looked up at the back of the house, at the window Aiden was studying. To their right, fire-fighters had already beaten back most of the blaze in the office. The brick was blackened outside, but aside from smoke damage, the house would survive to last another hundred years or more.

"You saw the way Winter was looking at Kennedy's desk. Like she could see straight through the wood to whatever he was hiding in there."

Noah shot him a sharp glance, and Aiden curled his lips into a smug grin. "You think you're the only one who knows what Winter can do?"

Noah scowled and took a step toward him. "I think *Winter* thinks I'm the only one who knows what she can do. How the fuck do you think you know anything about her? Her *now*, and not the scared kid she used to be?"

Aiden looked steadily back at him, almost pitying Noah. It was obvious the big guy had a thing for Winter. He didn't begrudge the guy his protective attitude. He was here for the same reason. And, like Dalton, he didn't trust anyone else to watch her back.

"I've known her a lot longer than you have," he finally said. The terse words were an understatement.

He'd watched Winter go from a skinny girl barely in her teens, struggling to find a reason to keep going after waking up from a coma to find her family gone. She'd struggled so hard to live, to thrive, after the attack. And he, the FBI agent she blatantly hero-worshipped? He hadn't managed to catch her family's killer. He'd never even come close, and it was a source of constant fury. But the child's adoration had never slipped.

Then, in a little over a decade, Winter had transformed herself from a young and grieving girl to a hardened and purposeful woman, but he could still sense her vulnerability. It still simmered just beneath the surface. It lurked in the intense blue of her eyes. Beneath the stubborn set of her jaw.

He also knew that she'd come out of the coma different than the way she'd gone in. That it was virtually impossible to be a normal kid, make it to a normal adulthood, after going through a childhood trauma like she had.

She'd come close. He'd kept tabs on her through the years. It had been rocky at the beginning, but once her grandparents moved her to Raleigh, things got better. Since her college days, though, Aiden had seen something different in Winter.

She had almost an eidetic memory. She could leap to conclusions that were impossible for most. She could see things no one else could, and he realized that sight went beyond the physical. She knew things she shouldn't. And he'd seen firsthand the toll that ability took from her when she'd passed out in front of him, blood streaming out of her nose.

He'd also seen something else she hadn't wanted him to see. Something he'd tried not to acknowledge in himself. Winter wasn't a child anymore. She was a strong, mysterious, intelligent woman. The years that had once distanced them seemed to have shrunk. The balance between them, mentor to student, had shifted into something new. She fascinated him, almost to the point of obsession.

Mentally, he shook himself. Dalton was still watching him with a mixture of dislike and suspicion.

"Kennedy got out of that room somehow," he said, nodding up at the windows of the corner bedroom. "When those guys are done, we'll see if there's anything left in his office, but whatever's in there won't include his body."

They went back to Winter, who was impatiently trying to get a heavyset woman in a blue uniform to let her up from the cot she'd been assigned to in the back of the ambulance.

"I'm fine," she appealed to Aiden. She was a little pale, still, and a bandage was wrapped around her hand, but her blue eyes snapped with annoyance. "Will you please get her to let me up? We need to get a look in that box." Her voice was muffled, but he could still hear the smoke-roughened rasp of it through the plastic oxygen cup over her mouth.

Aiden met the eyes of the paramedic over Winter's head. She rolled her own at the stubbornness of her patient but nodded reluctantly.

"The box is taken care of for now," he told Winter as she dropped lightly down from the back of the ambulance. "I locked it in the back of the car. Right now, we've got a different focus. I saw Kennedy in that house before I found you. As soon as we're cleared by the fire department, we're going in to look around."

Noah spoke with the Bethesda police officers that had arrived while Aiden called Max Osbourn to update him on the situation. It wasn't discussed, but as the ranking agent, Aiden had stepped into the de facto position of lead on the investigation. Technically, Winter remained AIC, and Osbourn was still officially overseeing, but they all knew what the real deal was.

Winter talked to the fire chief on scene, and after another few minutes, they were allowed to go in and conduct their search. The four Bethesda officers took the main floor, and Aiden led the way upstairs. They went over each room on both sides of the staircase and found nothing. When they entered the master suite on the second floor, Aiden went to the wall beside the fireplace. Looking up through the window outside, he'd been able to see that the north wall of the bedroom ended about five feet before the actual corner of the upper floor.

Knocking on the wall, he heard an echo instead of the solid thunk of plaster on brick. Noah joined him. "Secret passageway?" the younger agent said. "Kennedy is rapidly turning into a Scooby Doo villain." He tugged on a wall sconce, but it didn't budge.

Winter stood behind them without speaking for a moment, studying the brick. She reached out and ran the fingers of her uninjured hand under the mantlepiece. A section of the wall, formerly seamless, unlatched with a click. Aiden wedged his fingers into the crack that had formed and pulled it open. Instead of a dark, musty stairwell, there was a drywalled landing with a covered light fixture overhead.

Aiden flipped the switch to illuminate the staircase. A flight of narrow stairs went up to the attic, and the other descended to the main floor.

"It's not a secret passageway. At least it wasn't originally. This was retrofitted from the servant's stair that was originally built in the house."

"So it probably leads down to the main floor and maybe farther down into the basement."

Aiden nodded, starting down. "From the cool air coming up, I think it does. And there's likely another exit down there."

They bypassed the main floor and continued down. Winter took the lead at the basement level. Despite the beauty of the rest of the house, Kennedy's basement was a cold, cavernous space that ran the length of the home. She led them unerringly through the darkness, lit only by a penlight on Noah's keychain, her steps quick and sure.

At the other end of the basement was a short flight of steps that led up to the door. She pushed it open, and they found themselves a few feet from the garage. Woods—real ones, not like the manicured tree garden at the front of the property—stretched off into the darkness twenty feet away.

"We can have the Bethesda guys call in a canine unit," Aiden said, his face a blank mask of fury. "But Kennedy is likely long gone."

25

It was nearly midnight by the time they left the Kennedy house. The inside of Parrish's SUV stank like smoke, and Noah was just petty enough to hope that the fancy leather upholstery never lost the odor.

He glanced up at Winter, slumped in the passenger seat, her head against the window. She was out cold, her breathing steady and deep. Her black hair had come loose from its neat twist hours ago and hung down in a dark curtain, shielding her soot-stained face.

He'd hated Parrish for making him stay behind while she ran into danger.

Aiden met his eyes in the rearview, just for a moment with a cool, assessing glance, and then he looked back at the road. They'd come to an understanding. Not verbally. Noah didn't want to converse with the uptight prick any more than necessary. But they each understood their priorities, positions firmly established.

Winter would come first.

The fire investigator had determined the origin and cause

of the fire. Books and papers—presumably the incriminating contents of Kennedy's desk—had been piled up just on the other side of the office door. The whole mess had been doused with a mixture of gasoline and styrene, made up ahead of time. He'd been prepared for their arrival.

Winter was lucky to have not taken in any more smoke than she did. He had a very sudden and unprofessional urge to kill the man, just for that.

Kennedy had literally made homemade napalm by dissolving a Styrofoam plate in gasoline. It thickened the mixture, making it burn hotter and longer. He obviously didn't want any material left intact that could be read by anyone after the fire.

His tactic had worked. The gasoline he'd splashed around the room, coupled with the mixture on the papers, had created an initial explosion that settled into a nice, long-burning, hard to extinguish blaze. It had continued to eat at the floorboards of the office and nearly collapsed the floor beneath before it could be put out.

Kennedy himself had escaped through the clever staircase to the basement, and from there, who the hell knew. The canines hadn't been able to track him.

Winter shuddered awake as they pulled into the lot at Holiday Inn Express just outside of D.C., her eyes wide and dark. Noah had booked them three rooms earlier in the evening, figuring they'd have things to follow up on the next day. She glanced around quickly and seemed to relax once she oriented herself.

"Time to open the box," she said, wincing a little at what must've been a sore throat.

The Holiday Inn was a step-up from their little hotel in Harrisonburg. They trooped into the lobby and picked up their room keys at the front desk.

As soon as the cute desk clerk handed them over, smiling flirtatiously even though he smelled like a house fire, he dug in his pocket for change. There was a Coke machine in a little alcove outside the elevator.

"Hit the button for two and hold it, will you?" he asked Winter.

His mouth tasted like ash, and hers had to feel like she'd been sucking on an exhaust pipe. The machine whined and rattled after he put in the coins, but it did its job and spit out three cans. He shifted his small duffel higher on his shoulder and grabbed them, followed Parrish and Winter into the elevator. Winter had her own beat-up backpack, and Parrish sported a garment bag and a small overnight case. He also had the smoke-blackened box tucked under one arm.

Their rooms were all on the same floor, and by unspoken agreement, they used the senior agent's since it was the closest. After Aiden swiped the key card and opened the door, Noah handed Winter the Coke as she walked past. Aiden set his things down by the door and the box on the table, nodding in what Noah assumed was a thank you.

Sweeping the room was second nature by now, after the nights spent in Harrisonburg, and he hoped he wasn't catching a case of OCD. The fact that they were in a different hotel didn't make a difference. He did it quickly, ignoring Aiden's curious look.

Winter was already at the table, checking out the lock on the box. She dug in her purse and came out with a hairpin. At Noah's raised brow, she shrugged. "Sometimes clichés are cliché for a reason."

Within moments, she'd opened it. Inside, there was a passport. She looked at it briefly and handed it off to him. Scott Kennedy's picture was on it, but the name read James Parker. Beneath that were credit cards, traveler's checks and a handy assortment of things one might need if one decided to suddenly get the hell out of Dodge. "James" was all set to travel, probably to someplace with lax ideas on extradition cooperation.

Under those was a thick file. Winter pulled it out, but Parrish took it from her, glanced inside briefly, and set it down on the nightstand behind him.

"Before we get to that, Winter, there's something we need to discuss." He stayed standing, pinning her with a look, his arms crossed. Noah knew what was coming next, and he sat down on the edge of the bed, positioning himself to get the best view of the confrontation.

Grinning as he watched the realization set in on Winter's face that she was about to be taken out behind the woodshed —figuratively, anyway—he didn't know who to put his money on. Parrish, the sharp-eyed, experienced FBI agent with the spine of steel seemed likely. He was colder than an ice cube and intimidating as all hell. Winter, though, sat back calmly, her black hair tumbling over her shoulders and her eyes sparking blue fire. She looked like she was silently daring him to bring it on.

"If you ever pull an impulsive, selfish, shit move again like you did today, running into that house without backup, I will get you fired before you know what hit you and take absolute pleasure in it."

Noah stifled a snort. Parrish even made cussing sound sophisticated with that upper-crust accent of his. But as far as ultimatums went, it was a good one.

Noah watched for an explosion, a little disappointed when it didn't happen.

Instead, Winter gazed up at Parrish, looking like butter wouldn't melt in her mouth. "We've known each other for a long time, haven't we, Aiden?" Her lips curled into a small smile. Parrish looked wary but didn't speak. "Over the years, I couldn't help but start to think of you like a friend. Even a big brother."

Noah wanted to wince on Parrish's behalf, but he was enjoying himself too much. Even he could tell that Aiden's feelings toward Winter had taken a far-from-brotherly turn. She couldn't be oblivious to that, with all her powers of observation.

"Your involvement in my life could definitely be considered above and beyond your call of duty as an FBI agent, wouldn't you agree?"

She was laying down landmines left and right, but Parrish wasn't budging.

And here came the fire.

Winter stood up fast, knocking her chair back against the wall. She closed the space between them, and despite the fact that Parrish was taller, did a damned good job of getting in the man's face.

"Don't you dare throw around bullshit threats. You know damned well you wormed your way into this case because you can't separate Agent Black from Winter. Winter was a little girl who needed protection after having her parents ripped away from her. Agent Black can take care of herself, and this hovering is over the top, even for you."

Her face flushed and her voice went even rougher from the strain of yelling in his face.

"From now on, you can address me as a fellow agent, *SSA Parrish*, and treat me as you would a fellow agent. If you have any problems with my conduct, take it up with my superior and let him decide if I need to be fired. In the meantime, go fuck yourself."

Damn, the man was cool. During her entire tirade, Parrish's smooth, slightly sarcastic expression didn't slip once. When Winter roughly brushed past him to grab the file, Noah caught a brief, dangerous glimmer in his eyes.

"My apologies." His voice was soft and controlled, with a thread of stone underneath. "In the future, I'll go through Osbourne when you need a reprimand. In the meantime, you should work out what the definition of professionalism really means. I'm sure you've still got some college textbooks handy…graduation wasn't so long ago, was it?"

Without waiting to see if the dart had hit the mark, Parrish went to the door, opening it wide. "Six o'clock, down in the lobby?"

Parrish directed the question at Noah, who nodded with a hint of the respect he'd been holding back until now as he pushed to his feet. He was impressed, despite himself. The guy could deliver a helluva set-down. "Six o'clock," he agreed as he stepped into the hallway behind the seething woman.

"Seriously?" Winter burst out as soon as the door closed behind him. "You couldn't have backed me up on that?"

Noah shrugged. "Better coming from him than me. Parrish gave the classier delivery."

Her jaw dropped, and he chuckled.

She shut her mouth quickly and glared. "You agree with him?"

Sobering, he nodded. "I do. You had no right to go chasing off like that. Even though you knew something was there, dammit, you should have said something. You knew about the lockbox and its hiding place, but you didn't know if Kennedy was in there. He's a damn suspect, I think we can agree at this point, but you didn't know if he or anyone else who had decided to do a little spot of arson for some evening fun was lying in wait."

"I can't help but feel," she rasped out, not backing down, "that we would not be having this conversation if you or Aiden had run in there instead of me."

"Whether you like it or not, sweetheart, it was a shit move."

"Unbelievable." She spun around, grabbing her bag from where she'd dropped it. "You're both un-fucking-believable." She turned on him again, irate, her fingers digging into the manila file folder until her knuckles turned pale. "You need to drop this overprotective act just as badly as Aiden does. I do *not* need your protection."

The hell she didn't. Now, his own temper shifted into a slow simmer.

"I agree with Parrish. While we're all working together, none of us needs to go chasing off solo, leaving the other two hanging. I was trained to watch out for my partner and my team. Doesn't matter if that's in the military, on the police force, or with the FBI. So were you."

She flushed a little, knowing he was right.

He took a step closer to her, just like she had with Aiden not ten minutes before, knowing she wouldn't back down. "The main difference between Parrish and me, darlin'," he murmured, lowering his head until he was only a few inches from her upturned face, "is that you know damned well I'm not your brother."

Furious, Winter gave him a hard shove to the chest, and he let it knock him back a couple of feet. She was gone, seconds later, and he waited until the door slammed before he started laughing.

He had to remind himself that she was still new to this. Parrish had been pretty snarky about it, but he was right. She was barely out of college, no previous experience in the army or as a law enforcement officer. She'd get the hang of things and either learn how to be a team player or end up reassigned to a desk job.

Stripping off his shirt and heading for the bathroom to shower the smoke off, he glanced at the bed. Yeah, it'd be nice to sleep on something other than the floor for a change. But he was going to miss those cute little noises Winter made when she slept.

As well as Parrish and Winter knew each other, he'd still bet Aiden had never heard those cute little sleep noises.

26

Winter desperately wished she had coffee. She re-read the last section of the report in front of her. The words, already ten or more syllables long, were starting to blur.

She'd been exhausted the night before, falling asleep in the car on the way to the hotel, but after her confrontation with her "team" members, she hadn't been able to get to sleep. Instead, she'd showered, stewing in her own anger at overbearing, sexist males in general as she scrubbed at her hair with one hand. Then, she'd stayed up until nearly four in the morning, going over the file they'd lifted from Scott Kennedy's lockbox.

The information in that file was game-changing, she knew. She just wished she understood exactly what she was reading.

It had been a late night, but she was the first one down to the lobby. It seemed like a good idea at the time to her sleep-starved brain, but the extra few minutes left her angsty, wondering how Noah and Aiden were going to act after their separate blowouts.

The elevator doors slid open, and they both stepped out at the same time. Noah, his jaw still scruffy with stubble and his too-long wet hair slicked back, was dressed in a pair of jeans and boots with a black sweater that hugged his wide shoulders.

Beside him, Aiden looked like he was on his way to Wall Street. Tall and lean in a tailored blue suit with subtle gray pinstriping...not a hair out of place and shoes she knew she'd be able to see her reflection in.

Two men, so different, and both so important to her, even though they were almost equally infuriating. She didn't want the connection, but she had it anyway.

"Good morning, Agent Black," Aiden offered dryly. She rolled her eyes at him and looked to Noah, but he was no help. He just shrugged, as if to say *well, what do you expect?*

"I need coffee. Preferably the kind with a lot of chocolate in it. Can we come to a team agreement on that?"

Noah glanced at Aiden. "I think it's a reasonable request. What do you think, SSA Parrish?"

"Agent Dalton, I believe we have a consensus." Aiden turned back to her. "Yes, Agent Black. Let's go get some coffee."

"You guys owe me Starbucks for being such jerks about this." Winter turned to lead the way out to the parking lot. Behind her, she heard Noah ask Aiden if he was amenable to Starbucks as a possible destination. Aiden replied that he found Starbucks acceptable.

Winter lifted a middle finger so they'd both be sure to see it. She didn't turn around, though. The gesture would lose its effectiveness if they saw her grin. Separately, they were infuriating. Teamed up, they might just make her crazy.

※

THE LINE at the coffee shop drive-thru looked about three miles long, but it was still too early for an inside crowd. Winter got her mocha and took an appreciative sip. The soreness was mostly gone, but the hot coffee still felt good on her throat. She wound her way back to the table Noah had snagged.

Noah read the contents of the file, his brow furrowed.

Aiden was texting. "I've got a DNA specialist lined up," he finally said, looking up and setting his phone down. "Tracy Hooper. She works out of the Laboratory of Analytical Biology lab space at the Natural History Building, and she agreed to meet with us later this morning."

The file she'd retrieved from Kennedy's hiding place had been worth the risk, in Winter's opinion. In it were the results of test studies for the fertility drug that Scott Kennedy had applied for a patent for in the early eighties: Progesteraline Six. On several of those pages were names that Winter recognized immediately.

Tony and Belinda Collier. Darin and Joanna Bowman. David and Nancy Benton. Andy and Catherine Kinney. Betty and Jerry Talbot.

They were all listed as subjects who had been given the fertility drug, and judging by the fact that the information about Progesteraline Six hadn't surfaced until this point, none of them were aware they'd been dosed.

"I can't figure out why Kennedy wouldn't have taken this box," Winter mused. "He had to have known that the information in it was damning."

"I assume he has other aliases," Noah replied. "Maybe this one is a backup."

"So, are we watching airports? Is he going to split, knowing that we've got this information?"

Noah shrugged, but Aiden shook his head slowly.

"What are you thinking?"

"He doesn't know we have the information." Aiden started tapping keys on his laptop as he continued. "Kennedy is powerful, arrogant, and thinks he's a step ahead of us. You saw him during the interview. He thinks he's untouchable and we're idiots. It wouldn't occur to him that we have the lockbox. In fact, he's less likely to leave now that all the irons are in the fire."

"He's working with Rebekah Archer," Noah put in.

Aiden nodded. "Whether or not she's completely aware of what he's doing or not remains to be seen, but we can work under the assumption that the two are in contact. We'll get a subpoena for phone records, but in the meantime, we're going to look into Kennedy's other properties."

Within an hour, Winter came up with a rental condo in South Beach, connected with Scott Kennedy. Aiden had found two more, a luxurious house in Vail with easy access to skiing, and a townhouse in Boston, apparently rented out to an affluent doctor and his wife. Noah found a beachfront cottage near Savanna.

On the way to the Smithsonian to speak with the DNA researcher, Noah sent local law enforcement officials at each property location a picture of Scott Kennedy as a person of interest in an FBI investigation and posted a BOLO, requesting a phone call if he was spotted. Winter located a number for Scott Kennedy's brother, who agreed to meet with them that afternoon.

It felt like the investigation was finally gaining momentum, but where it would end up, Winter wasn't sure.

"WHAT THE HELL IS THIS?" Tracy Hooper adjusted her black cat-eye glasses and squinted down at the file she'd been studying for the last five minutes. "Where did you get this?"

She looked up at the three FBI agents lined up in front of her desk, one or all of whom smelled a little like woodsmoke.

"It's a—" Winter started.

"Sit down." Tracy pointed to the metal folding chairs she'd dragged out of the storage room earlier in the morning. One would think that in a facility as prestigious as the Natural History Building, the furniture would be better. "You're all making me nervous hovering like that."

Aiden sat but leaned forward. "Tell us what you think."

Tracy's path had crossed with Aiden Parrish's before, and she'd always liked him, despite his brusque attitude. She was the last person to hold anyone's attitude against them, and besides, he was hot. She had a thing for Tom Hiddleston, and Aiden looked like Loki's stunt double in a suit.

She sucked in her tummy a little and took a quick second to be glad she'd worn her favorite vintage red wiggle dress with the sweetheart neckline. Granted, she wore a lab coat over it, but that never seemed to matter to Jeremy, the college kid who interned with her in the afternoons. The dress showcased her assets.

"I think you've got someone trying to play God and doing an absolute shit job of it." She slapped the file down and crossed her arms, leaning back in her chair. "And I'm not going to elaborate until you give me some background on this."

The female agent across from her leaned forward, her brilliant blue eyes sharp with intelligence. "We think that's exactly what someone was—or *is*—trying to do. We know Progesteraline Six was a fertility drug, but does anything in those medical records lead you to believe that the person that created the drug was trying to influence personality? I did some googling last night, but you're the expert."

Tracy smiled wryly. "Flattery never hurts, but yeah, I'm

the expert all right. How much do you know about how personality is developed?"

"Nature versus nurture, you mean?"

"To be basic, yeah." Tracy reached into the top drawer of her desk and pulled out a bag of M&M's. She offered them to her visitors, but the only taker was the big, green-eyed agent. He gave her a surprisingly sweet smile and held out a hand for her to shake a few candies into. If Parrish was Loki, this guy was Thor.

"In early gene studies, researchers liked to follow twins through their growth and development. Basically, watch and see how much they grew up alike, sometimes through different upbringings. Those experiments established that, yeah, there was some genetic link that determined likes and dislikes, personality tendencies, things like that."

She popped a couple M&M's into her mouth and crunched thoughtfully. "That early research led to the study of different genes, trying to pinpoint which were responsible for what. I could go into neuropeptides and genetic poly-morphism and the debate over how effective DNA really is in deciding personality traits, but I don't need to watch your eyes glaze over. This drug wasn't designed to mess with DNA."

Tracy watched their faces fall a little, just because she had a little mean streak. She grinned. "Lucky for you, I double-majored in BBC. Brain, Behavior, and Cognition. Cognitive science."

Aiden didn't appear to be in the mood to appreciate her not-so-humble brag. He just raised one eyebrow and nodded for her to continue.

"P6 was designed to increase fertility. It was also designed to mess with brain development. I could rabbit hole into the technical stuff, but the bottom line is that P6 was meant to target the orbitofrontal lobe." She tapped between her eyebrows. "This part of the brain is linked to emotion and decision-making. Your mad scientist was trying to decrease brain matter in the orbitofrontal cortex to make nice, easy-going, malleable babies."

Tracy opened the file and flipped through the pages again. It was enough to turn your stomach if you knew what you were looking at. And she read enough dystopian fiction and sci-fi that she could easily see the possibilities in mass population control with a drug like that.

"Instead of nice babies, though, the moron who developed P6 somehow designed a drug that caused a whole lot of physical and cognitive defects. As a bonus, it essentially killed the mothers within five to fifteen years. I can't emphasize it enough: this stuff is bad. Not just the drug itself, but the fact that, judging by the dates on these records, even after results showed that P6 didn't work, they continued to tweak it and administer it anyway. Unethical, to say the least. Downright sadistic would be a better description."

Tracy didn't feel bad about building up the drama on purpose—it had been a slow day in the lab, and this was probably the most excitement she'd see all week—but none of the agents looked appalled enough by her bombshell.

She leaned forward, frowning. "Maybe I'm not being clear enough. Kids exposed to this could suffer all kinds of brain malformations and physical side effects. Depending on the dosage, it could be like a chemical lobotomy. And that's completely overlooking the fact that if a drug like this was successfully tweaked, developed, and mass-produced, it could create a whole generation of little Stepford children."

27

B rian Kennedy looked like he wanted to rub his hands together in glee when he saw them standing on his postage stamp-sized front porch. He looked around the same age as his brother should have, had Botox not intervened. He'd inherited the same good looks, but unlike Scott, he didn't leer at Winter, just grinned widely and welcomed them into his understated, two-story middle-class home.

"Tell me," he ordered with vindictiveness, "that you all are finally going to nail him for something. What is it? Tax evasion? Corporate fraud? Screwing his family out of their rightful share of the family fortune?"

Noah grinned back at the man. "Can we come in and talk about that?"

"Sure." Brian chuckled and stepped back, waving his hand for them to enter. "Sheri, will you bring our federal agents something to drink?"

A small, cheerful woman in her mid-fifties with steel-gray hair in a neat bob popped her head out of a doorway, presumably to the kitchen. "Brian insisted on chips and dip, like this was some kind of a Superbowl party." She rolled her eyes indulgently. "Would any of you like a Pepsi? A beer?"

Winter shook her head and gave the woman a small smile in return. Aiden declined too. "I'll take a Pepsi if it's not too much trouble," Noah replied, and Winter could see him fighting with his stomach about declining the chips and dip.

"Absolutely. Come on in," Brian urged them. "We can talk in the living room."

Not exactly a reluctant informant, Winter noted. They might have to sift through some bias, but hopefully, they'd learn something that would help them locate Scott.

The house was comfortable. Not overly expensive, but nicely decorated. No original Monet graced the walls, but there were tasteful art prints and inexpensive antiques that looked lovingly cared for. It was definitely more welcoming than the Kennedy estate had been.

Once they were seated on a set of plaid, cushy couches, Brian scooched forward in his chair expectantly. His eyes were a warmer shade of blue than Scott's, and his face was scored with natural laugh lines. But his eyes were hard. "What'd he do?"

Aiden took out his notebook and Montblanc pen. "Actually, we're still working on putting that together. We're hoping we can get some information from you. Can you tell us the last time you spoke to your brother?"

Brian's face fell a little, but he nodded. "I can tell you the exact date." His voice was bitter. "It was January 2, 1981. Scott informed me that I was no longer allowed through the doors of our family's company, just before he had security escort me from the building. He'd sold it. I'd sunk everything I had into that business." He snapped his fingers. "And I was broke, just like that."

Sheri entered the room with a tray and deposited it on

the coffee table. She hurried to her husband's side, her black flats making no noise on the carpet.

"Brian," she warned him, putting a hand on his shoulder. "Don't go there again."

His face softened a little, and he grinned up at her, placing his hand over hers in an affectionate gesture. "Trust me. I don't regret it. If I hadn't been kicked to the curb and ended up drowning my sorrows at the same bar every night for a week afterward, I wouldn't have caught the eye of a certain cute little waitress."

"Whatever," Sheri replied tolerantly, a twinkle in her eyes. "You were a sloppy drunk, crying in your beer. You asked me out, and I refused to date you until you quit feeling sorry for yourself, stopped drinking, and got another job."

"If that's how you remember it." He shrugged and chuckled. "But you'll all have to excuse me while I indulge in a little schadenfreude. Scottie's got this coming, whatever it is."

"Scott cheated you?" Aiden asked. "Did you take him to court?"

"You bet the bastard cheated me. I fell for it, too, along with a couple of cousins and an uncle who had inherited shares. We were all told that the company was going under, and he oh so generously said he'd do the family a favor and buy up their shares ahead of time." He snorted. "At a loss, of course, so we wouldn't be hit as hard. I refused, being young and idealistic. Instead, I talked him into letting me invest, and sold most of what I had to help turn things around."

"Which it didn't," Winter surmised.

Brian scowled. "I played right into his hands. He took my contribution, and slick as shit, sold the company to the highest bidder. I ended up with a piddly amount that didn't cover a fraction of what I'd put into the company. I threatened to sue, and he outlawyered me, knowing I didn't have the money to fight him in a long legal battle. Do you know, he had the nerve to laugh about how badly I got screwed on that? Said I should have done my homework first."

Even Sheri scowled at that. Scott Kennedy was not a well-liked man in this Kennedy household, as nice as the occupants seemed.

Noah eased the tension in the room slightly with a subject change. "Your father built himself a sizeable estate before he passed on. Do you know if he had any other properties besides your family home? Other houses or estates or vacation properties that your brother may have retained or still have access to?"

"Is Scottie on the lam?" Brian's face visibly brightened at the thought. "God, that'd be great if you guys found him in some crappy hideout and had to drag him out in cuffs. I know my parents had a cottage up in Michigan. And I know that when we inherited, before he fuc—"

He stopped at a warning squeeze from his wife, her hand still on his shoulder. "Language," she singsonged.

He cleared his throat. "Sorry. There was also a house in Florida. A little fifties beachside bungalow. We'd spend summer vacations there."

Aiden's pen scratched rapidly against his notepaper. "Can you think of any others? Anything in West Virginia, maybe?"

Brian shook his head. "Sorry, that's all I can think of."

"Does the name Wesley Archer sound familiar?" Winter tried not to let her growing frustration show. She'd been hoping for more, and they hadn't managed to come up with anything other than additional evidence that Scott Kennedy was an asshole. "He served in the military with your brother."

Again, Brian shook his head. "Scott and I were never really close, even though we were only three years apart in age. By high school, we were practically strangers. I didn't even know he'd gone to war until my dad told me he'd shipped out."

Noah reached for his glass of Pepsi and took a sip. "Have you ever heard of a drug called Progesteraline? Maybe developed back in your dad's day?"

There wasn't even a flicker of recognition on Brian's face, and Winter was watching closely for any telltale sign. "Could have been a variation of the fertility drug my dad built the company around in the fifties, but it doesn't sound familiar."

The rest of their questions went about the same. Brian couldn't provide anything helpful, and he didn't bother to hide his disappointment. They were getting ready to leave, with Brian much more subdued than he'd been when they arrived.

"It's probably wrong of me to want karma to catch up with him," Brian said as he walked them to the door, Sheri hovering behind him.

Noah shook Brian's hand, his expression sympathetic. "Don't take it too hard. He sounds like one of those guys that karma will catch up to eventually. Let us know if you think of anything else that you think might be helpful."

"I'll rack my brain," Brian promised.

Aiden and Noah had just climbed into the SUV and Winter had opened her door when Brian popped his head out of the house.

"Hold on," he called out, shuffling into a pair of slippers and letting the screen door bang behind him as he trotted down the sidewalk. "You mentioned West Virginia, and it made me think of something."

Winter felt a tingle at the base of her neck as she turned around.

"I don't know how helpful this is, and I have no idea where he went, but I know that Scott *did* travel there, at least a couple of times. The day I tried to get in to see him and security was called? As I was leaving the room, I heard his secretary say something about West Virginia. That she'd made his hotel reservation for three days, like he'd asked, and at the same hotel as before."

"Do you remember his secretary's name? The town? The name of the hotel?" Winter asked, finally feeling a little surge of excitement. If they could put Kennedy near Harrison-burg...but when?

Brian shook his head regretfully. "I wish I could. All I know is his secretary was a mean old bat even back then. She's probably dead by now. I know it's not much."

"It's something," Winter assured him. "And every little bit of information helps."

Especially when she felt like they were still ten steps behind the game.

AIDEN PULLED the SUV into a parking place in the hotel parking garage. The smell of fast food burgers from the bags they'd picked up wasn't the least bit appetizing, but his suggestion of Chinese had been voted down. It was looking like room service tonight. He hoped they had a decent wine menu.

He glanced up at the rearview mirror as he shut off the ignition. Winter was looking out her window, her face intent. "Hold on," she snapped as Dalton started to open his door. "Wait a second."

"What is it?" Aiden slid his hand inside his jacket, close to his weapon.

At Winter's tone, Dalton did the same. The ramp was crowded, with no spots free until the third level. It was likely there was a convention or a social event happening at the hotel that evening. A couple made their way off the nearby elevator, nicely dressed, laughing at something with enough enthusiasm to imply that wherever they'd been had an open bar.

They stumbled past the back of the vehicle and headed for a white Lexus a few spaces down.

"There's something wrong." The words were hesitant, but Aiden didn't doubt Winter's intuition for a moment. He scanned the lot, looking for anything out of place. Most of the cars in this section were expensive models, but an older, silver Toyota caught his eye.

Behind the wheel, he could make out the outline of a driver. It was raining outside, a slow, sullen drizzle, but his car was dry. He'd either been in it for a while, or he was just leaving.

"The Toyota?"

Winter nodded. "He's waiting for us."

"Let him wait," Noah said.

They watched as the guy behind the wheel shifted restlessly. Just over five minutes had passed when he opened his door and stepped out. He was trying to be subtle but was definitely looking in their direction.

The man was white, probably in his mid-twenties. Aiden couldn't see his eyes, but he had a scruffy beard and wore a black hoodie, pulled up over a red baseball cap. "Crimson Tide?" Noah murmured. "Must be an Alabama fan."

The guy was obviously nervous. He started moving toward the back of his car, and then stopped, hesitating.

"Y'all want to see what he wants?" Noah asked.

"Better than waiting here all night," Aiden replied. "It doesn't look like he's ready to come over here and tell us himself. I'll get out first, keep the vehicle between us. Winter, when I get past your door, go to the front of the car and cover me. Dalton, roll your window down while Winter gets in position, and create a distraction."

At their agreement, Aiden reached back and turned the

dome light off. He opened his door silently, just enough to slip out, and eased it closed without letting it latch. His adrenaline was already thrumming. He wouldn't admit it to anyone, but since he'd been holed up in the Behavioral Analysis Unit he'd missed the rare moments of action that came with being in the field.

He slipped past Winter's door, his weapon already drawn. She opened hers as quietly as he had. Their suspect, he could see through the back window, was watching their vehicle, his hands below the side of the car he stood beside.

Winter moved low, soundlessly into place and Aiden heard the whine of Dalton's window.

"Hey, there." Noah's voice boomed out cheerily, the Texas twang thick. "You need some directions or something, son?"

Aiden was already moving when the guy brought up his gun. It was a .9 mm Luger, semi-automatic.

"FBI," he yelled. "Drop your weapon and put your hands in the air."

The kid—up close, he looked like a sweaty, scared eighteen- or nineteen-year-old—swung around, wide-eyed, and fired wild as Aiden ducked. He heard the truncated thud of a bullet hitting concrete. Another single shot took out the tire of a car across the aisle before the kid howled. Aiden rounded the vehicle he'd taken cover behind to see that Winter already had him on the ground, her knee in the middle of his back, calmly twisting his arm to snap him into cuffs.

Aiden nudged the Luger farther out of reach with his foot as Noah reached them, already calling the apprehension into the local PD. When Winter had finished securing the handcuffs and reading him his rights, Aiden rolled the kid over and hauled him by the collar into a sitting position.

He looked defiant, belligerent, and scared enough to shit his pants.

"How much did he pay you?" Aiden asked sympatheti-cally, crouching down beside him. "Whatever it is, it wasn't enough," he added when the kid didn't answer.

"Don' know what you're talking about." He spat on the ground, near Aiden's feet.

"Did he tell you there'd be three FBI agents? Seems like a pretty big job for one person. Especially one who'd never actually done a hit before."

The kid, his face pale, glared at the pavement silently. Aiden could tell he was biting his tongue. His reputation as a hired gun was being called into question. A little more prod-ding would do it.

Winter made eye contact with Aiden over the kid's head. "At least he didn't use the same guy as last time. Jackass couldn't drive for shit. My grandma could have put us over that guardrail with no problem. Instead, he ended up almost running *himself* off the road."

"Fuckin' liar," the boy spat. His eyes glittered up at Winter with rage and his body all but vibrated with it. "You was the one that almost—"

He shut up quick, and his pale face flushed red. She smiled at him, her eyes hard.

Noah tapped his phone to disconnect the call and chuck-led. "Glad I didn't miss that part. Where'd he find you, kid? Craigslist?"

The boy didn't answer, but the deepening red in his face did.

28

A pparently, you *could* hire a hitman on Craigslist.

Noah had a hard time keeping a straight face when it came out in questioning the night before that the young man who'd been hired to kill them—twice—had in fact answered a sketchy job ad online. Even without the aspiring criminal's testimony, and the fact that he'd pulled Scott Kennedy's picture out of a lineup, they would have eventually tied him to Kennedy by tracing the encrypted Craigslist email associated with the ad.

A signed and detailed confession from the failed crook made things much easier, though.

Noah cracked his knuckles, one by one, grinning when Parrish took his eyes off the road to shoot him a dirty look. Noah couldn't help it. He'd been antsy the entire way back to Harrisonburg, and even knowing that the road trip was almost over wasn't helping. Winter was either sleeping or meditating in the back seat, and since he didn't figure he and Parrish had much in common, the SUV had been silent for most of the ride.

Plus, Parrish had shit taste in music.

He'd finished his knuckles and was starting on his finger joints when his phone rang. Florence Wade, the ME in Roanoke, sounded exhausted.

"You were right," she said peremptorily. "I found an unidentified chemical compound in the remains of the soft tissue on our teenage Jane Doe. What the hell is going on up there, Dalton?"

"Still not sure," Noah replied. "But it's coming together. How are things down there, Wade?"

She snorted. "No thanks to you guys, I've got a helluva backlog. You got any other unreasonable requests to throw at me?"

"Nope. We appreciate you, Florence. Let us know if you find anything else. I promise, we almost have everything nailed down."

"You'd better. Don't send me any more bodies. I've got vacation time coming."

Noah disconnected, and Parrish glanced over at him. "Nailed down?" His tone was dry.

"Sure. I've got a feeling about it." As if in confirmation, Noah's phone buzzed with a text. "See? I bet this is good news right now."

His grin fell away fast when he read the terse line from the Harrisonburg police chief.

We have media.

"Well, shit."

Aiden flipped on the turn signal for their exit. Behind them, a Fox News van did the same.

"Good news, huh?" Aiden's eyes went to the rearview mirror, assessing.

Before he could come up with an answer, Noah's phone rang. He picked it up, assuming it was the chief without looking at the display. "Has the circus come to town, Chief?"

But it wasn't Gary Miller. It was Tom Benton, and he sounded like a man dangerously close to the edge.

TOM PACED THE FLOOR, his mind in turmoil. He ignored the mess that cluttered the living room. The open pizza box on the table, surrounded by a dozen empty beer cans. The fact that he hadn't taken a shower in days...and smelled like it.

He couldn't get Sam out of his mind. He had a growing, horrible certainty that the day of their fight would be the last time he'd ever see her. He wanted to howl. He wanted to break something. He wanted her home safe. He didn't care if it was just the two of them and they never had the family he'd always wanted.

He loved Sam. That was the most important thing.

Her family didn't know where she was. They blamed him. Her sister was even making noises about something having happened to her. Who better than a cop to commit murder and get away with it, after all?

His dad was no help. He'd retreated into some kind of depression after whatever had gone down when the FBI agents had gone to see him. Maria, his long-time house-keeper, could hardly get him to eat.

Tom kicked viciously at a shoe lying in his path. It hit the paneled wall, dangerously close to the TV, and thudded to the floor.

The doorbell rang.

He still hated the thought of asking them for help, but now that they were here, he felt something within him ease.

Agent Dalton and Winter were waiting on the front porch, along with another man Tom hadn't met. He had the stereotypical look of a ranking federal agent. Crisp suit, looking freshly pressed. A sharp-eyed, searching stare. A face that looked like it would break if it smiled.

Self-consciously, Tom raked a hand through his uncombed hair and stepped back so they could enter. He felt his face flush as the third agent studied the room. Tom knew it was a mess, but he had bigger fucking problems to worry about than housekeeping.

Winter stepped forward, her blue eyes looking dark with sympathy. "There's been no word from her?"

To his horror, Tom felt a lump clog his throat. He cleared it. "No. I've checked with all her friends. Borrowed a car from my dad and drove around everywhere, looking for the Subaru. It's like she just disappeared." He clenched his jaw so tight his teeth squeaked inside his head. "Her family thinks I did it. Did something to her."

"Sit down, man. Let's talk it through." Noah casually plucked a pair of dirty underwear off the back of the La-Z-Boy with two fingers and tossed it down the hall before moving a pile of newspapers off the couch so they could all sit down.

Tom couldn't even find it in himself to care. He sank down on the chair and put his head in his hands.

"I just want her back," he choked out. He felt a small hand on his shoulder, the warmth comforting. Winter. He almost lost it right there.

"This is killing me," he ground out, looking around at the three of them. Pleading for understanding. "Chief texts me regularly, but I'm fucking suspended. I can't even be in the office. Out on the street. Involved in searching for her. They're so wrapped up in the stupid cult case, they can't be giving Sam their full attention."

"I'm SSA Parrish. Agents Dalton and Black gave me the backstory on your wife's disappearance," the clean-cut agent said, his voice cool and emotionless. "But I need you to tell me in your own words what happened."

Tom rubbed his forehead. "My wife, Samantha...she and I fought. She took off almost five days ago, and I haven't seen or heard from her since. I've been calling her cell constantly. Voicemail every time."

Parrish pulled out a small notebook from the inside of his jacket and uncapped a fancy-looking pen. "What did you two fight about?"

"We've had a lot of shit going on. Both of us stressed. I've been drinking a little too much lately. She snapped on her boss and got let go from her job. She's pregnant. Kind of hormonal. She's—*we've*—been trying to have a baby for a long time. She's had a lot of miscarriages. It takes a toll, you know?"

"When did you last see her?"

Tom sighed. "I got suspended from my job. Two weeks, no pay. She started in on me, and I snapped back, and next thing you know, we're screaming at each other. She locked herself in the bathroom. Said she was having cramps. I was so afraid she was losing another baby..." His voice broke. He scrubbed his face so hard with his hands he expected to see blood when they dropped back into his lap. "She wouldn't let me in. She called somebody. I didn't know if it was her mom or her doctor, but—"

"Did you try to get her phone records?" Parrish interrupted, his eyes sharp.

"I...no." Tom couldn't help it. He felt himself getting defensive, but the guy was a cold fish and it was pissing him off. "Chief told me to let him handle it."

Parrish pinned him with a look. "It would be easier to get your own wife's phone records for you, wouldn't it?"

"Yeah." Tom's jaw ached, he was clenching it so tightly. He could see Winter and Agent Dalton out of the corner of his eye. His temper eased a little. They didn't look like they were enjoying this, and he wouldn't have blamed them if they had been.

"What do *you* think is going on, Tom?" Winter asked.

"I think she's with Rebekah Archer."

Dalton leaned forward, and even Parrish seemed to go on alert.

"I tried to tell Chief Miller that, and he couldn't see how it would fit. But Sam, she'd been *so* convinced that this baby would be the first she'd carry to term. I watched her go through each miscarriage like it would break her. Afraid each time that it would. She'd be so down afterward, so depressed."

He pressed the heels of his hands against his temples, feeling a stress headache pulsing from the base of his neck to the center of his forehead.

"This time is different, though. She's had this fearful, intense hope. She kept promising me, *promising* me that this time would be different. She lied to me. She told me her doctor was keeping a close eye on things, and she had appointments almost every week. But when she left, I called her doctor, and they hadn't seen her in months. Not since the last pregnancy."

"Tom, why do you think she's with Rebekah?" Winter asked gently.

"We've talked about it before, but the Archer's place came up again not long ago. We'd heard rumblings for years about babies and fertility drugs, and Sam asked a bunch of questions about it."

Winter frowned. "And you think that's how she got pregnant?"

He pushed out of the chair, frustrated. "It's the only logical conclusion I can come up with. And if she's with that Rebekah, will I see her again? Will she end up like that girl that was found in the burial site? Abandoned in some unmarked grave? You have to find her. You have to make her come home."

His eyes burning, Tom stared at them each in turn. Parrish was watching him like he was some kind of a bug under a microscope. Dalton looked concerned. Worried. Winter, though. Her face was intense. Focused. Determined.

Of the three, her expression was the most reassuring.

She stood up, and the other three followed suit. "We'll find her, Tom. We'll bring her home."

He believed her.

But when they left him in the trashed house, he felt more alone than ever.

As their car pulled away, Tom caught a glimpse of himself in the mirror in the entryway. His eyes were bloodshot. His hair stood on end. His face was pasty and puffy from too much alcohol and too little sleep. Stubble roughened his cheeks, and there was a dark stain on the front of his dingy white t-shirt. He looked like a stranger.

Hell, if Sam walked through the door right now, she might turn around and leave him all over again. And he wouldn't be able to blame her.

He headed to the back of the house, to his bedroom to grab a clean set of clothes. He was going to shower and shave. Then, he was going to call the phone company and have them send over the record of calls from their cell phones. And while he was waiting for them to do that, he was going to clean the house.

He had to get his shit together. He wanted Sam to come back to a man a little more like the one she'd married.

TWO NEWS VANS had been set up in the parking lot of their

hotel. CNN and MSNBC. Chief Miller had his hands full fielding media inquiries. He was furious that someone saw fit to tip off the big networks on the investigation after they'd been lucky enough to keep things quiet up until now. He warned them to stay away from the station. Their presence would just add fuel to the fire.

Thankfully, "their" hipster coffee shop was deserted. The pierced barista with the big headphones gave them an almost friendly nod when they walked in, and Winter felt like a regular. But once the girl handed them their coffees, she was completely uninterested in them. The rap blasting out of her headphones was audible all the way across the room.

"So, I think we can operate under the assumption that Kennedy took advantage of a friend's depression and disillusionment." Aiden had his little notebook out and was going over his notes.

Winter would have liked to get her hands on that thing. He wrote in it constantly. It would likely be an interesting look into the workings of Aiden's brain.

"He probably talked Wesley Archer into going along with it, feeding him the 'better living through chemicals' line," Noah agreed. He'd stretched out on the beat-up couch he'd claimed, his eyes half-closed. His mind, though, was firing on all cylinders.

"Kennedy didn't give a shit about peace, love, and happy babies," Winter tossed in.

Noah snorted his agreement. "He would have had the long game in mind, with dollar signs at the end of it. A marketable fertility drug that promised miracle babies with sweet, easygoing personalities. It would be a PR dream."

"The dream went bad, obviously," Aiden replied. "Birth defects. Physical impairments. Cognitive problems. And later on, what looks like an almost one-hundred-percent chance of cancer for the mother."

Winter shivered, though the coffee shop was almost uncomfortably warm. Steam fogged the window behind the plants that lined the sill. If Sam was mixed up in this, had she signed her own death warrant?

"So, how does he tie in with Rebekah?" Noah asked.

"That's the real question." Winter shifted in her chair restlessly. They needed to parse everything out that they'd discovered so far, and she was dealing with a nagging feeling of exhaustion, but she was itching to get back out already. "Is Rebekah the pawn? She seemed to have a real affection for her father, but enough to want to carry on his efforts? Or is she interested in the monetary implications, too, no matter the cost?"

"The body of the teenager would indicate the latter. That's recent work, well within the time she's lived at the farm." Aiden flipped a couple of pages back in the notebook. "Samantha Benton went missing the same day as Rebekah. Nearly the same time."

"She's pregnant," Noah pointed out. "And desperate to have a baby. Seems weird that she'd go to someone who had no solid percentage of success. We're missing something. Some connection between the two women."

"We'll find it," Aiden said calmly. "But the connection between the two women isn't as important as locating them at this point. I don't think Samantha is in any danger yet. As long as she stays pregnant, and she's not far along yet."

"If anything," Winter corrected, "that makes finding her *more* urgent. Benton said her doctor told her she has a weak uterus. If that's a symptom of a congenital reproductive issue, she'll miscarry. If she's of no use as a test subject, she could be disposed of."

29

The rest of the afternoon was starting to look like a total loss. Winter was having a hard time holding back her frustration. They needed to find the missing players, and they were running into repeated dead ends.

It didn't matter what Aiden thought or whether Noah agreed. Winter knew with cold certainty that they were working against the clock.

David Benton refused to meet with them. The housekeeper turned them away at the door, telling them that they'd been inundated with phone calls and that he had gone to bed with a migraine. Someone had leaked David's name to the press, and from her tone, it sounded like she was holding them fully responsible for both the headache and the phone calls.

They went to Tony Collier next. He wasn't home. The van in the driveway was gone, and the shades were pulled.

Darin Bowman was the last revisit on their list before they turned around and headed to the station to meet with Chief Miller. To her surprise, he opened the door almost immediately after Noah's knock.

"Mr. Bowman?" Winter asked. "I'm Special Agent Black, and these are Agents Dalton and Parrish. Could we speak to you for a moment?"

Darin Bowman was a man who looked like he'd taken every kick life had dealt him and still bore the bruises. He was stoop-shouldered and sad-eyed. All of him seemed gray and lifeless. His hair, his eyes, his lined face. He nodded, unsmiling, and let them in.

His house was small and outdated, but tidy. As he led them into the living room, Winter immediately noticed the framed photos on the mantlepiece. On the far left was a picture of a pretty woman in her twenties, smiling brightly, holding a little boy on her hip.

Without consciously meaning to, Winter moved closer to the picture.

It had been taken at the Archer farm. She recognized the location from the background of the photo. The woman looked carefree and happy, her smile full of love and light. Her long red hair drifted around her shoulders and the boy she held gripped a handful of it in his small fist.

"Patrick," she murmured, touching the glass.

The boy must have been around five years old at the time of the photo but looked smaller and younger. The curve of his back was pronounced, almost question mark-shaped. His jaw seemed crooked, but it didn't dim the beauty of his playful grin. His hair was red and tousled, and she could make out a smattering of freckles across his smushed-looking pug nose.

Winter experienced a quick flash of memory, seeing the small bones on the cold metal examination table in Florence Wade's lab. For a moment, the bones were superimposed over the child's features in the picture. Her throat tightened with a combination of anger and sadness.

"My wife and son." The voice to her right shook with

emotion, and Winter turned to look at Darin. His eyes were fixed on the picture, filled with unshed tears. "God, I miss them every day. So much."

"Tell us."

The story came out in fits and starts, and several times, the man had to stop, overcome. Through most of it, silent tears slid down his face. As the three of them listened silently, Darin painted almost the same early picture of peaceful commune life that David Benton had. He and his wife were so excited when she became pregnant. So sure that they were doing God's work.

"Patrick was such an amazing child," Darin said, his eyes soft with memory. "So happy. He may have come in a different package than other babies born without his handicaps, but he was a ray of sunshine. He had so much love bottled up in that tiny body of his. He was a gift."

His face darkened, and he looked down at his hands clenched together in his lap. "But later on, when other babies were born like him, it seemed like everyone started thinking of those beautiful babies as more of a curse. We hadn't been good enough. Pure enough. We were doing something wrong. God was angry with us."

"But you knew your son wasn't a curse," Winter put in, stiff with anger. "Why didn't you leave?"

Noah nudged her subtly. Telling her without words to cool it.

Darin looked up at her, his face heavy with the guilt that he'd carried for decades.

"I know that now!" The words sounded like they were being wrenched out of him. "Don't you think I know that? You don't understand what it was like. We were a group, disciples united by a higher purpose. A higher power. And Wesley was our Bishop. He was closest to God. When he told us these things, we *believed* him." He dropped his head again, and his shoulders shook. "Even when he told us that God had taken our babies back as punishment."

"But God didn't take your babies." Aiden's voice was quiet. Calm.

In the face of the unemotional statement of fact, Darin seemed to pull himself together.

"No. God didn't take our babies. Wesley did." His voice hardened. "I told myself otherwise for many years afterward. Joanna and I, we kept up the pretense of believing Wesley Archer's lies. The alternative was too unbearable. The guilt was just too much. But when Joanna died..." He swallowed hard. "The cancer took her quickly, but at the end, she would talk about Patrick in her delirium. Crying. Screaming. Apologizing."

Winter struggled under conflicting feelings.

She'd read enough about cult leaders to know that they could hold their subjects in a kind of thrall. The outside world could cease to exist, or the followers would be indoctrinated so completely that everything about it would be taken as a lie. The leader's word would be taken as gospel, and individual thought took a distant second place or was stifled altogether.

The man's grief was genuine. But the thought that a defenseless child could be murdered in cold blood and left to rot in a grave alone, his parents not even questioning his disappearance? She couldn't forgive the man for that, indoctrination or not. It cut too close to her own wounds.

"Why are you willing to cooperate now, when you wouldn't even see us last week?" Winter asked.

Darin smiled for the first time. It was almost beatific, the way it lit his entire being. "I'm dying," he said simply. "Late-stage prostate cancer."

"So, this is like a deathbed confession?" Noah asked. Winter could hear the skepticism in his voice that he couldn't fully hide.

Darin shook his head in the negative. He must have heard it too, but he wasn't offended.

"Not at all. My sins are between me and God. I still believe in Him, even though I faced up to what Wesley Archer was years ago. Patrick didn't fit into Wesley's plans, but Patrick fit into God's plans."

Darin leaned forward, the smile falling from his face.

"When I saw on the news last night that those bones had been found, I knew there was only one thing that could make everything right. Bring Patrick home. I want him buried between me and Joanna, and hopefully, we'll all find each other in Heaven.

His glittering gray eyes fixed on Winter. Something about them looked transparent. Ethereal. Like he already had one foot in the hereafter and couldn't wait to finish the plunge.

"Please," he said, ignoring Noah and Aiden. "Please. Bring my son home to me."

"I FOUND IT."

Winter's voice was weary, but triumphant.

She'd been quieter, much more subdued than normal, since they'd left Darin Bowman's house. Aiden had watched her in odd moments, as they met with the Harrisonburg police chief. Later, when they'd set up a kind of command center in one of the conference rooms.

She hadn't touched the pizza they'd ordered in to feed everyone who was working on digging into Scott Kennedy's background. Instead, she'd just kept her head down, her focus laser sharp, her fingers tapping at the keys of her laptop. The rest of the people in the room might as well have not existed.

Now, it was past midnight, but her eyes were bright with renewed determination. A loose lock of black hair contoured her pale cheek in a silken curve. Aiden had to stifle the jolt of pure need that went through him at the sight.

"Found what, darlin'?"

The jolt died as suddenly as it had hit him. Dalton was looking at Winter, too, in the same way he was. And Dalton, always grinning idiotically, as irritating as Aiden found his country-fried brand of charm, was better for Winter than he could ever be.

Darkness needed light to balance it. Not more darkness.

"They're here." She turned her laptop around so everyone else at the table could see it. On it was a close-up satellite image of a rundown old home. Four columns held up a sagging portico. Large, arched windows lined the front of the house, and thick woods crowded against the rear.

"It looks like a plantation house," Noah said. "Where is that? How do you know that's where they are?"

Winter glanced around the table. Three officers and the chief were watching them with hopeful curiosity, waiting for her answer.

"I had a hunch," she finally admitted. "This is the original home farm of the Abbots. Helen Abbott was Scott Kennedy's mother. Her family built it in the early 1800s. According to property records, it's never been bought or sold in all those years. It must still be part of the Kennedy estate." She looked at Aiden directly, and then Noah. "It's in North Carolina. Literally just over the border. About three and a half hours from here."

"You guys going to go check it out?" Chief Miller sounded

hopeful. Aiden knew they were shorthanded. The few offi-cers seated at the table showed as much, and Benton wasn't due back for at least a week.

"We'll head out in the morning," he agreed, speaking for the three of them.

30

I t was a gorgeous afternoon. The sun shone through the trees, dappling the leaf-covered ground. The temperature had climbed to nearly sixty degrees, with only a slight breeze that hardly disturbed the air. Birds chirped in the oaks overhead as Aiden secured the straps on his Kevlar vest.

After studying terrain maps of the area, they'd chosen a spot on a little used dirt service road that ran directly behind the Abbot house. From there, they'd cut through the quarter-mile stretch of forest to come up on the back of the property undetected.

The plan was recognizance. Determine whether Scott Kennedy and Rebekah Archer were using the property as Winter had guessed. Hopefully, they could also get a visual of Samantha and Jenna, and make sure they were both safe and healthy.

Dalton hummed lightly as he tightened the straps on his own vest and tugged on a dark brown windbreaker. Without the bulletproof vest visible, he looked like a guy getting ready to go for a walk in the woods. He wore a long-sleeved dark green shirt and dark jeans, along with a pair of beat-up hiking boots.

Winter, too, was ready. She'd pulled her hair back into a high ponytail. A loose gray zip-up sweatshirt hid her gear and the black tank top she wore beneath. Black leggings and a pair of black boots completed her outfit. She looked young and just a little edgy, like a nature-loving college kid. Not someone you'd shoot for trespassing on your land.

"I'm glad you found something other than a suit to put on," Dalton commented with a grin. "Didn't picture you as a camo guy, though."

Aiden didn't look up from the map he had spread over the hood of the car. "Always be prepared."

"Boy Scout?"

He glanced up, ready with a sarcastic response, but Noah wasn't laughing at him. He had his arm bent at the elbow, holding three fingers in the air, giving the Scout salute.

"Yeah. Eagle."

"Me too."

So, maybe they did have something in common, after all.

"Are we going to do this or what?" Winter asked. She was pacing restlessly. "Or do you guys want to plan a campout with s'mores instead?"

Aiden almost asked her if she'd been a Girl Scout, but then he remembered. She hadn't had a normal childhood. Instead, he folded the map neatly and put it in the glove compartment. "Cell phones off?"

The other two nodded. More than once, an ill-timed ringtone had spelled disaster for a law enforcement official. They left the two-track, naturally falling into a single file line behind Winter as she followed what looked like a deer trail through long grass. Her steps were sure and swift, and she seemed to know exactly where to go.

She'd have done well on the Orienteering merit badge, Aiden thought irreverently.

There was a quick rustle nearby. A startled squirrel chittered at them in irritation and disappeared into the branches of a pine. Aiden didn't jump, didn't even react to the noise with anything but a flick of his eyes, but his nerves felt scraped raw, trying to take in everything around them at once.

They moved quietly through the trees for about ten minutes, dodging low-hanging branches and rotted logs. Deep carpets of moss underfoot masked all but the barest crunch of footsteps. Surprisingly, Noah was the lightest on his feet, despite his bulk. The trees grew denser near the back of the property, and black raspberry brambles snagged on his pants every few steps.

Through the underbrush, he could see where the forest ended and gave way to a back lawn, overgrown and scraggly. A child's high giggle rang out, and a bright red flash moved through the grass. The little girl was playing with a ball. No one else was in sight.

Using hand signals to communicate, the three of them moved beneath the overhanging limbs of a pine tree within sight of the edge of the woodline. The cover was thick enough that their movements wouldn't attract attention and the dull colors they wore wouldn't immediately show to anyone who might glance out into the woods. The carpet of pine needles beneath their feet muffled their footsteps as effectively as the moss had.

Aiden scanned the yard again. The old house was a tall, boxy square that left much of the yard in the shade. Winter put a light hand on his arm and pointed. A hammock was slung between two maples. A woman's leg hung out, her sneaker clad foot on the ground, swinging it gently. It was either Rebekah or Sam. She was hidden in the folds of the canvas material, so it was impossible to tell.

With a hollow, echoing bong, a big red rubber ball bounced off a tree and into the underbrush. It rolled down a small slope, coming to rest against a hollow log about ten yards from where they crouched.

The little girl, unnoticed by the woman in the swing, started picking her way through the undergrowth. She studied the ground in front of her tentatively, her tongue caught between her teeth in concentration. She didn't see them.

Noah nodded at Winter, jerked his head in the girl's direction, and then motioned back toward the direction of the service road. He wanted her to take the girl and run.

She shook her head in the negative and pointed back at him, then drilled one finger in her cheek. Dimples? What the hell did those have to do with anything?

Aiden interrupted the silent argument, holding up a hand. The child might respond to a female better, but if the woman in the hammock was Samantha Benton, he was going to need Winter. They knew each other, and Winter would need to convince Sam to go.

He gestured for Noah to take the girl. The other man's eyes hardened. For a moment, he looked like he badly wanted to argue, but he finally nodded.

Jenna had successfully navigated the thicket and spotted the ball. She was toddling toward it, her short, pudgy legs a little unsteady on the rough terrain. The woman in the hammock was now motionless, her foot resting against the ground, not moving. It looked like she'd fallen asleep.

Aiden nodded to Noah.

"*Go*," he mouthed.

The resentful look disappeared from Noah's face as if it

had never been there. He moved out from under the tree, and his face softened into a nonthreatening smile.

"Hi, Jenna," he said, his voice a quiet, friendly rumble. He was good. The sound barely carried, but the little girl looked over at him immediately.

Her blue eyes went wide, and she grinned. "Pretty!" She immediately changed directions, the ball forgotten. "Pretty man!"

Aiden shot a quick look at the sleeping woman, in case the child's crowing had woken her. Winter shook her head slightly, her eyes trained on the yard. When Aiden looked back, he had to stifle a grin. Dalton looked uncomfortable at being called pretty, but he smiled at the little girl and held his arms wide for a hug.

She went straight to him and jumped into his arms. "Denth," she lisped solemnly, pointing at his cheek.

"Want to go for an adventure, princess?" he whispered.

She nodded and lowered her voice too. "Walk in the woodth?"

"Yep."

"Dragonth," she warned, her eyes wide.

"We'll move fast," he promised. "I'll keep you safe."

She nodded and latched her arms trustingly around his neck. Dalton threw him a warning look over Jenna's head that he read loud and clear. *Take care of Winter.*

Aiden nodded once in acknowledgment.

As Dalton seemed to melt into the woods, only the child's quiet giggle marked their exit.

By the time he turned around, Winter was already moving, focused on the hammock. They needed to get closer, to see who was in it, but he needed her to work with him. He hissed out a breath and went after her, trying not to make any sound. Despite the effort, a twig cracked underfoot. In his ears, it sounded like a gunshot.

Winter didn't slow. She'd almost reached the treeline, and he made a furious lunge for her, to stop her from stepping out into the open. He got hold of her sleeve and yanked her backward. She looked at him with a surprised expression, but before he could react, there was the echo of another branch breaking, and he stumbled forward.

And then came another sharp report.

This one was louder, and he felt a punch of impact high on his shoulder. At the same time, he registered a dark stain spattered across the front of Winter's sweatshirt.

It still wasn't until his legs crumpled beneath him that he realized he'd been shot.

WINTER HADN'T REALIZED Aiden was behind her until she felt the jerk on her sleeve. Samantha was in that hammock, and they had to get to her before Rebekah came looking for Jenna. Her heart was pounding, and her stomach was tight.

Something was going to happen, and they needed to get her out of there. Instinct was telling her to go. Now.

Aiden spun her around, his face furious, his eyes narrowed and jaw set. She knew she should have waited, but she couldn't ignore her instincts and now wasn't the time to explain.

In the next instant, a shot cracked in the stillness of the afternoon, sending birds shrieking and scattering from the trees. Aiden lurched forward, like he'd lost his balance. She moved toward him automatically to brace him, and there was another shot. Nearly in slow motion, she felt his body jerk against her, and a ragged hole appeared in his shirt above his right shoulder, just outside of where the Kevlar covered. Blood spattered against her cheek in a fine mist.

She took the brunt of his bodyweight and spun quickly,

baring her own back long enough to get him down on the ground.

A scream ripped out from the left of her.

She brought her gun up in the direction from which the shots had been fired.

"Stop screaming, Sam," said Rebekah Archer, who stood a few yards behind Winter, her porcelain face pale and tight. She was pointing a compact little G45 in Winter's direction.

"Where's Jenna?" Rebekah's voice was cold and calm, but her eyes burned with rage.

"Safe." Her mind spun through possible actions she could take. It didn't take long. She tried not to wonder if Aiden lay dead at her feet. He'd been hit in the shoulder, but where else?

"Sam," she called out. "You need to get out of here. You're in danger."

"Winter." Sam's voice shook with rising panic. "You're wrong. Rebekah's my friend."

"No, there's a lot here going on that you don't know about."

"Don't say another word, Agent Black," Rebekah bit out, "unless it's to tell me where the fuck my daughter is."

"Jenna's not your daughter. She's Kayla Bennett's daughter, a poor dead teenage runaway. What would Jenna think if she knew you killed her real mother? She likes fairy tales, but that's pretty dark for any child to take in."

Rebekah's face flushed red and then went white again. There was anger in her eyes.

There was also uncertainty. "You're lying. Jenna is *mine*, and Kayla Bennett isn't dead. She gave up her baby. She didn't want to be a teenage mom."

"Sam, you need to get out of here," Winter repeated, not taking her eyes off the gun. "Rebekah is not your friend. She used a runaway girl as a guinea pig. Injected her with a fertility drug that did God knows what to her. Kept her in a cage, like an animal. Then she killed her and took her baby. We found her body near the Archer farm."

It was a risk, pushing so hard. Winter felt sweat slick her palms and her arms trembled with the effort to hold her gun steady. "How'd you get her pregnant, Rebekah? Artificial insemination, like your cattle? Or did you find someone to rape—"

"Shut up!" Rebecca shrieked. "Sam, go in the house. Get Scott. Now. Damn you, Kayla *isn't dead*. You're lying!"

Near her feet, Aiden groaned softly.

"I'm not lying. We found her. She's been identified." Winter took a small step toward Rebekah. "Drop the gun," she ordered quietly.

"Winter, you don't understand." Sam spoke quickly, her voice pleading. "You have to be wrong about this. Rebekah is a miracle worker. I'm pregnant, and this time it's going to be full-term. I *have* to have this baby."

Rebekah's eyes shifted to something behind Winter at the same time she sensed movement. As she started to turn, a few feet away, Sam pressed one hand to her mouth and the other protectively to her belly. Her eyes were wide in horror.

Winter caught a glimpse of Scott out of the corner of her eye, a grimace pulling his handsome features out of shape, just before something slammed down hard on the side of her head. As she fell, through the gray curtain that dropped over her vision, she thought she saw Sam disappear into the trees.

31

"You need to be careful, Winter."

Gramma Beth, wearing one of her signature 1950's-style house dresses, was fixing pancakes. Aside from her tightly curled white hair and softly lined face, she looked young and attractive, the spring green of her dress contrasting prettily with her creamy skin.

Winter was overwhelmed for a moment with emotion. Since she'd graduated from Quantico and taken the job in Richmond, she'd hardly had any time at all to spend with her grandparents. She'd missed them.

"Where's Grampa Jack?" Winter asked as her grandma expertly flipped one of the pancakes.

"Oh, he's off somewhere." She waved one manicured hand absently. "But you're not listening to me. You need to be *careful.*"

"When I'm making pancakes?" Winter teased. "I know that. I need to be careful whenever I'm in a kitchen. Things tend to catch on fire."

Beth nodded sharply and turned again to the griddle. "That's exactly what I'm saying! Fire is dangerous."

She reached into the pocket of her gingham-checked apron and pulled out a long lighter, the kind she used to light the gas burners on the stove when they went out. Clicking it, she reached over and held the flame to the dainty white curtain over the kitchen sink. The lace edge smoldered for a moment and then caught.

As the flame greedily licked upward, Beth turned again. Her pretty face was contorted with fear. "See? Be careful!"

An unreal amount of smoke billowed outward from the curtains, filling the kitchen almost instantly and blocking Gramma Beth from her sight. It was thick and choking, and Winter coughed hard, feeling a burn in her chest.

She struggled, trying to get to the beloved woman, but she couldn't move.

Her head hurt too.

She coughed again, hard, coming fully awake.

She wasn't in Gramma Beth's kitchen. She was in an old-fashioned parlor. From the claw-foot, horsehair couch, to the long moth-eaten curtains covering the dusty windows, everything was on fire. Flames were even licking up the side of a spinet piano in the corner of the room. The plaster was blackening, old wood trim was smoldering, ancient varnish crackling and peeling.

It wasn't a conflagration yet, but there were so many points of origin, it would be soon.

Winter rolled to one side. Her hands were numb, the circulation weak from being tied uncomfortably tight behind her back. Next to her was Aiden, lying on his side, as still as death. His eyes were closed, his complexion bone white. She tugged and pulled at the ropes around her wrists, but they wouldn't budge.

"Aiden!" She shimmied up close to him and thunked at his head with hers. "Wake up."

She didn't want to hit him anywhere else. She wasn't sure where he'd been shot.

She pushed at him again and yelled his name, louder this time. His eyes flew open, icy blue and clouded with pain.

Winter let out a shaky breath. "Shit, Parrish, I thought you were dead." She could have wept in relief at seeing him still alive.

"Just mostly dead," he rasped out, his lips twisting wryly. "There's a difference."

"Can you untie me? Your hands are bound in front."

"No. I'm having some trouble moving the fingers of my right hand. But I've got a knife in my boot."

She rolled again, grateful that at least her feet were free, and backed up against him. He drew in a sharp breath when she reached his thigh, and her fingers brushed against him. They came away slippery.

"I'm sorry. The other hit?"

"At least she didn't get an artery," he pointed out, the words coming out between coughs. "Or I'd be all the way dead."

She found the knife and managed to undo the snap on the nylon strap just above his ankle.

"Careful," he said. "It's sharp."

"Are you going to be able to manage the blade with one hand?"

"Don't have much choice." His voice sounded weaker. "I'll try to leave you a few fingers."

He managed to leave her all ten.

The flames eating away at the curtains had reached the ceiling by the time she shook her hands loose, her fingers prickling as the blood rushed back into them. They tingled painfully as she set him free.

"Come on, SSA Parrish," she ordered. "Open your eyes. We need to get out of here."

As she spoke, the old piano collapsed to one side with a discordant clang of keys. A few feet away from where they were tied up lay their service weapons. She grabbed hers and slid it into its holster. She checked the safety and put Aiden's in the back of her pants.

"Go ahead," he replied, not opening his eyes. "I'm right behind you."

Growling, she grabbed him under the arms and dragged him toward the archway that led into a main hallway, staying low and hoping that the parlor was the only room that had been set on fire. Scott Kennedy was apparently a closet pyromaniac, lucky for them.

Using bullets to kill them would have been much more efficient.

The hallway was cooler and a little less smoky, and it was easy to find the exit with the shotgun-style layout of the house. She was wheezing by the time she got to the front door, from breathing in smoke and dragging two hundred pounds of passed out male, but she was glad he was unconscious. There were drag marks from where his wounds had bled that led back down the hallway.

She wiped her hands on her sweatshirt and looked out the window at the side of the front door. She could see the back end of a Mercedes SUV parked to the side of the house. Moving to another window, she saw Scott Kennedy standing beside it, looking polished and handsome in a trim suit. He was arguing with Rebekah, gesturing for her to get in. She'd crossed her arms, looking mulish.

She crouched down next to Aiden. "Parrish. Parrish, I need you with me. Come on."

He shook his head, groggy. In pain.

She pushed back her fear for him and smacked his cheek lightly. "Open your eyes, Aiden."

With a heavy indrawn breath, he did.

"Here," she told him, putting his SIG Sauer in his hand. "You have to stay alert. I've got to go out there, and you need to get yourself out of this house as soon as it's safe. Crawl your ass out if you have to. This place is on fire, remember."

He nodded his comprehension, his mouth pinched at the corners with pain.

Winter opened the door, drawing her own gun. The hinges, thankfully, didn't squeal as the heavy door swung inward.

She slipped out onto the porch and crept against the front before moving behind one of the heavy columns that lined it. From there, she could see both targets more clearly.

Rebekah's voice was shrill. "You told me that Kayla went home. You didn't tell me you killed her."

"Why would I kill her?" Scott asked, his hands lifted almost reasonably. "She was ready to move on. You know she didn't plan to take a newborn baby with her. She wanted to go to Hollywood."

Rebekah faltered. She clearly wanted to believe him. "The FBI agent said they found her buried up on the ridge. They know about Jenna."

"Sweetheart, come on." Scott's voice was patient, but with an edge that Winter could hear clearly. "Let's talk about this in the car. Speaking of Jenna," he added, throwing the little girl's name out like a carrot, "we'll find her, and then we can move on. Start someplace new."

"Not until you tell me what happened to Kayla," Rebekah shot back stubbornly. "This time was going to be different. You promised me."

Scott sighed, looking his age for just a moment. As he inhaled his next breath, he reached into his coat and pulled out a handgun and leveled it at her, his smooth, youthful façade slipping back into place. "I can always finish this project solo, you know. I already have bidders lined up. It has to be finished, with or without you."

Rebekah took an automatic step back, the absolute shock on her face almost comical. "What are you doing?"

"You're just as bad as Wesley was." Kennedy shook his head mournfully, and his voice was nearly kind. "Easily manipulated. Going along with everything in pursuit of some lofty goal and pretending the dark side that came with it doesn't exist." He paused thoughtfully. "Except that your father never shot an FBI agent. The love of a mother, am I right?"

"Drop the gun, Scott." Winter stepped out from behind the post, deliberately making herself a target to divert his attention away from Rebekah. She wanted them both alive. This story was going to be convoluted enough to figure out as it was.

When he swung the pistol around, his face hard, she could see the soldier he'd been under the pampered veneer he'd created. Still, she dropped her aim, going for nonlethal force and fired, hitting him in the right leg, below the knee. He wouldn't be driving out of this.

On a roar of anger and pain, his shot went high and took out a chunk of plaster from the column about three feet above her head. She thought she heard Aiden curse behind her. At least he was still conscious. She moved fast, staying low and using the scattered pecan trees in the yard for cover as Kennedy dragged himself behind the car, through the gravel, screaming constant, almost incoherent profanity.

He was still a threat. Likely a bigger one now.

She monitored Rebekah out of her peripheral vision. The woman looked torn, watching Kennedy bleed and writhe in the gravel, swearing viciously. She hesitated in the center of the driveway before self-preservation won out and she backed away.

Winter focused on Kennedy, keeping one eye on Rebekah. She could run. They'd find her.

She almost had Kennedy in sight. She could see one of his shoes, a brown wingtip. He'd gone quiet. She darted for another tree, and two shots rang out in quick succession. She stumbled, a hot welter of pain exploded in her arm, just above the elbow.

Holding her hand tightly over the wound, she crouched behind the thick trunk of an oak.

Distantly, she heard the sharp crack of wood, followed by a crash and a scream. It came from the back of the house. She stood as something collapsed, and she hoped Aiden had been able to do as she'd asked him to. Smoke hung heavy in the air now.

Winter focused on evening out her breathing. In and out, through her mouth, like she was warding off a panic attack. The throbbing pain in her arm receded a bit as her heartbeat slowed.

A woman's piercing shriek broke the pregnant stillness. Rebekah. Had Kennedy gotten to her? She struggled to her feet, still shielded by the tree, but she didn't see the other woman. Then, warm metal touched the back of her neck, almost caressingly, near the base of her skull.

"Gotcha," Scott whispered before another shot boomed out.

She staggered forward, a heavy weight dragging her down. For several terrifying seconds, she couldn't breathe.

Abruptly, the weight was lifted away, and she rolled over. Noah's wide grin made his warm green eyes crinkle at the corners. "How's that for timing?" he asked as he kicked Scott's gun away and handcuffed the dead man, just in case.

"Good…" The world was growing darker, and it was almost impossible to keep her eyes open. "Time…"

❄

SHE WASN'T sure how long she'd been out when she opened her eyes again. Noah was still there, and he looked relieved that she was awake. "Hey there," he said.

She tried to smile. "Hey."

He helped her up as sirens sounded in the distance, pretending not to notice her tears. In return, she pretended not to notice how badly his hands were shaking.

"Where's Aiden?" she asked hoarsely. "Jenna? Sam?"

"Everyone's fine," he assured her, taking her good arm with a grimace and leading her away before she could look down. "Sam ran into me. She took Jenna. She also called for backup, and they're trickling in now. Apparently, they had a hard time triangulating a location since that service road was showing as the middle of a forest, and Sam couldn't give them an address. Plus, she was panicked. A little incoherent."

"I can imagine." Winter was feeling a little panicked and incoherent herself. "Where's Aiden?" she asked again.

"They had to wait for local officers to clear the scene. They're getting him loaded into an ambulance now. Which is where you're going, so don't freak out on me. You'll see him in a second."

Two of the paramedics that were loading Aiden onto a stretcher looked up at her. One frowned abruptly. "We've got another victim."

"I'm fine," she snapped back. "I just need stitches. Let me see him."

Aiden had no color. He was also unconscious again.

They'd already started him on oxygen and had slit his pants open to the thigh. A hole oozed blood sluggishly as one of the paramedics wrapped a bandage tightly around it. Another removed a blood-soaked pad of gauze from his shoulder and replaced it with a fresh one.

"What happened?" Noah's voice was grim.

This was her fault.

Winter reached out a hand to touch Aiden's still face, but she looked like she'd bathed in blood. It was crusting and cracking on the back of her hand. She dropped it back to her side. "He took a couple of hits for me." Her voice sounded broken.

A second ambulance crunched up the gravel drive. "We need to go now," one of the paramedics said. "Step back, please, so we can get him loaded in."

"I'm going."

The man started to argue with her but seeing the vicious light in her eyes and the FBI badge she shoved in his face, he thought better of it. "Fine, but we're triaging, so wherever all that blood of yours is coming from, it's going to have to wait. You're upright and talking. This guy needs our attention more."

Winter turned on Noah, daring him to argue, but he just nodded. "I'll finish sorting things out here."

She hardly felt the pain in her arm, but with every bounce and jiggle of the stretcher, she flinched for Aiden. He was so silent and still. Only once she was in the back of the ambulance, staying out of the way as the paramedic worked, did she start to feel the burning ache in her own injury.

"What kind of blood type are you?" the paramedic asked almost casually, not looking up.

"O positive."

"Good," he muttered. "I know you've already leaked a little, but we might have to borrow some more. Bad wreck out on the highway and the local bank is running low."

Winter didn't hesitate.

"Absolutely," she murmured. "It's my fault he's there."

32

"That'll teach you to stay in the BAU where you belong."

She was shot a scathing look. "I told the nurse I didn't want visitors."

"I flashed my badge and a smile, and he let me in. Security around here sucks."

Winter carried two little pots of Gerbera daisies and set one on Aiden's bedside table. He didn't seem like the Gerbera daisy type—he didn't seem like the flower type at all—but she liked them. They were bright and cheery and red, so that's what he got.

Aiden looked irritable and very unlike his normal self. His light brown hair was mussed, a lock of it brushing his brow instead of being smoothly combed back. There was a day's worth of dark stubble on his normally smooth cheeks. He was propped against the white hospital sheets, shirtless, the blankets draped across his waist. She tried not to look, but there was a lot of lean and rippled muscle on display, and averting her eyes was surprisingly difficult.

A white bandage wound around his shoulder, and he

awkwardly tried to pull the sheet up higher with his other hand.

"Don't be modest," Winter teased. "You'll just hurt yourself." Sitting the second flower pot on the floor, she helped him tug the sheet up with her good arm. She was careful not to bump his leg as she leaned over the bed. She could make out the outline of another thick bandage on his thigh.

"You know, it's kind of nice seeing you helpless, on your back. Probably pretty hard to do your bossing and interfering from there."

Aiden's frosty eyes glinted in temper. And warning.

She held up a hand. "Be nice to me," she ordered. "You've got some of my blood swimming around in there."

"Is there anything I can do for you, Agent Black?" he bit out. "I'm hoping for some morphine soon, and I'm fairly sure the nurse won't let me have any until you leave."

"I'm sorry," she said, genuinely contrite. "I'm being a bitch. That's not why I came here."

He smiled a little. "Could have fooled me. You were doing such a good job of it."

"I'm here to apologize." She sank down into the chair beside his bed while he watched her. "I'm sorry," she repeated, shifting uncomfortably under his scrutiny when he didn't respond.

"For going off on your own again? For blowing cover and running straight into the line of fire?"

She flinched. "That was a mistake."

"Damned right it was," he burst out. "What the fuck were you thinking?"

Open up a little, she told herself. He deserves that much.

"You know I operate differently than normal people. I rely on instinct and feelings." She swallowed hard, the truth clogging her throat. "And visions. I mistook the tension out there for something that wasn't real. That almost got you killed. Almost got me killed."

Understanding dawned on his face. He opened his mouth to reply, but she held up a hand.

He nodded for her to continue.

"I shouldn't be out in the field." The admission was like a knife slicing up her throat. "You were right. I need to be behind a desk, where I can't get anyone hurt. I should be in the BAU or out of the FBI altogether."

"Will you please quit your self-flagellation and shut your damned mouth for two seconds?"

At his tone, she bristled. Aiden at his most arrogant was one irritating son of a bitch. Wounded or not. Sitting back in her chair, she crossed her good arm over her chest, cradling the aching arm, and nodded for him to go on.

"Before you get all noble and tell me I was right and quit your job, scrapping your...quest, I'd like to apologize to you."

She let out a short, surprised laugh. "Right. For what?"

"I almost got *you* killed," he admitted, scratching at the stubble that roughened up his normally tailored appearance. "I was half out of it and feeling like a dead weight laying there, waiting to be rescued while you swapped gunfire and handled the situation on your own. I saw Rebekah trying to get away, and instead of letting someone else get her, someone capable, I dragged myself up and tackled her over the railing of the porch. She screamed when I fell on her. When you stood up to look, Kennedy got the drop on you. If Dalton hadn't taken him out with that sniper shot of his, you'd be dead right now."

She looked at him for a long moment. He seemed sincere, but his lips twitched. Just slightly, but she noticed. "That's a stretch. Not very believable."

"It's the truth." Aiden shrugged and winced. "But I'll deny to my dying breath that I did anything as idiotic as fling my bleeding carcass off a porch to catch a suspect." He arched a brow. "And if you tell anyone else, no one will believe you. You're a hotheaded rook. I have dignity and credibility."

She opened her mouth to reply, but what the hell could she say?

"Anyway," Aiden went on. "You're not turning in your resignation. You're staying where you are until I can *legitimately* talk you into coming over into the BAU. I'm going back to my desk when I heal up. And we'll never discuss this afternoon again."

Her mouth was still opening and closing, so she snapped it shut, still unsure of what to say. The silence stretched between them, the atmosphere growing heavy.

"Okay, then," she finally said after what seemed like decades of just looking into his eyes. She launched to her feet. "I guess I'll go. You need your morphine."

"No." His voice was emphatic, and she automatically sat back down. "I passed out like a true damsel in distress and missed the final scene. You need to tell me how everything shook out."

Winter didn't want to think about it. Even Aiden's unexpected understanding and self-deprecating humor couldn't dim the impact of that experience. For a horrible moment, when she'd felt that gun pressed to the back of her neck and heard the gunshot, she'd been convinced that Kennedy had shot her and the only reason she couldn't feel it was because he'd severed her spinal cord.

But Noah had neutralized Kennedy with a headshot…she couldn't think about that, either. It would come back in her nightmares, soon enough. She hadn't even realized the extent of the gore that covered her until one of the ER residents, a newbie, had almost puked on seeing her.

It was not an experience worth repeating.

"By the way, I forgot. You got a little revenge on

Rebekah," she told Aiden to lighten the mood, "in case no one has mentioned that to you yet. When you took her down with your swan dive, she broke her leg. She's going to be wearing a cast when she hears the laundry list of charges against her."

"The irony," Aiden responded in a dry tone. "So. The story?"

"After Wesley Archer killed himself, Rebekah found his journals. He laid out the entire story. From his time in the war to the start of the Disciples, to the realization that he'd been deliberately blind to the terrible things that were happening around him. At the end of his life, he recognized Kennedy for what he was. Then, when he was drowning in remorse and grief for the wife he'd lost, he decided to end it. Rebekah was a teenager when she learned the whole story. She loved her dad, idolized him, faults and all. She shaped her life to carry on his legacy."

"But she couldn't handle Scott Kennedy."

"No. She knew what he was and thought she could use him. She contacted him with the idea that they carry on her father's legacy. He agreed to meet with her. Her bargaining chip was that she gave the journals to Elbert Wilkins, her father's old friend, for safekeeping. It was her leverage over Kennedy, and he didn't like jumping to her tune, but he went along with it for the long con."

Aiden's eyes were sharp with interest, and he nodded occasionally. Winter wondered how much of this he'd already figured out for himself.

"Rebekah got the original Progesteraline formula from Kennedy, along with the money to buy her family's old farm. She tweaked the drug on the cattle she raised, messing with the formula until she was fairly certain she'd figured out what was causing the genetic issues. By this time, Kennedy had visited several times to check her progress, working on changing her mind about him. His latest wife had died, and he turned his swagger on Rebekah. She'd let her guard down, and she fell for it."

"He'd have been the same age as her father." Aiden's lip curled. "I get younger women and older men, but that seems drastic."

Winter shrugged. "You're the behavior guy. You should be able to give a Freudian explanation for that, right?"

The nurse chose that moment to poke his head into the room. "You ready for some more painkillers, Mr. Parrish?" the young man asked.

Aiden waved him off impatiently. "Later, please. Go on."

"Rebekah swears she knew nothing about Kayla Bennett's death. Supposedly, the girl showed up at the farm one day, looking for work. She took her in and fed her, got the story that she was a runaway who wanted to go to California to be an actress. Rebekah invited her to stay on for a while and help out around the farm, so she could save some money. Then, the story gets weird. Rebekah started drugging her food with sedatives, injecting her with the fertility drug, and then turkey-basting her with sperm she got off the internet." Winter shrugged, wrinkling her nose. "That's a thing, apparently, fyi—to make sure the girl got pregnant."

"Even digging into the minds of messed up humans for a living," Aiden interjected with disgust, "I still don't understand why some people have no problem justifying depraved behavior."

"She swears it was Kennedy's idea, but I agree." Winter made a face. "It's one thing to listen to someone's crazy, gross idea. It's another to implement it for them. According to Rebekah, after Kayla realized she was pregnant, she just figured that a guy she'd hooked up with before she left home got her that way. The pregnancy gave Rebekah more leverage to 'take care of her,' until Kayla disappeared late in her third trimester. Rebekah was upset when she told us this, and said it happened shortly after Scott Kennedy had come for one of his visits. He showed up with Jenna, the perfect little newborn, a week later, and said he gave Kayla money to continue on to California."

Aiden shook his head slowly. "In reality, *he* locked her up."

"There was a cage in the old carriage house at the Abbott place in North Carolina," Winter agreed. "It backs up her story. I had the cage right, but the location wrong."

"So, Rebekah didn't question it," Aiden said, "because it already felt like the baby was hers, in a twisted way." Winter didn't need to answer that, because it wasn't a question. They'd both seen firsthand how devoted, almost to the point of obsession, Rebekah had been with Jenna.

"She'd started to turn a blind eye to Kennedy's actions, like her father had. It probably seemed justified to her because the new variation on P6 looked like it worked. You only saw that little girl briefly. Spend some time with her, and you'd see what a special kid she is. Imagine an army of little Jennas, lisping their way into everyone's hearts."

Aiden shook his head with a twist to his lips. He was starting to look tired, but he laughed. "I'm not a kid person. I'll take your word for it. So, fast forward a few years, and the bones are found. Kennedy starts clipping loose ends."

Winter nodded. "Rebekah denies it, but I think she must've let slip to Kennedy at some point that it was Elbert Wilkins who had the journals."

"What about Samantha Benton?"

"Rebekah met Samantha at a support group for women who'd had miscarriages. She was trolling for another mother, this time in a more legitimate-looking way. Samantha was desperate and must've seemed like an easy mark."

Aiden's head sank back on the pillow, and he was

blinking slowly. "She was an easy mark." When he blinked again, it was a long time before the eyelids lifted.

She stood. "I'm leaving. You need to rest."

"Okay. If there's more," he said, closing his eyes, "it's going to have to wait. I need that morphine after all. How's your arm doing, anyway?"

"It's just a flesh wound. I'm hoping to use the sling excuse to get out of writing my reports for a while." Winter grinned, wiggling her arm a little. "They owe me, back at the office."

"Yeah, I heard about the rookie who fell for the paper-work prank."

"Remind me to tell you about how you were quoting *The Princess Bride* after you'd been shot twice," she teased back. "You're a closet nerd, SSA Parrish."

Winter took a step away but felt a pang, looking at him stretched out in the bed, ghostly white and so obviously in pain. She wondered for a moment if anyone else would visit him. She'd known Aiden for so long. He'd always known every detail about her life and her family but had kept tight-lipped about his.

Sensing her pity, Aiden closed his eyes against it. "Get out of here, Agent Black."

"Take care of yourself," she ordered softly and picked up the second pot of daisies. "Let me know if you need anything. I'll see you back in Richmond in a few days."

Before she made it to the door, Aiden said her name again, quietly, and she stopped. He was watching her with an unreadable expression on his face. She was struck again by how un-Aiden he looked.

"Thanks for the flowers," he finally said, giving her a half-smile. "Can you work your magic out there and send the morphine fairy back in?"

She nodded, blinking back sudden tears, and left.

Winter was getting tired too, but after sending the nurse back to Aiden's room, she had one more stop to make.

Tom Benton was in the hall outside of Samantha's room, his phone pressed to his ear when Winter stepped off the elevator. He looked better than he had since she'd first seen him again. He'd lost probably fifteen pounds nearly overnight—the stress of having a missing wife could apparently do that—but his eyes weren't bloodshot, and his clothes were clean. Instead, it looked like he'd gone to some effort with his appearance. Maybe the time he'd spent around the perfectly polished SSA Parrish had made him self-conscious. Or maybe he figured his wife deserved better.

She gave Tom a little wave, and he nodded, smiling. She tapped on the half-closed door and heard Sam's voice, quiet and sad, telling her to come in.

Samantha didn't look better. She was hooked up to an IV and looked small and insubstantial against the hospital sheets. The room was dark, the blinds drawn against the late morning sunshine. Machines quietly beeped.

"Hi, Winter." Her voice was thin, whispery, and everything about her looked dull. Beaten down. Her hair lay lankly over her shoulders, and her eyes were red-rimmed from crying.

"How are you?" The words felt inadequate.

It was obvious she wasn't well.

"I've been better," Sam replied with a ghost of her old humor.

Winter set the daisies on the counter—a cheerful yellow—next to a few other bouquets and a balloon with an even more inadequate sentiment. "Get well soon." A pot of tiny white roses had Noah's bold handwriting on the card. She didn't read what he'd written, but it was so like him to have thought to send something.

"I'm getting ready to go back to Richmond, and I wanted

to stop in to tell you thank you. You kept your head together, and if you hadn't run for it when you did…things could have ended up much worse. You were brave."

"You were always the brave one," Sam corrected. She shifted on the uncomfortable mattress and put her hand to her stomach on a little gasp of pain. Winter was halfway to her bed before Sam waved her back.

"It's okay," she said. "It'll pass. They had to do a hysterectomy."

Winter grimaced in sympathy. "I'm sorry. Was it because of…everything that happened?"

Sam shook her head, looking past Winter, toward where sunlight edged around the blinds.

"There was a reason I couldn't carry to term, and I knew it. My doctor knew it. Rebekah didn't know it. With or without her miracle fertility drug, I wasn't going to be able to have a baby. I had Polycystic Ovarian Syndrome and a weak uterus that simply wouldn't house a pregnancy."

Her face contorted in pain, and tears pricked Winter's eyes in sympathy. "I'm sorry."

Sam waved a hand in front of her face, struggling to pull herself together. "Anyway, after I saw Scott Kennedy hit you, I ran. I don't know how I found Noah. He must've already been on his way back to you. He practically shoved Jenna into my arms, along with his cell phone. He'd already called the Mount Airy police. When we were waiting in the car, and I was playing games with Jenna to keep her calm…I started getting cramps, and I knew it was over."

The door swung open, and Tom came back into the room. He instantly gravitated to Sam's side. The look he gave Winter was welcoming but full of warning too.

"You don't have to hover," Sam told him. Her voice was listless. Uncaring. "Why don't you go home and get some sleep?"

"I'm not going anywhere." He took her hand. She didn't pull away.

The moment felt too private, and Winter wanted to get away from it. "Noah's waiting in the car. I'd better head out before he leaves without me."

They were an awkward tableau for a moment. Three adults whose lives had seemed so intertwined as kids. Now, they were strangers.

"I wish you guys the best."

"You too." The words from Sam were simple but held a wealth of unspoken meaning. It was an apology.

Winter felt something in her lighten as she walked out of the room. Behind her, she heard Sam ask if Tom could open the blinds. She needed to see the sun.

33

Noah studied Winter where she sat beside him in the crowded bar. She was quiet, but that wouldn't have mattered. The music at Louie's could drown out all but the most determined conversation.

They'd come home to the FBI's idea of a hero's welcome from their unit. Max Osbourne had unbent enough to almost smile at them when they'd walked into the office. It had lasted all of twelve seconds before they'd been sent to their desks to work on their debriefing. The rest of the Violent Crimes squad, over the course of the afternoon, had stopped by to congratulate them. Even Sun Ming, a bitchy agent who had been auditioning hard for the role of Winter's work nemesis since they'd first met, delivered unsmiling praise.

"Nice job not fucking it up, rook. Try not to get shot next time."

Everybody was talking about their first big case. Winter, especially, took a lot of ribbing, especially about tasting a little lead so soon in her career. She took it without complaint, but there were times when her eyes glittered dangerously, and he had to change the subject fast. There were a few curious questions about SSA Parrish—mostly why he'd been involved at all—and his injuries, but he'd noticed that Winter always glossed it over and avoided the subject of Aiden.

"Want to dance, darlin'?" he raised his voice to be heard over the crappy band that was giving it their enthusiastic best on stage. "I'll teach you the Texas two-step."

She grinned at him. "You think you could dance to this? It's only fit for a mosh pit. And I'm not ready for that, yet."

She moved her arm a little gingerly. She'd gotten rid of the sling already, and her stitches were probably pulling. He didn't want to think about how she'd gotten them. Seeing her frozen by that tree, with a gun to her neck...he'd been too far away to do anything. She was already covered with blood that he hadn't been aware was mostly Aiden's. He'd taken bigger risks during his time in the military, but he'd been more scared to take that shot than he wanted to admit.

He shrugged. "I'll get you out there next time then."

She drained the last of her beer and started digging around in her purse for her keys. "You should have let me pick you up," Noah pointed out. "Didn't make sense to take two cars when we live a few doors down from each other. Where's your concern for the environment?"

Winter rolled her eyes. "You know, we're not going to be joined at the hip anymore. It's back to business as usual, comrade."

"Oh, I know. I'll be glad to sleep in a bed again."

She punched him lightly. "You liked the floor, and you know it."

He stood up when she did. "I'll walk you out."

She narrowed her eyes at him. "Keep that chivalrous, old boy from Texas stuff for someone who doesn't carry a Beretta under her coat. I'm going home to visit the grandparents. I'll see if I can bring you back a meatloaf."

"Make it two, and I won't follow you down there like a desperate, hungry puppy."

She tossed him a smile and a wave and headed for the door. She looked like a shadow, weaving her way through the Friday night crowd. She'd worn her black hair loose, and it waved over her shoulders. In a black, long-sleeved top, dark jeans, and high black boots, she was an exotic contrast to the other women in the bar dolled up in their Friday night best.

He was going to miss being in such close quarters with her. She needed him. She was too serious, too wrapped up in herself. But for his own peace of mind, some distance was probably a good thing. She was damaging to his equilibrium.

Still worth it, though. He snorted to himself. Maybe.

Noah grinned as he polished off the last of his Corona. He lifted the bottle slightly, catching the eye of a cute waitress with a lazy wink. Little Jessie, according to her nametag, had short, curly blonde hair and brown eyes with just a little bit of wicked in them. When she dropped him a slow, deliberate wink, Noah decided that Jessie wouldn't mess with his equilibrium at all.

You got a spare bedroom free?

She texted her grandma in the parking lot, knowing that Grandpa Jack was useless with technology and messaging Beth would be easiest. Even though it was close to nine, her grandma texted back almost immediately.

For you? I guess we could make some room.

She chuckled, slipping her phone in her purse and crossing the lot to her little Civic. She could still hear the band playing inside, an offbeat rendition of the Stones' "Satisfaction," and wondered if Noah had gotten the phone number yet of the waitress who had been eyeballing him all night.

She smiled, thinking about it, but it hurt a little.

It didn't matter, so she pushed it away.

The moon hung low and bright in the sky. A hunter's moon, she thought it was called. That, or a harvest moon. Whatever it was, it was beautiful, bathing the parking lot in a pale, chilly glow. She shivered a little and wished she'd opted for her heavier leather coat instead of a light fall jacket. She clicked the remote to unlock her door and opened it awkwardly with her left hand, sliding into the driver's seat and automatically hitting the car locks.

Tucked beneath the windshield wiper was a note on lined yellow paper that fluttered in the light evening wind. At first, it looked like someone had gone around putting fliers out on every car. But the note was pinned face down so that she could see what it said. Just two words were handwritten in big, masculine-looking letters. *Hello, girlie. You look beautiful tonight.*

It could have been from anyone. But the paper glowed faintly red, and her hands trembled, just once, on the steering wheel in response. She stiffened, her hand automatically easing inside her coat to touch the reassuring weight of her gun. The parking lot was brightly lit. Except for a couple making out a few cars away, there was no one else around. No shadowy figures lurked, waiting to see their message received.

She started the car and waited, still scanning the parking lot. Instinct told her the man who had left the note was gone, but still, she waited until the car slowly warmed, pumping lukewarm air out of the vents.

She'd left a stretchy pair of knit gloves on the floor. She slipped one on and unlocked her door, opening it just enough to reach out and grab the paper. Shutting the door and locking it again, she didn't spare the note another glance, just stuffed it in the glove compartment and closed it. The red glow wasn't visible, but she could still feel its presence.

No big deal. Just a serial killer checking in. Reminding her that he was out there somewhere, doing whatever serial killers did in their retirement years.

Winter reminded herself that she wasn't scared. This was what she wanted. The Preacher obviously remembered her. She could draw him out…and do whatever came next.

She put the car in reverse and checked her rearview, backing out of the parking spot, and pulling out on the main road.

Then she drove home. Not to her little apartment with its beige walls and cheap furniture, but to her real home.

She kept watch for a tail, but no one followed. To make sure, she drove an extra five miles, then backtracked several times. She even stopped on the side of the road to check for any GPS devices under her car when the feeling that she was being followed wouldn't leave her.

When she was certain she was safe, she turned into the familiar driveway. The front door with its diamond-shaped window panes was unlocked when she arrived, and a table lamp burned brightly near the front window in welcome. She stepped in and caught the scent of fresh chocolate chip cookies immediately. Sliding the deadbolt and kicking off her shoes, the knot of tension easing in her chest already, she walked through the quiet house to the kitchen.

Her grandma, dressed in a quilted, baby blue robe, her snowy white hair in little pink curlers, was just pulling a cookie sheet out of the oven. She had matching blue slippers on her tiny feet, and she was still as small and trim as a doll.

"Seriously? Cookies? At this time of night?" Winter spoke softly, not wanting to startle Gramma Beth. But Beth turned around, her face already lit bright in welcome.

"I heard your car in the driveway. C'mere." She held her arms out wide, and Winter went to her. She breathed in the scent of Worth perfume that always lingered around this most loved woman. The rest of the knot in her chest unraveled.

"I missed you," Winter breathed, her eyes filling with tears. She blinked them back before Gramma Beth released her. "Where's Grampa? Isn't there a UFC match on tonight?"

Grandma sniffed. She didn't approve of Grandpa's "fights," but he'd been watching them for years and wasn't about to stop now. "He went to bed early. He's been feeling a bit punky the last few days." She waved off Winter's immediate look of concern. "Just a cold. You'll be a welcome surprise to him in the morning, but don't hug him. Germs. Coffee?"

She was already moving briskly to the cupboard, pulling out two white glass mugs with delicate blue flowers on the front.

"Decaf?"

"Of course. What are we, heathens?"

Seated at the little pink Formica kitchen table, her grandma across from her, she was reminded of the dream she'd had at the Abbott farm. Her grandma's expression as she'd calmly lit the curtains on fire. She shivered a little.

"How's life as an FBI agent?" Beth asked, watching her closely. "You know, I've started watching *Criminal Minds*. It's very...bloody. But that Shemar Moore." She sighed and fanned a hand in front of her face. "He's so yummy." She dimpled and winked cheekily. "I think your grandpa is jealous."

Winter couldn't have been more shocked if her grandma had told her she'd decided to embark on a career as a UFC fighter. "*Criminal Minds?*"

Her blue eyes softened. "It's pretend. Just a television show. It doesn't make me think of...you know."

The murder of her daughter's family.

"FBI life is interesting," Winter answered, recovering a little.

"Is it like in the shows?" Her grandma's eyes were bright with interest. "Shootouts and sarcastic banter and all that?"

Winter laughed. "It's not supposed to be."

Her face fell in disappointment.

What the hell was with her Grandma? The sweet, brusque woman who still wore heels and a full skirt daily and lived for her weekly bridge club meetings?

As if in answer to her unspoken question, Beth smiled. "I'm trying," she explained simply. "I know that this is what you've wanted to do with your life forever. I've been terrified, waiting for the day you'd achieve your goal. Because I never doubted you would. The day you left for your new job...I smiled and waved, and then your grandpa and I cried like babies."

She'd known that. Even though her grandparents had acted so happy for her, inside, she'd known they'd also been afraid.

"Then, I pulled my shit together," Beth went on delicately. Winter snorted a surprised laugh. "I decided that I had to have faith in you. You're the toughest, smartest, most resilient girl I know, and if anyone could do a job like that and keep herself alive while she did it, you could. You compartmentalize, fitting what happened into one box, and putting the things you need to do to get by in another. Now." She narrowed her eyes. "Why don't you tell me what happened to your arm?"

Winter told her.

From the beginning with the bones, to the end, and her near death.

She paled when Winter described the final confrontation with Scott Kennedy, but Winter didn't hold any details back as she told the story. Her grandma surprised her again by jumping in with insightful comments and smart commentary throughout.

"I'm going to call you in as a consultant," Winter said with more than a little awe. "You're brilliant."

Beth gave her a smug smile. "You know I'm brilliant. Where do you think you inherited those brains of yours? I used to devour Agatha Christie novels...before. It didn't seem right, later on."

Winter nodded. "Before. It's always before and after, isn't it? I went to the house while I was in Harrisonburg."

Beth let out a long breath. "Did you? I wondered if you would."

Tentatively, because the past had always been a taboo topic in their house, Winter went on. "I just sat outside. Noah was with me. I...remembered some things."

Beth's eyes clouded with pain, and Winter almost stopped. She'd never tell her about the camera and the photo of Justin, or her belief that her brother had survived after the attack, at least for a little while. She wouldn't let her share the knowledge—and fear—that The Preacher had been in her hotel room. Had been in contact as recently as this evening.

But there was one thing she wanted to get Gramma Beth's opinion on, since they were sharing this new closeness.

"I'm thinking about going back. Going in."

Rather than immediately trying to dissuade her, Beth nodded, a very slow up and down of her head. "I can imagine you would. You think it could help?"

Winter let out the breath she'd been holding. "I do. I might remember something else."

"Do you want me to go with you?"

"No." Winter laughed a little, surprised at the offer. "You stay here and solve crimes on TV."

"Stop in and see how poor Sam is doing too. I'll send her flowers. And find out what happened to that little girl."

Jenna. Would Kayla Bennett's parents take her in? It would be a form of closure for them, and Jenna would need a strong and secure foundation. After losing their daughter, they would at least have a piece of her that would live on in the form of a sweet, beautiful little girl who couldn't help the horrific way she'd been brought into the world.

Her grandma looked at her steadily, and Winter knew she was drawing the comparison. Jenna was the Bennett's link to Kayla.

"I'll find out," she promised.

34

It felt a little cowardly, but Winter stopped to see Sam first. She left her grandparents' house on Sunday afternoon with the intention of going straight to her old home, but her courage failed on the drive to Harrisonburg.

Tom Benton answered the door, his face creasing in a tired grin. "Hey. Back already? Far as I know, all your work here is done."

"I had something to wrap up. I came to check on Sam. Is it okay if I come in?" She held out a bouquet of tulips. "My grandma asked me to give her these."

"Come on in. I'm cooking. She's in the living room."

She followed him into the open space where Sam was tucked up on the couch in a nest of blankets. A quick glance around showed that someone had been making an effort. The house was spotless, even the glass on the picture frames on the walls clean and shining.

"You'd better not be up and around cleaning," Winter said by way of greeting. Without thinking about it, she'd fallen into their old way of snarking at each other.

"Do I look like a moron to you?" Sam shot back. "Tom did it. I'm milking this surgery recovery for all its worth."

They both laughed, and years of bitterness dimmed a little.

"Those are pretty," Sam said. "Did you bring them for my housekeeper?"

"He'd probably appreciate them, but these are for you. From my grandparents. They send their best wishes. And did Tom say he was cooking?"

Sam leaned over carefully and shut off the television. "Pot roast," she whispered, her eyes wide. "With carrots and mashed potatoes. Apple cobbler for dessert. He says I'm too skinny."

Winter shook her head in mock disbelief. "Who would have thought that you'd have grown up and married Tommy Benton. And he cooks pot roast now. You look good," she added.

It was true. Sam had lost some of the transparency she'd had just a few days before in the hospital. There was a little color in her cheeks now, and her eyes weren't so sad. "I'm getting there. I've got something to keep me going now. Do you have time to sit for a minute?"

Winter set the flowers on the table and sat down on the edge of the recliner.

"I'm going to be a mother." Sam shook her head and laughed at Winter's immediate expression of concern. "Not biologically. I'm not crazy, I promise. We're going to try and adopt Jenna."

Winter wasn't able to hide her surprise and immediate concern. "What about her grandparents?" she asked carefully.

Sam shook her head, her eyes dark. "They don't want her. They're devastated by what happened to their daughter, and who could blame them? But they're blaming that little girl and see her as evil because of the way she came into the world. Plus, they still have children at home, school-age. We want to adopt her but leave the option open for the rest of the family to get to know her later. In case they change their minds. In the meantime, she'll have a mom, dad, uncle, grandparents..."

It was hard to see a tiny three-year-old with a sweet angel face and an adorable lisp as evil. But everyone reacted to grief differently.

"How soon will you know?"

"Soon. The process could maybe start as early as next week. We have a social worker coming by on Monday, and we'd do a foster period first. That's why Tom has the house looking so good."

"I'm happy for you." It was true. Sam looked like she was glowing with the same inner light Winter had seen in women who were pregnant. The only difference was that the child she was expecting had already been born. "I hope it all works out. How does Tom feel about it?"

"He can't wait," came a voice from the door. Tom crossed the room and sank down into a crouch next to Sam. She took his hand and held tight. "We're thinking that if this works out, maybe we'll try and adopt a sibling for Jenna. Sam was meant to be a mother."

Winter studied him thoughtfully. He did look happy. Much different than the Tom Benton that had confronted them when they'd arrived in Harrisonburg.

Sam grinned at him. "And you know you'd like a little boy too."

He grinned back. "Sam's going to be a stay-at-home mom," he told Winter. "Chief wants me back next week. Next thing you know, we'll have a houseful of kids to keep us busy."

Winter left soon after, promising to keep in touch. She

wondered if she would. She thought instead that that chapter of her life would be closed. Resolved.

She sat in her car for nearly five minutes, gripping the steering wheel and trying not to cry. The painful hope she'd seen in Samantha and Tom was so fragile. Based on a long shot, forged out of trauma, and so easily shattered.

She thought about Jenna, an innocent kid. Too young to understand how her life had been upended. The mother she thought was hers would go to prison, and her biological family hated her, sight unseen, because of the tragedy that marked her beginning in life.

Another innocent for Winter to mourn.

The tenuous threads of family and fierce love that bound everyone together seemed to always be threaded through with dark strands of tragedy. Sometimes, too, with hatred and evil. She knew that too well.

Winter started the car and made the short drive to the house that had been the setting for her encounter with evil. She hadn't bothered to make arrangements to go in and look around. The house sat empty, and a records search showed that it had eventually been forfeited back to the city for back taxes the last time it had failed to sell.

No one wanted to live at the site of a homicide, apparently.

She parked in front and got out.

The house itself didn't look evil. It looked sad. Abandoned. The faded green paint was peeling away in long strips. The windows were dingy, some cracked or missing. She moved toward it, sensitive to any headache or threat of a flashback, but her mind was clear.

The porch steps creaked more loudly under her feet than they had that night so many years ago, but the structure still seemed sturdy. She moved to the door, where a no trespassing sign had been posted. The knob turned easily under her hand and swung inward.

It was musty inside and smelled like mice, and maybe a raccoon had taken up residence. But the hardwood floors were the same. They stretched forward toward the upstairs staircase, the dining room on one side and the living room to the other. She ignored the piles of clutter and empty boxes a previous tenant had left behind and climbed the stairs, trailing her fingers along the plaster wall.

For a second, she was thirteen again. The wall above where she brushed her hand was hung with pictures. Her brother, grinning proudly in his kindergarten graduation cap. Her mom and dad on their wedding day, stuffing cake in one another's faces. Mom with big, teased hair, and Dad with his plastic-framed nerd glasses. Her eighth-grade smile, teeth white and straight, but too big for her narrow face. Thank god she'd grown into them. The last family photo they'd taken at a studio at the mall. A solid unit of four. Unbreakable.

She came back to herself at the top of the steps. Something skittered away in the shadows at the end of the hallway. The bathroom door—one bath for four people was a constant complaint when she was a teenager—hung crookedly on its hinges. As it had that night, her parents' bedroom door was open a crack.

A shadow moved across the wall. There was a noise.

She stepped forward, put her hand on the cold wood, and pushed gently.

A breeze wafted past her, stirring her hair gently. It swirled through a window, broken during a storm. The air smelled fresh and hinted at rain, not clotted with the coppery scent of fresh blood. A branch lay half-in and half-out, broken glass glittering as it lay scattered across the floor.

She could almost see her parents' bed in the empty room.

A quick flash of staring blue eyes, frozen wide. An arm draped over the side of the bed like a doll's. A hand hanging free from the tangle of covers, index finger poised, pointing, just above the floor.

A thin, dark stream ran down the back of a motionless hand, and a droplet of black dripped into a small puddle already gathered on the floorboards.

Blood was streaked across the walls, the ink of a madman. Red crosses took center stage while *Jude 14:15* was scrawled in several places.

The crosses were what had pegged the killer as The Preacher by the media. The Bible verse was specific for Winter's family.

"Behold, the Lord came with many thousands of His holy ones, to execute judgment upon all, and to convict all the ungodly of all their ungodly deeds which they have done in an ungodly way, and of all the harsh things which ungodly sinners have spoken against Him."

Winter wondered if she would ever learn why The Preacher had found her family ungodly. Why they had been targeted for his executed judgment. She hoped to find out. She hoped to one day look into the killer's eyes and understand.

She blinked, and the room was empty again, except for a thick layer of dust and a few leaves piled in the corner by the wind. She blinked again, wondering if it was possible to mourn forever.

A scraping sound came from behind her, and she spun, a little dizzily, expecting the blow that would knock her into months of unconsciousness. But superimposed over the empty hallway, just above her eye level, was a man's face.

It was a normal face, not the face of a monster, and it burned itself into her brain in a millisecond.

It was a soft and round face, with a neatly clipped white

beard. Balding, the top of the head shone in the moonlight that leaked in from the hallway window. What hair was left on it was cropped short into a soft, white fuzz. A prominent nose, red as if from the cold, rounded at the end. Dark eyes rested like raisins in a doughy, pink-cheeked face, as unlined as a child's.

The eyes were all wrong. They should have been light blue, like a cloudless sky, or maybe a gentle gray. Instead, they were so black that the iris was nearly indistinguishable from the pupil.

The face smiled. The voice, quiet with a Southern accent, was oddly sympathetic.

Sorry, girlie. I'm not here for you. Just him.

A sudden jolt against her sore arm set off a sharp star-burst of pain, and she blinked again. She'd sagged against the doorjamb. In the clarity of the sudden pain, she saw that the face was gone, but the echo of the voice seemed to linger in the room.

Sorry, girlie...just him.

Mind focused again, she looked around the room. There was no more bed, or blood, or black-eyed monsters disguised as regular, grandfatherly looking men. But in the empty fire-place, among the ashes, there was a piece of paper.

Winter crossed the room on feet that felt numb and heavy. When she saw it more clearly, she took in a shud-dering breath.

Crouching down, she picked up the picture of her brother, carefully covering her hand with her shirtsleeve first, and grabbing it by the barest corner of the thick photo paper. Careful, this time, of fingerprints. Justin's face looked out at her from the woods where she'd seen him in the last photo.

She turned it over.

And stared at the same bold handwriting as the note she'd found on her car.

See you soon, girlie. XOXO.

The End
To be continued...

Want to Read More About Winter?

Will the "gift" The Preacher gave Winter destroy her before she can solve her next case? Find out in Book Two, *Winter's Curse*. Now available! Find it on Amazon Now!

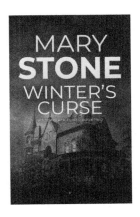

ACKNOWLEDGMENTS

How does one properly thank everyone involved in taking a dream and making it a reality? Let me try.

In addition to my family, whose unending support provided the foundation for me to find the time and energy to put these thoughts on paper, I want to thank the editors who polished my words and made them shine.

Many thanks to my publisher for risking taking on a newbie and giving me the confidence to become a bona fide author.

More than anyone, I want to thank you, my reader, for clicking on a nobody and sharing your most important asset, your time, with this book. I hope with all my heart I made it worthwhile.

Much love,
Mary

ABOUT THE AUTHOR

Mary Stone lives among the majestic Blue Ridge Mountains of East Tennessee with her two dogs, four cats, a couple of energetic boys, and a very patient husband.

As a young girl, she would go to bed every night, wondering what type of creature might be lurking underneath. It wasn't until she was older that she learned that the creatures she needed to most fear were human.

Today, she creates vivid stories with courageous, strong heroines and dastardly villains. She invites you to enter her world of serial killers, FBI agents but never damsels in distress. Her female characters can handle themselves, going toe-to-toe with any male character, protagonist or antagonist.

Discover more about Mary Stone on her website.
www.authormarystone.com

Printed in Great Britain
by Amazon